Praise for Joseph Massucci's Novels

"A great and amazingly atmospheric story! The writing is wonderful and achieves a captivating melding of historical and supernatural fiction."
—*Chris Beakey, author* DOUBLE ABDUCTION

"Amazing stuff, really trippy and very imaginative writing. And suspenseful!"
—*Ann Collette, Rees Literary Agency*

"Loved the characters, the action and the adventure!"
—*Dan Barbier, author of* JUST 4 CHILLS

"A real page-turner."
—*World Entertainment*

"A perfect adventure."
—*Tulsa World*

"Truly frightening material."
—*Huntsville Times*

"Scary and mind-expanding."
—*Fredrickson & Friends*

"Joseph Massucci does an excellent job in combining New-Age literature with an action thriller."
—*Ron Callari, Editor, y-two-k.com*

ALSO BY JOSEPH MASSUCCI

GORGON
AMAN (Extinction)
The Millennium Project
The Sabbath Experiment

THE RESURRECTION OF
ANDREW FINSBURY

JOSEPH MASSUCCI

Safari Multimedia, LLC

ISBN-13: 978-0692489116
ISBN-10: 0692489118

Cover artwork by Kentaro Kanamoto
Book design by Safari Multimedia, LLC – v01.10_r20

To my Mother,
who believed in me as a writer
but never saw me published.

My Dear Eben,

However bizarre this story may seem, I assure you every word is the truth. My faculties are still acutely sane, and the details of my extraordinary adventure are etched indelibly upon my mind. It is only now in the winter of my life that I feel compelled to share this story with my son. Your mother and I agreed that you are ready. You see, I fear the Almighty will soon see fit to take my soul into his own for the final time and forever silence the account of one mortal's journey through the Otherworld of the Dead.

—Your Father

My Death

"Now comes the mystery."
Henry Ward Beecher

"They groaned, they stirred, they all uprose,
Nor spake, nor moved their eyes;
It had been strange, even in a dream,
To have seen those dead men rise."
Samuel Taylor Coleridge

CAPTAIN MYLES EDWARDS ACCOUNT OF THE LOSS OF THE *H.M.S. TIMONIUM*

The beast had returned. Captain Myles Edwards, master of the frigate *Timonium*, could no longer see the creature, for the encroaching night hid it from him like a black veil. Despite the darkness, he could sense its presence, its cold, malevolent spirit, watching him from behind the mounting waves off his ship's starboard beam like a snake waiting to strike. He knew nothing of its origin, but he did not doubt the creature possessed the power and the purpose of crushing his ship and dragging its twisted planks along with his passengers and crew to the bottom of the North Atlantic.

The night droned with rolls of approaching thunder. Captain Edwards pulled his oilskin jacket around his neck but found no warmth on this black night. The pallor of his hands matched the color of the ship's bone-white canvas. Although he had just passed his forty-fourth birthday, those who saw him on this hellish night would declare him at least half again that old.

Edwards watched the mast's brass oil lamp swing and turn as though shaking its glowing head in warning. The weather stalks me as well, he thought. Very soon his ship would be in the midst of a North Atlantic storm. Intent on the lantern's pendulum lurching, he tried to calm his pounding heart and staunch the twisting in his bowels. *For chrissake, do something!*

A hand fell upon his shoulder and spun him around with a start. A black seaman, his first officer, stood uneasily before him. Something terrified him beyond reason. "Myles ... it's come back. I seen it."

Edwards looked deeply into the Negro's sea-weathered face. What he saw—those terror-filled eyes, sunken cheeks, twisted mats of gray hair flecked with dew-like sleet— made him shudder. "C.J., tell the others that this foul weather will delay our arrival in Baltimore."

"Myles," the old mate whispered, moving closer, his glistening eyes reflecting the lantern's glow, "I seen it clear tonight. That thing ... *it ain't of this world*. What harm does it mean us?"

The captain closed his eyes to shut out the image of the frightened seaman and shook the lingering dread from his mind. "I cannot tell you the future, C.J."

The old mate stammered, "Myles ... Myles..."

"Come below with me," Edwards said, anxious for something, anything, to distract them. "I want to record the new sighting in the log," and added under his breath, "and pray it won't be my last."

Edwards opened the hatchway and descended the ladder into his cabin. His first mate followed. The captain waved the sailor into the cabin's only chair and sat down heavily on his cramped box bunk.

C.J. sat down at the desk and brushed several charts and maps to one side to clear the blotter. He slid open the drawer and withdrew the bound log, treating it with peculiar reverence as though it were a holy book. His stringy, rope-worn fingers riffled through the pages until he found the last entry. He uncorked the ink, dipped a quill pen and dripped a trail of black dots across the page. Ready, he looked at the captain, awaiting his dictation.

Edwards rubbed a hand over a week-old beard, gathering his thoughts. "Supplementary log entry," he began, feigning calm control, "this … this…" He snapped his fingers. "What day is this?"

"It's Sunday … the sixteenth of March."

"This sixteenth day of March," he continued, "in the year of our Lord eighteen hundred and ninety-four. Sighting confirmed at approximately 1830 hours. The bastard appeared again off our starboard beam as black as evil, lurking, matching our speed and course, watching us—waiting for…" he paused and shook his head "… only the devil knows for what. The weather is deteriorating, and I can see nothing now that night has fallen. All decks secured, and passengers confined below."

Edwards closed his bloodshot eyes and rubbed them hard with his thumbs, nearly mashing them into the back of his skull. "Make one more note, C.J."

The mate dunked his pen and held it over the page, spotting the last entry with black droplets.

"I will ready the lifeboats as a precaution." He added in a whisper, "God be with my passengers."

C.J. stiffened, his face a mask of unchecked fear, an expression that sent tremors of dread through the captain. "What is it, man?" Edwards hissed.

C.J.'s terrified gaze shifted to the captain. "I smell smoke." He threw a trembling finger at the cabin door. *"There!"*

Edwards sprang from the bunk and saw a tail of smoke slithering under the door like a serpent. He drew a deep breath and winced at the acrid smell.

"What the hell—" Edwards threw open the door, drawing in a thick cloud of smoke. His eyes burned terribly, and he began choking. The passageway outside was impassable.

"Move," the captain shouted between fits of coughing. *"Move!"* He could no longer open his streaming eyes. "Get to the lifeboats."

C.J.'s vague outline groped for the ladder. Before he could secure a foothold, a violent crash jarred the ship, hurling both men to the floor. The corridor resounded with screaming passengers. Edwards felt his way to the old sailor and pulled him into a sitting position.

C.J.'s breathing came in short huffs. "We can't launch boats in this weather. We're dead men—"

"Listen to me, C.J.," Edwards implored. "I want you to get my passengers off this ship."

The mate's eyes widened. "But the storm, Myles. We'll be washed under."

"Have you another suggestion?"

C.J. stared at the captain and then finally shook his head, conceding the obvious that they had no other course.

"Then see to it ... and *quickly.*" Edwards knew the old mate would perform his duty as long as a breath remained in him.

Before C.J. could carry out his captain's order, another crash sent a violent quake through the ship, then another. More shouting and screaming resounded from the corridor. The planks shook and splintered as blast after blast pounded the frigate.

The first mate's eyes darted wildly about. "What's happening, Myles? *What in God's name is happening?"*

"C.J.—"

The cabin exploded in an upheaval of wood and

shrapnel.

Edward's eyes fluttered open. A frigid blast of air mercifully purged the compartment of the foul smoke and roused him back to his senses. He could hear sobbing far off and, worse, the sound of the sea roaring into the ship's hold. He knew the *Timonium* would soon make her final journey to the bottom of the Atlantic.

He lay on his back staring up at an inferno of burning rafters. Beyond the fire, he could discern the ship's shredded sails flapping in the raging wind against a black sky. *I am peering through a hole into hell.*

Then came the pain.

Edwards shifted his body amidst the debris and cried out from the agony of shattered ribs. He could feel nothing below his waist. He glanced down and saw his lower torso twisted at an angle severe enough to sever his spine. He grabbed a beam and struggled to pull himself into a sitting position. Wiping his eyes, he scanned what remained of his quarters and spotted a fist jutting from the broken timbers.

"God, no..."

The hand remained clenched.

Fighting back the bile boiling in his throat, Edwards dragged his shattered legs over the debris and pushed away the beams to reveal the crushed remains of the man who had served faithfully at his side for more than two decades. Emotion swelled in his throat.

"I'm sorry, C.J."

Edwards spotted the ragged edges of the ship's log half-buried beneath his body. He wrenched the book free and held close to his chest the only record of this night's horror. Somehow this must reach British naval authorities.

But how?

"Who is in there?" called a voice with a heavy French accent.

Edwards cocked his head towards the source and listened—someone was moving through the rubble.

"In here," the captain shouted. "*Quickly.* I need help."

A shadow stumbled over the debris, and a face appeared over him, the face of a slight French merchantman whose hundred casks of wine were stored in the ship's hold. He couldn't recall his name. *DuMont?*

The Frenchman's eyes were fixed on the logbook pressed against the captain's chest. His nose wrinkled in repugnance when those eyes shifted to the remains of the first officer. "A dead colored."

Edwards reached for him. "For the love of God, help me out of here, DuMont. I've been crippled."

The Frenchman sat upon a fallen beam. "Ducreux," he corrected me. "My name is Ducreux."

Edwards thrust the logbook at the Frenchman. "Take this. You must give it to Admiral Joshua Finsbury in Potters Bay."

Ducreux made no move to assist me.

By the light of the burning timber, the captain saw a twisted look of lunacy on the Frenchman's face. He appeared oblivious to the ship's sinking and showed no regret for the fading sounds of dying women and children topside. Was he injured? No, he saw something more sinister in his dark features … madness? His tone became desperate. "Save yourself. Get to a lifeboat. You must take this to Admiral Finsbury. *Please.*"

The little man's lips broadened into a grin. Edwards' gaze shifted, and his eyes widened. The Frenchman's right hand rested in the flames of a burning section of beam. Yet there was no trace of pain in Ducreux's eyes or any sign of corruption of his flesh.

The sight left him stunned.

The Frenchman removed his hand from the fire and took the book from the captain's trembling fingers. He leafed through the pages, pausing to read the last few entries, his manner casual, as though browsing the morning news over tea. Water foamed through the door of the compartment while he read and washed over the debris— icy claws that had come to drag the *Timonium* to her grave.

The little man shut the book with a snap and offered his broadest smile. "Thank you. I can assure you that this will be read carefully—although not by the man you had hoped." He waved the book at him. "It will bring a smile to his face, as it has mine."

Ducreux rose, bowed awkwardly, then ducked under the beams and vanished into the fire's haze like a ghost.

Anger broke the captain's incredulity. "Joshua, you son of a bitch." He rammed his fist hard against a fallen beam. "Where are you?"

No one could hear him. The ship listed heavily to starboard, dumping debris, fixtures, and furniture onto the walls of the cabin. As the fast-rising black water swirled around him, Edwards vowed to survive this night. He would return to Potters Bay and tell the admiral how his ship was destroyed.

Fending off the debilitating cold, Edwards groped among the flotsam until his hands found a shattered beam. He embraced it in a desperate bear hug. He found a frayed rope and tied his broken torso to the beam until he and the improvised raft were inseparable.

An explosion in the ship's hold tore the doomed vessel in two. The compartment turned over and the planks burst inward, admitting a raging sea. He managed a final, shallow breath before the thick, icy water enveloped him.

Tied to the beam, he rode submerged into the cold blackness, fighting the insistent hand dragging his wrecked ship to the distant seabed.

The water transformed his arms into useless boards. Further struggle became futile. His mind grew numb, and he lost all bearings. He prayed that the beam on which he rode would break the surface in the next seconds before his lungs collapsed. But fate decreed that Captain Myles Edwards would die with his vessel. Only one meter from the surface, reflex forced him to inhale deeply. Black saltwater imploded into his lungs.

Teetering on the rim between life and the unknown, Edwards came to the stark realization that his ship had been lured into a death trap—for its cargo. He felt the spirit of each doomed passenger and crewmember rush through him like a sacred wind. Dead—all of them murdered because of a cargo only he knew had been stowed aboard.

Their spirits cursed him bitterly, holding the ship's captain alone responsible for this massacre. Edwards water-swelled throat emitted a bitter cry of despair.

<u>MY GRAVE</u>

Blackness. I could not move. Where am I? Only silence, absolute and frightening. I flexed my fingers and felt damp, pliable earth. A swell of terror overtook me when I realized my predicament.

I was buried alive. I clawed my way through the soil in a panic, pushing loose clumps past me like a rodent. My hand grasped a tuft of grass, and a breeze laced with pine flowed over me.

And light.

Summoning all my strength, I hoisted myself up through the earth and thrust my head above ground with a deep breath like a swimmer surfacing after a dangerously long plunge.

I stared soberly at my surroundings. This was a neglected graveyard with hundreds of crooked headstones that reminded me of a field of hunched and crumbling men. The dark, overcast sky turned the landscape into an eerie twilight.

What was this place? And how did I get here? I had no memories of this, only swirls of puzzling images.

I pulled my feet clear of the earth and sat down beside the hole from which I had just crawled. There were no freshly dug plots in this old cemetery, only long forgotten headstones of souls laid to rest long ago.

Was I dreaming? Impossible. Never before had I experienced a dream of such clarity, far more real than waking life. I felt no discomfort, hunger or thirst. A strange serenity settled over me. I could not deny that a profound change had befallen me. But in what way? And why?

I grabbed the towering stone crucifix and climbed to my feet. My stomach knotted when I read the inscription on the cracked and faded marker:

Here lieth the Body of Andrew M. Finsbury,
faithful Christian and proud Captain.
Born on the second day of August in the year
of our Lord Eighteen Hundred and Sixty One,
departed on the twenty-third day of April
Eighteen Hundred and Ninety Four, age 32 Years

Reading the chiseled words describing my life unsettled me. Was I to die in four weeks hence? I turned away with a shiver. I desperately needed to know the name of this place and how I had come to be here.

I heard a muffled groan, and then the earth next me began to crack and rise from a pressure beneath. As I watched, breathless, a hand reached through the soil and began pulling himself from the clinging earth as I did moments before. This was no corpse. I watched a tall, lean man dressed in a muddy sea captain's uniform pull himself free of the ground and rise to his full height before me. At first I didn't recognize him. His eyes, bright brown, radiated warmth and kindness. His solid angular features hosted a trimmed beard, and a full head of curly hair topped a blithe expression.

"Myles," I gasped. "By all of God's glory..."

My old friend Captain Myles Edwards, master of the

merchant frigate *Timonium*, offered me a broad grin of greeting. He appeared more handsome than I had ever seen him without the hard lines that in later years etched cynicism and weariness onto his noble features. Despite his youthful appearance, his eyes revealed an intensity that humbled me.

Myles scratched a dirt-smudged nose and said to me, "I traveled a long way to meet you here, mate." His voice, deep and resonant, lacked the hard rasp of age.

"Where ... did you come from?"

He waved his hand at the disturbed soil over the grave next to mine. "From the same place as you." He gave my shoulder a friendly slap that startled me. "What'd you expect? That I'd leave you to wander this land alone? I've been racing to catch you. We have much to do in a very short time."

I could scarcely find the words to respond. "What is this place? Why are we here?"

"You're joking, are you not?" His grin faded and he looked at me quizzically. "You don't know yet, do ya, mate?"

"Myles, I don't remember anything. I don't know where I am ... or how I came here."

"Would it spook you to tell ya we're dead, mate?"

I let out a huff of incredulous laughter. "*Dead!?* Impossible. I am alive and real as you are."

Myles offered me a sympathetic look. He beckoned me to sit, and then he sat down beside me, his back propped against the giant stone crucifix, his legs stretched out before him. His eyes fixed on some far off point as he peered into his past.

"The beast came in the night and devoured my ship, my crew and my passengers," he said. "I died in the North Atlantic, the sixteenth day of March."

Before Myles could tell me more, his voice trailed off, and the air grew quiet. I looked up. He was gone. I felt a profound sense of loss and foreboding.

I was on my feet in an instant, charging down a hillside to find him. I had no destination in mind, only a need to run. Unlike the dreary graveyard at the top of the hill, this beautiful valley hosted rolling meadows and thick groves of trees all bathed in the warmest sunlight. As I ran, more wonders overtook me. I discovered that my body did not experience the usual fatigue after such exertion. I could run forever.

The field gave way to a lovely garden at the edge of a tall forest that seemed to beckon me. The blend of sight and smell was indescribably delightful. What was this place? If it were possible, I would remain here forever.

A strange sight brought me to an abrupt halt. I found my friend sitting in an ornate wooden chair in the center of the garden with a young boy, hardly more than an infant, seated in his lap. Like Myles, the child possessed an aura of wisdom far beyond his first years. From their expressions, I knew we were in some sort of danger.

"It's not your time yet, mate," Myles said to me. "Be patient. You will understand."

A strange transformation began taking place. The vast blue sky darkened. I watched immense black clouds roll across the heavens as though a great storm was approaching until ugliness consumed this beautiful land.

When I returned my gaze to Myles, fear as I had never known it seized me. My friend no longer was human. His face bore a look of the dead. His receding skin appeared white and pulpy, his eyes empty and dark.

His mouth opened and out croaked a warning, "They will come for you. Be ready."

The garden vanished. In the retreating blackness, I

heard him say, *"She is alive."*

POTTERS BAY

Potters Bay, England
Twentieth of March, 1894

A sound, shrill and menacing, jolted me awake. I sat upright, a frantic heart pounding in my chest. What had happened? That awful image of Myles' ghastly face still reverberated through my mind. Surely I had been dreaming. Myles … the graveyard … my tombstone … the beautiful garden—all of it just a dream. But, somehow, I knew the visions were much more.

I came to realize that the sound dragging me back to the smells of my workshop was the blast from a docking steamship. Captain Porter's steamer. The sustained whistle also aroused my neighbors; the usually quiet alley outside my workshop buzzed with their voices.

I threw off the paint-stained sheets and rolled off the cot, my mind still reeling with the nightmare. I was fully clothed. My eyes focused on the varnished rib-ends of my unfinished schooner, her skeletal fingers reaching for the rafters. The dust and paint fumes permeating my workshop helped rouse me. Still, my limbs felt heavy like iron, my movements stiff as though my body were not yet mine to command. Grooming this morning consisted of a quick rub of each eye, then several jabs through my thick hair that always seemed too long. Deprived of female prodding these past weeks, I had fallen into the habit of working well into the night with a disregard for my morning appearance.

I flung open the door to my workshop and inhaled the frosty March air to purge the fog from my mind. A steady stream of people flowed past my shop, their faces a blend of alarm and curiosity. Merchants huddled in small groups on the street and in doorways, conferring in hushed tones.

I joined the flow of foot traffic moving towards the waterfront and saw a crowd gathering on the pier next to Porter's steamer. The port's residents shouted questions up the steamer's gangway, demanding to know every detail of the old waterman's find. Then I heard it, someone shouted something about another ship lost. I stood still in the dampness and the cold and watched the dockworkers melt away from the pier one by one, shaking their heads in dismay at the news.

"What ship?" I asked a stranger dressed in a suit. His hollow cheeks huffed in and out, and his blank stare, fixed well beyond me, registered the bewildered look of a man who just lost his fortune. He pressed past without acknowledging me.

When I came upon Harrison, the butcher, I grabbed his bloodied apron and shook him to a halt. "What ship?"

He stared dumbly into my eyes for a moment, before his dull expression tightened into a grimace. "No need to lay your hands on me, Mr. Finsbury."

I released him with a muttered apology.

"Damnable bit of news," Harrison said, adjusting his apron. "Just damnable. Captain Porter found wreckage southwest of Wight and brought back pieces. And this time he's fished out a body. Damnable business, this. Will it never end?"

I broke away and ran towards the pier in long strides.

"Just damnable," the butcher shouted after me.

I pushed along the front line of dockworkers jammed before the steamer, hoisted my one-hundred-and-sixty pounds over the rail of the gangway and leaped up the plank. Captain Porter owed me several favors for the patches I made on short notice to his ship's rusted hull. This morning I intended to collect in full.

" *Porter.*"

An eager young man, standing without a coat despite the morning's chill, appeared atop the gangway. "Andrew, where in God's name did you spend the night?"

The young man was my brother, Eben—born Ebenezer, though no one had called him that since his baptism. He helped himself to a breakfast of Porter's catch of oysters heaped on deck. Eben was the image of me at nineteen, the sort most women found attractive, with a solid face and cascading layers of wavy hair. Another decade on The Bay and he, too, would sport my rugged complexion.

"You spent the night in your shop again, didn't you?" Eben said. He used a knife to pry open another oyster shell, sucked the raw mollusk into his mouth, and then drank the briny fluid from the half shell. He snatched another. He always ate quickly when he was excited—or frightened.

I flashed him a severe look. "What ship, Ebby?"

He finished another oyster, refusing to look at me. " Porter's heard queer noises in the hold ever since he fished out the body."

I began to shout. "Damn it, boy, was it the *Timonium?*"

Eben could no longer hide his distress and showed me

a glistening pair of blue eyes that threatened to melt into tears. "I refuse to believe that, Andrew...."

I bolted along the quarterdeck towards the coach with Eben at my heals. A hatch burst opened, and only a quick sidestep kept it from slamming into me.

Out stepped Captain Porter, a short goat of a man, studying me with squinting eyes. "Who gave you permission to board my boat? First your brother, now you."

"Show me what you found, Porter."

The goat frowned, muttered something that sounded like "You Finsburys," then waved me through the hatchway. "Can't wait to get the pieces off my ship. Haven't sleep since I found it. Damn noises all night. Footsteps mostly ... in the hold. Very persistent, very agitated. Grew worse each night. Searched the entire ship a dozen times. No one else is aboard, I promise you. Couldn't wait to dock."

Porter led us ten paces down a passageway and lifted a glowing lantern from the wall.

"Where is it?" I asked.

"Cold storage."

Porter opened a bulkhead door, releasing a waft of cold, fetid air from the hold below. The three of us stepped over the sill, down the ladder and entered a compartment that would have been black as pitch were it not for the glow of Porter's lantern. The air felt cold down here, colder than the wintry air outside. The rank stench of decay permeated every corner, mixed with a burnt, acrid odor I couldn't identify.

Debris from a wrecked ship covered the floor of the compartment. The twisted cordage appeared to crawl and twist beneath the anxious flicker of Porter's lantern. A chill much more frigid than the room swept through me; I could hear voices whispering just beyond my ears. I knelt down, turned up my collar, and motioned for more light. Porter drew closer. My fingers touched a piece of wood, a plank from the aft deck of a sailing brig—one end burned, the other splintered.

I knew this plank, I knew its workmanship. I spilled backward onto the cold metal floor, my head in a swoon. "The *Timonium*," I whispered, the words scarcely registering in the thick, dead air.

There followed a moment of reverent silence, a prayer for the fate of the ship's passengers and crew. Then Porter said, "That makes four since the first of the year. Are you still holding to the admiral's storm theory? One lost perhaps ... but four? There's evidence of a fire here. Who would risk war with England by blockading Her Majesty's islands?"

My throat swelled with grief and my hands clenched in despair. *God ... damn you.*

Eben's voice drifted over my shoulder. "We can't be sure these pieces are from the *Timonium*. No sense getting yourself all worked up 'til we know for sure."

Porter swung the lantern at him. "Who told you to come down here half dressed? I'll not be liable for a fool dying of pneumonia aboard my ship. Get your arse topside and find a coat."

Eben wrapped his chest with crossed arms.

I screwed my neck around. "Do as you're told, Ebby."

Eben obeyed, although with reluctance. When Porter and I were alone, I stood and looked questioningly into the old man's hard, gray eyes. Porter crouched beside a spread of tarpaulin that hid something stiff and bulky.

"The boy shouldn't see this," he said, drawing back the sheet and releasing a strong waft of stench.

Porter waved me forward and held the lantern over what at first looked like another piece of cordage. But no flotsam possessed features like a man. I covered my nose with a handkerchief and knelt before the corpse. My eyes squinted, and my mouth tightened involuntarily.

Myles.

What remained of my friend stared up at me with a look of horror, his once intense eyes now deep, empty holes. I recognized that awful face from my dream of the garden. His skin, white and pulpy, left a feast for the fish. His corpse below the waist was gone, eaten away in a single bite.

Despite the near-freezing temperature in the hold, sweat poured over my forehead. I forced my eyes to study the corpse. Myles had lashed his torso to a section of a charred beam, his shriveled hands still clutching its edges, refusing to give up the *Timonium* even in death. His lips were drawn back in the rictus of death, and he looked as though he were trying to speak to me from beyond the grave. He bore a look of outrage as though something far more sinister than a storm had taken his vessel and, with it, his life—just as he told me. Who did this to you, my friend? What do you want from me?

I touched his hard, withered hands and was at once struck by an extraordinary vision.

I saw my dear Vanessa aboard the *Timonium* during the ship's final moments. The decks burned with large plumes of thick smoke. She rushed to a cargo hatch, threw it open and scampered down the ladder into the hold as if to hide. From what? When she reached the bottom, she spotted a young girl crouched in the corner. A man, possibly the girl's father, lay face up on the floor before her, his unseeing eyes open, a bullet wound in the center of his forehead.

The thick, acrid smoke caused unending tears to stream down Vanessa's cheeks. She rushed to the girl. "The ship is burning," she said. "We need to find a way off—"

Vanessa whirled when men with rifles began clamoring down the ladder. She seized the girl by the arm and disappeared with her behind one of many rows of barrels. The first man off the ladder fired a revolver after her, but the two were gone.

The gun-toting pirate stormed among the kegs until he reached the back of a hold where he found Vanessa trapped in the corner, clutching the child. She swept the girl behind her. The attacker thrust his revolver into her perfect face.

"No," a voice barked. A large boar-like man, all hair and whiskers, shoved the pirate aside. He towered over Vanessa, appraising her as though deciding the worth of livestock. He would not take his eyes off her.

"I want the woman," he said, his voice deep and hard. His accent was French. "Do what you wish with the girl."

I released Myles' hand and fell backward onto the floor, stunned.

Porter covered the remains. "Sorry 'bout Myles. I know you and he were close. A good man."

I looked up at him in awe and said, "She's alive."

Porter, his eyes narrow with suspicion, lifted his flattened cap and scratched the patch of thinning hair beneath. "Who's alive?"

"Myles was taking Andrew's fiancée to Baltimore," Eben said from the hatchway.

The ancient cracks on Porter's face widening with surprise. His mouth opened and out came an incredulous, "Vanessa ... aboard? God damn the bastards who did this."

Eben buried his hands in the pockets of his jacket and stepped into the compartment, his eyes fixed on the bulging tarpaulin. "I'm so sorry, Andrew." Eben's moist blue eyes glistened in the lantern's light. "She didn't deserve this."

Eben drew back the tarpaulin. His eyes no sooner made contact with the corpse when he doubled over, vomiting oysters onto the floor between his legs.

"Cover it," Porter yelled, his order reverberating around the dark compartment.

I kicked back the canvas and pulled my brother away by his collar. Eben flopped about the hold's slippery floor, kicking himself far away from the corpse. A full minute passed before he retched his stomach dry.

I pulled my brother to his feet. "Is *The Dolphin* empty?"

Eben, his face drawn in distress, responded with a cough and a dry gag.

I shook him by his collar. "Have you unloaded *The Dolphin?*"

His head bobbed twice. "I'll finish by noon."

"Finish it now."

Eben looked at me, unsure. "You're not considering taking uncle's largest ship before market day?"

"I'm past considering it."

"And where do you think you're going?" Porter hissed. "Out there with the ghosts?" His expression softened. "I know it's hard to accept this loss. When I lost my Deborah—"

"Vanessa is alive," I repeated.

Porter lowered his eyes and shook his head. "I'm afraid we'll never see the *Timonium's* passengers and crew again."

"I saw her just now," I said. "She's alive, and she needs me."

"Uncle will want to investigate," Eben said, some color returning to his cheeks.

I grimaced, refusing to waste precious time courting a

tedious naval investigation. "Find Charles and tell him to fetch Joseph. I'll double their usual wages."

Eben stared at me, unsure whether I was inviting him to be a part of my crew.

"Well, hurry, boy. We've got days of work to finish by dusk."

"Yes, sir." Eben sprinted through the hatchway.

"Employing children, are you?" Porter said. "Must be hard times for a captain without a crew."

"He's nineteen years old. Hardly a child."

"Some men are always boys." His cynical eyes bore a note of sadness, a look rare for him. "God help you."

Porter blew out the flame of the lantern with a huff, and we left Myles alone with the remains of his beloved ship.

ADMIRAL JOSHUA FINSBURY

Dusk gave way to a thick, starless night, and I cursed myself for not leaving hours earlier as planned. I hurried down the darkened pier, my arms aching from the weight of my sea chest filled with personal effects, topped with a wooden case containing my sextant.

Eben bounced down *The Dolphin's* gangway and ran the length of the pier to meet me, his boots knocking the damp planks. He could not contain his excitement, his youthful energy infinite. "Charles will be back directly with the last of our supplies. Then we can go. There's a ten-knot breeze to take us out."

I gestured to my armload. "Would you mind?"

Eben grabbed my sextant from atop the chest and dashed down the pier. He raced aboard *The Dolphin*, shouting something to his fellow shipmate, Joseph securing the clewlines, and then disappeared below. I never saw my brother so excited. Who could say? Perhaps he would prove himself a fine seaman.

I gazed proudly across the ship and assessed her with my artist's eye. *The Dolphin*, a two-masted, fore-and-aft-rigged schooner—the first ship of my own construction. A perfect masterpiece to begin my shipbuilding career. Three could handle her with ease; four would be a holiday. The soft orange of the stern lanterns turned her masts into two grand pillars that appeared to support the night sky. I vowed that when I returned I would take up my brushes and pallet and capture her beauty on canvas.

There I stood, surrounded by the smell of the sea and the land equally blended when a deep voice startled me from my musing.

"Goin' somewhere in a hurry?"

I nearly dropped my sea chest in surprise. I hadn't noticed the large man sitting beneath the dock lamp watching me. "Williams? Can I trust my eyes?"

The huge Negro jumped to his feet and showed me a grin as wide as the dock. Although he possessed the strength to break a man's back with an easy flex of his muscles, Williams' soul was good-natured, and his eyes radiated only kindness.

"Word's out you're gonna chase the devil," he said in a deep drawl. He cocked his thumb at the open sea. "I hear you're plannin' a run out there."

"Then you also heard that the *Timonium* was lost."

His eyes glistened. "Yes, sir. 'Tis why I'm goin' wit you."

"If you're trying to get back to the States, I should tell you I'm not going across this time."

Williams belted a laugh. "I likes this place just fine. Really. I ain't tradin' what I gots here for what I left behind in the land of the free."

I balanced the chest on my shoulder and offered him my hand. "Welcome aboard."

Instead of taking my hand, Williams grabbed my free shoulder and gave it a confident shake. "'Tis the least I can do. We're gonna find that woman of yourn. Yessir." He lifted the chest from my arms, nodded a salute and said,

"We gonna find her, Cap'n."

The strong seaman trotted up the gangway with my sea chest perched on his shoulder, his beautiful baritone voice rendering a favorite work song handed down through generations of American slaves. I did not want for a crew. I would have with me a friend as well as the toughest hand in England.

Boarding *The Dolphin*, I looked out across the black ocean beyond the harbor lights, and I thought of Vanessa. My heart raced with anticipation. "I know you're alive, my love," I whispered. "I can feel your loneliness. Wherever you are, I will find you and bring you home. I promise."

Williams left my trunk by the hatchway. I heaved the chest onto my shoulder and maneuvered the steep companionway down into my cabin. An oil lamp with a low flame had been left burning for me over the desk. I swung my trunk around and dropped it with a bang at the foot of the box bunk.

"Can't you wait until morning?" came a gravel voice from beyond my desk.

I whirled. The sea officer rocked his chair forward and leaned into the glow of the lamp.

"Uncle..."

My uncle—better known throughout England as Admiral Joshua Edward Finsbury—fixed his penetrating gray eyes on mine, his white beard quivering with irritation. He no doubt had spent the afternoon arguing with Her Majesty's Naval Security Council about how to respond to this latest sinking. Despite my precautions to be discreet with his property, Uncle knew I planned to take his schooner without permission.

"We have much to talk about," he said, rocking back in his chair.

"We'll talk when I return." The sharpness of my voice

caused Uncle's white eyebrow bushes to rise.

"We'll talk now," he shot back. He folded his weathered hands on the desk in formal military fashion as though presiding over a court-martial—mine. "I don't like this. If you intend to be reckless with your life, I can't stop you. But I forbid you to involve one of my ships in this madness. Kill yourself with a vessel you can steal from someone else."

"Steal? She's our ship. Or have you forgotten how long I labored building her for you?" A weak retort, but it was my only rational explanation.

Uncle's eyes studied me coldly. Finally, he allowed those eyes to soften. "Vanessa's dead, Andrew. Nothing you do now will change that fact. If you don't let go of this foolishness, you'll soon be joining her."

I placed my hands on the desk and met his gaze. "I don't believe Vanessa is dead. The ships lost this year were deliberately sunk. Revenge, profit, war, I don't know. But they were sunk. I intend to find out who is responsible and where they've taken her. A fortnight from now, she will be back here safe with me."

Uncle's steel eyes matched my intensity. "This is madness. You saw what happened to Myles. Why in the name of God kill your crew who have no stake in this affair, including your brother?" He raised his voice. "I cannot allow that to happen."

"I need a fortnight."

Uncle shifted uncomfortably in his chair. "A fortnight from now, Captain Porter will be fishing your bones from the sea. Then it will be your corpse we bury in the churchyard alongside your parents."

"I don't intend—"

"A captain with any sense would not use this … this…" He gestured to the rafters, groping for the right word. "… this vessel."

"This ship is perfect. And I know every line and sheet on her."

"You will be defenseless."

"I built her for speed and maneuverability, not for fighting."

"A sensible sea captain would fear those lofty masts and cut them down to naval standards," Uncle rasped. "I suggest you strengthen those spars and put up bulkheads."

"*No*. She would lose her advantage of speed—"

"Damn you," he spat. "You've grown reckless. The years you spent in Baltimore learning shipbuilding from those blockade-running friends of yours will get you killed."

"Baltimore shipyards are superior—"

"And what about your crew?" he hammered, building his case. "You have a convict, an old man and your brother who, I might add, has never been out of sight of land? A sad bunch of fools."

"They are more than adequate. And I will have Williams with me."

"Good," he mocked. "And a Negro who would have a better life in America in servitude like his father."

"They are good men—"

"Cheap labor," he hissed, "no better off on your boat than in prison."

I heard voices and the slap of feet along the deck above as the last of my supplies arrived.

"There is another side of this business you should know," I said, deciding to tell him everything. I drew in a deep breath and said, "Vanessa is with my child. Myles was taking her to Baltimore while she still could travel. We would be married there without shaming the family."

Uncle's eyes fluttered, but he betrayed no emotion.

"Try to understand, Andrew, I fear for the lives of my nephews—the only sons I have. You do not appreciate the trouble you're inviting."

"I've outrun trouble before."

"This is different. There are sinister forces at work here. Until we understand what it entails and who is responsible, no ship is safe. I don't want you involved."

"Vanessa and my child are missing. I am involved."

Uncle and I stared at each other, and I suspected he now regarded me as more than just a mischievous boy. Perhaps he saw me as a resourceful seaman who could make his own decisions.

"I believe you know more about this business than you're telling me," I said.

He looked away and let out a long, weary sigh. "Yes, perhaps you should know everything."

Uncle picked up a rule from the desk and stared thoughtfully at its graduated markings. "After the *Timonium* left Potters Bay a week ago," he began, "Captain Edwards docked in Portsmouth for one day to pick up additional passengers and cargo. The passengers were of no consequence as far as we know, but the cargo was of monumental importance to this country's security. Keenly aware of the dangerous stakes, Myles knew better than to utter a word about his cargo to anyone, least of all to his passengers."

I shook my head. "What cargo?"

"He carried Her Majesty's gold for payment to a private concern in the United States, the best shipbuilding outfit in the world. The funds were to finance a prototype of a new warship with steel hulls, a diesel propulsion system and revolving turrets. With a fleet of these ships, Her Majesty would again command the strongest navy on the seas."

"How much gold?"

"Almost a ton of gold bars. A treasure worth one million pounds sterling."

I stared at him incredulously. "Good God, why take these risks with passengers aboard? Why didn't a naval armada transport the gold?"

"Her Majesty wanted the funds transferred discreetly aboard a commercial vessel. We could not afford a hint of a military transaction."

"But why the *Timonium*?"

He shrugged. "Myles isn't the only captain Her Majesty trusted in this venture. There is another merchant vessel underway—The *Burlington*—carrying a similar cargo. She left Portsmouth yesterday. God help them." He slammed his fist on the desk. "There was no way word of these shipments could have leaked to anyone. Not even during the war has there been a more closely guarded secret."

"So much for Naval security."

Uncle stood up, a flicker of hope lighting his eyes. "Her Majesty ordered half her fleet to find out who is responsible for these atrocities. If Vanessa is alive, I promise we will find her."

"I appreciate your offer," I said. "But you won't find a pirate within a hundred miles of a fleet of British warships. Let me do this my way. A lone merchant schooner just might be able to spot something."

"Leave Eben behind. As his guardian, you have a responsibility for his safety and his welfare."

"He's determined to go. Eben has a good mind and will make a fine language professor at the University if that's what he finally decides he wants. But he also needs to learn about life in ways only the sea can teach him. You and I must stop sheltering him. A harbored ship is safe, but that's not what ships are built for."

Uncle looked worn and beaten. "Then may God be with you on this death hunt." He grabbed a small wooden box from the floor by his chair and set it on the desk. His mariner's compass. He knew all along he would not dissuade me. "I want you to take this with you."

"Uncle ... that belonged to grandfather—"

"Trusting you with it is my one guarantee that you will return. Take it, and may it bring you luck as it has for me. Sail south by west—the *Timonium's* course when she left port—and heed the air movements of the North Atlantic. Winter squalls are still reported in the northern streams. Keep to the warmer currents. If you spot anything, I want you to return immediately to report." A forced smile lifted his pure white beard. "And may God bring you back to me."

Admiral Joshua Finsbury was well known for his cold and meticulous execution when blasting a ton of twenty-four pounders into an enemy's hull and watching the warship sink with all hands. But despite his stone exterior, Uncle was at heart a sentimentalist, willing to give everything he owned to those he cared for. I offered him my hand. "Thank you, sir."

Uncle shook it with both his weathered hands, his eyes aglow with a blend of love and sadness that threatened to yield tears. Then, without another word, he ducked under the beams and climbed up on deck. I followed, wanting to say something more to him, but the time for talk had passed. Without looking back, Uncle walked briskly down the gangway and crossed the pier.

My crew watched me, their eyes begging to know about my conversation with the rightful owner of this vessel. Eben broke the awkward silence. "We've loaded the last of the provisions."

I nodded. "Proceed."

These four good men scattered to their positions for getting underway.

I moved to the rail, the brisk wind filling me with a cold I could not shake. I watched Uncle disappear into the blackness beyond the glow of the dock lamps.

I couldn't rid myself of the awful feeling that I would never see him again.

THE BURNING SEA

Ship's Log . . . Twenty Third of March
2000 hours
Lat. 41.28 Lon. 61.07 SW by WSW

I hesitate to put in writing the details of this evening's strange incident, and I have told no one. However strange this may sound, I am compelled to document the episode while the details are vivid in my mind, in the happenstance that a future sighting will give it credibility.

After three days of high winds and rough seas, the unpredictability of the North Atlantic this time of year did its best to convince me to give up this search. A rising northeasterly poured frigid winds into our faces throughout the day, and each man kept one eye on the bleak sky as he worked, fearful that a sudden storm might put a tragic end to the careers of five good seamen. Despite our good intentions and high expectations, we found nothing. Perhaps Uncle was right; maybe we didn't belong out here.

Just before dusk, as I sat alone in my cabin, I heard heavy footsteps up on deck—someone pacing. I went above to investigate. The sky was overcast, the afternoon growing ever dimmer. I saw what I believed to be my crewman, Joseph, sitting next to the quarterdeck, staring at the horizon, perhaps lamenting the unfavorable weather conditions. However, when he turned to look at me, I realized my mistake. To my utter astonishment, the man sitting not ten feet from me was my friend Captain Myles Edwards.

He looked pale—a trick, perhaps, of the early dusk. Even the pigments of his garments lacked color. He appeared otherwise healthy, far better than the corpse I found under Porter's tarpaulin.

Myles stood before me and offered an apologetic smile. I sensed that my friend wished to tell me volumes but, to his regret, he could not. I cursed myself now for saying nothing to him, but at that moment I could do nothing more than stare at a man who came to me a second time from the grave.

He turned away from me and looked to the northwest where something had roused his keen interest. I followed his gaze but saw nothing but the barren sea. Then, without a word, he began walking towards the forward deck. I followed several long steps behind. When he reached the ship's forward rail, he did not stop at the bulwark as I expected. Instead, he passed through the railing and stepped onto the waves. I thought he would vanish then, swallowed by the sea that had taken his life. But he did not. To him, the water felt solid like a field of sod, and he continued his walk among the waves, his attention fixed on the northwest horizon.

I decided to alter the ship's course so that I might follow my friend. Telling no one, I shifted The Dolphin to a new compass heading twenty degrees to the northwest, away from the course my uncle had advised. But for as much wind as I could put into the sails that evening, the ship could not overtake his apparition. Myles stayed ahead, always beyond my reach, his eyes gaze fixed on the horizon.

Then, at precisely midnight, the darkness enveloped him, a cruel veil that hid my dearest friend from me.

* * *

Twenty Fourth of March

"Coffee, Chief?" a voice rasped at my side.

I looked down into the crinkled face of old Charles, my most-seasoned able-body, his white bristles of beard glistening with droplets of sea and rain. The tightly-wrapped hood of his sea jacket made his head look like a dangerous projectile. He held a pot in one hand and a steaming cup in the other.

"Thanks," I said, accepting his proffered cup.

Eben spotted Charles with the steaming pot and joined us. "You're a godsend, Charles. This cold is trying to kill me."

Charles filled another cup and gave it to my brother. Eben's features wrinkled in repugnance with the first sip.

"Damn you, Charles. You've heated a pot of bilge water." He flung the contents over the rail and shoved the empty cup back into the old man's hands.

Charles grimaced. "A waste of good brandy."

Eben looked at me. "Brandy?"

Charles smiled slyly. "Aye, ever taste brandy before, son? A shot in your coffee takes the bite out of the wind."

"Perhaps I was too hasty." He grabbed for the pot, but Charles pulled it out of his reach.

"Sorry," the old mate said. "Won't be enough for the others."

Eben suppressed a sulking expression and stuck his

hands deep into the pockets of his oilskin jacket. "Can you heat a bowl of broth? I'd sell my soul for a steaming bowl of soup."

"Kitchen's closed 'til we're past this weather."

"How long?"

Charles cast a queer look at the skies. "Maybe by supper. Maybe longer."

"We'll starve out here." Eben stomped off, heading aft.

With Eben gone, Charles moved close to me and whispered, "You heard it last night too, didn't you?"

"Heard what?"

"Footsteps. Pacing the decks."

His strange change of subject caught me off guard. "One of the crew—"

"Don't talk crap. I stood on watch last night while the rest of you slept. Heard someone walk right past me. Didn't see nobody, though—"

Charles grew still, his narrow eyes fixed on something across the sea. He shoved the pot of coffee and mug at me. "Take this."

I took the items, puzzled. Charles helped himself to the ivory telescope fastened to my belt and, squinting, directed it out to sea. I used the pot to shield my eyes against the brisk, salty wind but saw nothing.

"What is it?"

He did not answer me. The old seaman scanned the restless water off our windward bow, his body pressed against the rail to steady the glass. I left him alone; his astonishing visual acuity bordered on the psychic. I studied the sky. Dusk would be upon us in an hour and with it another miserable night of thirty-five-knot winds. A great swell lifted the ship into the air then dropped her into a foamy valley. A chilling foreboding raised the hairs on the back of my neck: we were heading for rough weather just over the horizon.

Charles closed the glass with a snap.

"What is it?" I asked, squinting. "A storm wall?"

"A light."

My head snapped around to look at him. "How far?"

"Three fingers from the horizon." He handed the telescope back to me. "See what you make of it, Chief."

I exchanged the coffeepot and cup for the glass. With the aid of the telescope, I spotted what every seaman dreads—an orange glow that would appear and then vanish like a mischievous sea spirit behind the mountainous waves. A ship. I lowered the glass and saw a thin column of smoke stretching from the glow to the low cloud cover.

The others came to the rail. "What is it?" asked Eben.

I pointed off our starboard bow. "A ship's afire."

Charles gave the rail a slap. "We can tack north into this gale and make a good seventeen knots."

"Eben," I said, "I want you to man the tiller."

My brother followed me to the helm while the others scrambled to bring our ship about and prepare for a rescue. Eben removed the lashings that secured the tiller and pulled to execute a change in course. The schooner leaned leeward amid the flapping of sails losing their grip on the wind.

"Maybe it's sunlight reflecting off calmer waters," Eben called, wrestling with the tiller that bucked and kicked in his inexperienced hands.

I pressed my shoulder against the wood to steady the helm. "We're headed for rougher waters, not calmer. We'll be in the middle of a storm when we reach that ship."

Eben looked at me, his eyes betraying his apprehension. "Yessir."

"Tie yourself down."

I left my brother alone at the helm and joined the rest of my crew scrambling to secure the vessel and position the sails to make whatever speed possible under these conditions. As we proceeded, the curious speck of light with its black tail of smoke soon became readily visible off our starboard bow.

Williams' voice cracked over the ripping wind. "She's blazin', Cap'n. Blazin' like hell and the hereafter!"

I stationed the crew starboard as lookouts, then made my way to the forecastle for a better view. I pondered the logistics of reaching the vessel before she went down and prayed that luck would be with us and we would find survivors.

Charles appeared by my side, a rope in his hand, his weathered face contorted against the icy wind. "Her sails and masts are gone."

"Can you make out if she's a merchant ship?"

"Aye, a brigantine—a far nobler vessel than ours. The sort built for the wool-run from Melbourne. A waste. She's listing badly. Her hold's flooded."

With each plunge of our vessel, the island of fire drew steadily closer. Soon we were able to identify her as a two-hundred-ton brigantine merchant ship. Once proud and triumphant, the brig was mortally crippled with her heart burned out. Doomed. I returned to the helm. Eben, his white fingers stretched around the tiller, stared transfixed at the great plume of black smoke billowing from the wreck.

"Haul over to windward," I said.

Eben nodded and complied.

I grabbed Williams' arm as he rushed by. "Prepare to lower the lifeboat."

Williams called for Joseph's assistance and then headed aft.

My plan was straightforward: we would go windward of the wreck, lower a boat, then guide the schooner leeward to pick up survivors. But time was our foe. The northwesterly grew to a strong gale with unremitting squalls and high seas. My concern was getting the boat clear in these waters. If we failed to carry out the maneuver with absolute precision, the small boat would be washed under with the first swell. To complicate matters, the overcast sky forced an early dusk on us, inviting a rescue on a black sea.

The Dolphin labored heavily, pitching port to starboard, dipping her rails with each roll. With my attention divided between the spectacle of the burning ship and managing the constant rolling of the schooner, I failed to notice someone tugging my arm until a hand pulled me abruptly about—Joseph, a young, rough seaman who spent the best part of his teen years in prison for his compulsion for theft. Typically fearless, tonight his eyes were wide with fear.

His expression caused my heart to race. "What is it, Joseph? What's wrong?"

Before he could speak, a heavy wave crashed over the deck, drenching both of us. The cold water did little to rouse the seaman from his unsettling look.

"Something's out there," he said, water dripping from his pale features. "Following us … a beast!"

I looked over the stormy sea but could see nothing beyond the burning wreck. "Joseph, for the love of—"

"Didn't believe it myself. Charles saw it too. Ask him. He'll tell you … three-hundred feet—"

Another stinging sheet of spray smashed over the bulwarks. "Get back to your station before we run this vessel under."

The seaman clenched his fists and said sharply, "By

God, there's something out there. Watching us."

My heart began pounding. "Tend to this ship."

Joseph, shaking his head, made his way to the foredeck with one eye on the dark waves, as if fearful that a long tentacle would suddenly surface to snatch and drag him to the bottom of the sea.

A hard crash against the hull turned every man a shade paler. Charles bent over the rail, his feet off the deck. "Piece of timber."

The others joined him and began racing along the deck while shouting and pointing out cordage and debris that littered the rolling waves. Another crash, more severe than the first, struck our hull. The remains of a ship's mast spun away into the inky waters.

Williams grabbed a boat hook. He dipped the long pole into the sea and pushed a piece of flotsam clear before it could pound our hull. The rest of my crew hastened to follow his example.

Charles slid along the rail next to me. "Part of the brigantine's forward mast." He jabbed his boat hook at a splintered piece of wood. "Look at the way the timber's split. If I didn't know better, I'd swear something bit it in two."

We were within hailing distance of the burning brigantine, yet there wasn't a trace of life on or about her. The wind pulled the heavy smoke across our decks, a noxious plume that made my eyes tear.

Suddenly, the doomed ship exploded in a blinding fury. My heart rammed against my ribs. A great fireball shot skyward, and I threw up a hand to shield my eyes from its brilliance. The shock wave slammed into the schooner, tearing the breath from our throats and sending hot hurricane-like winds shrieking through the ship's rigging.

"Good mother of Christ," I gasped.

The hellish fireball rose and rolled into the black sky. Bits of burning wood and ash rained down on us, leaving faint glowing trails.

"She blew her magazine," Williams shouted.

"She's no warship," I hollered.

A thick, caustic cloud overtook *The Dolphin*. I could hear the others fighting off convulsive coughs. I winced and groped from one handhold to another.

"It's the devil breathing over our decks," Charles shouted between fits of coughing.

"One of your ruined suppers," Joseph called.

"It's lime, Cap'n," Williams shouted, "lime slaked with water. She must've broke a seam in these waters. Must've soaked her cargo of lime."

Then it became clear to me. I smelled that pungent odor almost ten years ago when the decks of the four-hundred-ton Japanese merchant ship *Mineko* burned from under two-hundred seamen. All because three kegs of lime became soaked with bilge water causing combustion. The same telltale odor I noticed in the hold of Captain Porter's steamer.

None of it made sense. Why would her captain carry lime knowing his course might take him through a winter squall?

"Turn about?" Eben called from the helm.

All at once the screams of hundreds of dying women and children rose from the sea and filled my ears. An appalling sound.

"Men overboard," I shouted. "Williams, get to the lifeboat. Hurry, man!"

Charles jumped to the rail and blew his rescue whistle. The shrill sound cut through the night, while his keen eyes scanned the waves for survivors.

I rushed forward, my ears filled with screaming children, dozens of them, desperately calling for help. I couldn't bear the terrible sound. "For God's sake—*hurry.*"

I noticed Joseph's puzzled stare. He just watched me, making no move to assist.

"*Damn you,*" I roared. "Children are dying!"

Williams made his way forward, abandoning the lifeboat.

"Have the lot of you gone mad?" I shouted.

"Cap'n," Williams said, "there's no one out there."

Charles ceased blowing his whistle, listened, and then shook his head. "If someone was out there, they're gone now."

I jumped to the rail and listened, my eyes wild. As abruptly as it started, the screaming faded, replaced by the howling wind. No more shouting, no cries for help. Only the roar of hard waves.

But we were not alone.

I caught the barest glimpse of a shadow moving off our starboard bow—it was impossible to distinguish anything against the black swells. An instant later it vanished, swallowed by the night. But a glimpse was enough. This wasn't one of Joseph's tales. Something of extraordinary size was lurking out there, stalking us.

"Bring her full about," I shouted to the crew. "Get us out of here."

The men scrambled to their stations.

I sprang to the helm and helped Eben pull the tiller hard to port. Together, we brought *The Dolphin* about and quickly had her running for the southern horizon, sweeping foam past her sides.

"Chief," Charles shouted, making his way forward in the blinding rain. "We have an escort off our port bow. As big as a whale."

"I saw it too," I said. "Now help me get us out of here."

"No argument here." Charles headed for the stern.

I pushed back my soaked hair and pulled the collar of my sea jacket around my neck. But despite every effort to keep warm, a heavy chill swept through my soul. Another piece of wreckage spun past our bow, trailing lines and cables that flopped about like living tentacles. What in God's name could have done this?

A flash of lightning lit the ugly sea astern. In the fragments of light, I saw a large black shape splitting the high waves as it labored after us. I swore under my breath. The beast that claimed the brigantine had taken a keen interest in our vessel.

THE BEAST

"**S**omethin' comin', Cap'n," Williams' voice roared over the storm. "Fast astern."

My crew jumped to the aft rail to watch a colossal object fast closing the distance between us. A black mass unimpeded by the high swells and winds.

"Set sails," I shouted. "I want five more knots out of her."

"We're carryin' all the sail she can handle," Charles hollered. "We'll lose a mast if we run up more."

"Not my masts. Rudder amidship. Prepare for speed."

The men leaped across the deck and ran up every inch of canvas we could carry. The twin masts groaned as *The Dolphin* rose from the sea and began pounding the heavy waves that crashed over our decks with each plunge, washing overboard anything not fastened down.

Charles beckoned me with a wave. "There's something you should see."

I slid along the bulwark next to the old mate. "What is it?"

Charles thrust a bony finger at the beast moving past our port bow. "There."

I squinted against the sea spray but could not make out specifics. "What?"

"Smoke."

I stiffened. Indeed, a string of smoke, nearly hidden in the spray, trailed the object. I let out a low whistle. "What have you found, old man?"

"That's no beast, Chief," Charles spat. "It's a machine. A steamer."

I watched the object by the intermittent flashes of lightning. The old man was right. We weren't dealing with monsters. I stared at a strange vessel, unlike any European or American naval barge I had ever seen before. The two-hundred-foot craft was enclosed with no sails or other means of propulsion, with a low, flat deck and a queer tower amidship.

"Chief," Charles said, "this schooner ain't a fighting vessel and we ain't soldiers. We wouldn't stand a chance against a warship."

I removed a storm lantern from the mizzenmast. "Put out all lights—"

Before I could finish my order, a flash appeared above the mysterious vessel's waterline, followed by a muted thump. A howl replaced the ripping wind, then a geyser leaped up on our port side and poured water over the quarterdeck. *Cannon fire.*

The men fled from the rail in terror.

Eben released the tiller. "It means to sink us!"

I placed my back to the wind and shouted, "Hold your stations ... all of you."

Eben, his eyes wild with fear, stood staring at me.

"Hold that rudder," I ordered.

Eben shook his panicked stare, the man in the boy emerging. He reached around, grabbed the tiller and struggled to keep us on a course due south, running dead before the wind.

"Charles," I called, "put out those lanterns. We'll outrun the bastard."

The men leaped to their stations. As we worked to maintain speed, a cold realization gripped me. A ship that size could carry thirty guns, most likely thirty-four pounders. Charles was right—we wouldn't stand a chance against it. A single, well-executed broadside from her would transform *The Dolphin* into an inferno of tangled rigging and howling, mangled men. What have you led us into, Myles?

I raced amidship and called for Williams. He lumbered to me, his eyes wide and glistening. I beckoned him to join me beside a bulging tarpaulin and threw back the sheet. "How's your aim, mate?"

"Jesus in heaven." Williams knelt before a disassembled six-pound Napoleon III bronze field cannon and let out a long, low whistle. "You split your moorin's this time, Cap'n."

"You haven't seen a cannon before?"

"I can handle a cannon." He patted one of the cannon's wagon-like wheels. "But we's on a boat, not facin' a field of infantry."

"The best I could secure on short notice. I'll entertain alternatives if you have another suggestion."

His anxious eyes stole another glance at the black shape lurking not one hundred yards from our starboard quarter. "Nossir. I surely don't."

Williams and I lifted the bronze barrel onto the carriage and drove in the mounting pins to fasten it in place. A moment later it stood ready—a European field artillery cannon, ludicrously out of place on the deck of a schooner. I shrugged, well aware of the absurdity of this attempt. Our schooner had but one six-pounder to respond to a well-executed barrage of iron from a warship. One gun. Christ—pathetically little. Our one hope lay in surprise.

The commander of that warship would not expect a strike from a merchant vessel. A sudden bite might just stun the hellhound long enough to give the rabbit a chance to flee.

Another loud banging filled the night. There came a hiss followed by a wrenching concussion beneath our feet. Our forward jib exploded, throwing up a spray of splinters and sleet as it blew across the deck. The unsecured jib flapped in the storm like a tattered white flag waving surrender.

I said to Williams, "Let's go."

We wheeled the cannon along the deck into full view of the crew.

"Uncle's cannon," Eben shouted from the helm. "I'm surprised he trusted you with it."

"I'll have it back before it's missed," I hollered back to him.

Staggering to the heave and pitch of the icy deck, Williams and I rolled the gun up to the bulwark. But, alas, its barrel failed to clear the schooner's bulwark.

I pounded the rail in defeat.

Williams scratched his bald pate. "Should'a measured before leavin' port."

"I need an ax." I cupped my hands and yelled forward. "*I need an ax.*"

A moment later, Charles staggered forth with an ax slung over his shoulder. I snatched it and began chopping away at the oak bulwark, while Williams and Charles lashed the cannon to either edge of the rail. In a moment, I finished carving an adequate breech in the rail for the barrel.

"Load and run out fast," I yelled.

The hollow boom of more cannon fire caused each of us to duck instinctively. Several geysers erupted directly behind *The Dolphin*. We exchanged stupid stares, amazed the barrage hadn't produced a direct hit. We had the advantage of speed.

We were ready. I used the glowing beacon atop its tower to calculate the black vessel's distance. "Range: one hundred yards." I slapped the bronze barrel for luck. "Prime and stand ready."

Williams nodded and brought the cannon to bear. Charles hoisted a lantern.

"Fire!"

Charles opened the lantern and lit the fuse. The cannon fired, bellowing a plume of blue smoke. The blast's recoil drove the gun backward and ripped the rail from the deck. Williams leaped clear with cat-like agility before the full weight of the artillery piece could fill his lap.

I scrambled up to the shattered rail. Our shot flew over the high waves and struck the vessel squarely on its flat deck. *Yes!* My euphoria vanished an instant later. Instead of crushing wood, a thick, metallic clang rang out over the wind as the ball bounced off the vessel's black hull.

"She's an ironclad." My voice betrayed alarm.

The next broadside came an instant later. Two huge geysers hissed up an arm's reach from *The Dolphin*, and several thumps sounded overhead as the projectiles tore gaping holes in our canvas. Forward, there came a jarring impact as a ball crashed through the schooner's hull and into our galley.

Damn. I leaned over the rail to inspect our damaged bow. Water collecting in the hold threatened to run *The Dolphin* far too deep forward. The men fought for secure footing on the slanting deck, coupled with a taut rope around them. More cannon shots ripped through the night, followed by hissing geysers astern.

I raced to Eben. "We're leaning to starboard. Can you feel it? Shift the rudder before we travel in a circle."

Eben pulled hard on the tiller and moved the rudder several degrees to starboard. I felt the schooner swing about, but she still listed dangerously windward.

I jumped from the helm and met Williams amidship. "How bad is she?"

"I seen worse—we's still floatin'. The galley's awash and water's fillin' the forward hold. Have we lost the bastard?"

"She's coming up fast astern," I said. "Means to ram us in the ass. We've got to lose that extra ballast. Joseph, I want you working the bilge pump."

The mate scrambled below to draw out the water.

I slid across the deck and inspected the overturned cannon—a split carriage and several wheel spokes missing. But I could still count on it to fire again.

"Williams, for God's sake, I need you."

Williams scrambled across the slippery deck to join me.

We lifted the overturned carriage onto its damaged wheels, then pushed the cannon aft, ignoring the spray of water smashing over the bulwarks. Charles, carrying another shot and powder, added his shoulder to the effort. I divided my attention between the task of readying the gun and watching the black vessel fast closing the distance to our stern. I saw lights beaming from portholes on the ship's pilot tower. The others stood watching in awe.

"Secure yourselves," I snapped.

Charles handed me a double plug of powder, but instead of an iron ball, the old mate presented a sack of nails.

"What the devil is this?"

"Carpenter nails. It'll give you a wider blow—like buckshot."

"Brilliant!"

I pushed the powder charge and bag of nails down the barrel and rammed it home, while Williams secured the cannon to the aft rail post to absorb the recoil. Charles passed me the ax, and I chopped away another section of bulwark until the barrel cleared.

Finished, I squeezed Williams' shoulder. "Wait for my signal. Aim for that tower. Blow it clear off!"

Williams pulled at the rope. "Recoil will tear her loose again."

"Forget the rope. We'll have one shot, so by God hit it square."

Williams peered through the tube site atop the gun. I scrambled down the length of rail to gain a better view. The bastard charged our stern, a specter of death pouncing to crush us. In a moment we would be dead men. *Tell me what to do, Myles...*

Eben's piercing cry cut through the wind. "Hurry, Andrew!"

The immense black hulk lunged ahead, crushing our davits. The impact hurled our longboat across the helm, missing Eben by a breath. I raised my hand, waiting in agony for the right moment. My heart pounded painfully, and my stomach felt as though it had been kicked by a huge boot. Williams kept one patient eye fixed on me. Charles stood ready with the lantern.

I swung my arm down fiercely, my voice a desperate cry. "*Fire!*"

Charles lit the fuse.

Whomp.

The cannon's recoil ripped the rail from the deck, hurling me backward. For a terrifying moment, I thought the shot had gone wide. Then, in the next instant, I heard the unmistakable clang of metal striking metal and the sound of glass shattering.

"Good shot!"

But it did nothing to stop the iron vessel's considerable momentum. Before any of us could move, the warship veered sharply and grazed our port side with an awful crash. All in one wild commotion, the terrible impact knocked every man off his feet while the schooner rolled and shuddered like an earthquake beneath us. Each of us jammed fingers into the planks of the slanting deck as the warship slipped under the hull and pushed our stern out of the water. And there we hung for a dreadful eternity.

Finally, the iron vessel slipped from beneath us, dropping our keel into the sea with a force that should have split every mast in two. But *The Dolphin* refused to go under, her well-crafted hull intact. She rolled evenly, defying the rage of the devil.

Williams and Charles lay spread-eagle beside the overturned cannon. We all were too bewildered to move, stunned that the sea hadn't swallowed us.

I staggered to my feet and, rubbing the pain from my shoulder, steadied myself against what remained of the aft bulwark. The warship wallowed behind us, aimless, her blazing pilot's tower a testament to the accuracy of William's shot.

My men let out a chorus of cheers and laughter. *The Dolphin*, pushed by the stiff wind against her torn sails, drew steadily away. I shook my head, astonished. *Well done.*

The rabbit had blinded the hellhound.

HENRI LA GALLIENNE

Ship's Log . . . Twenty Sixth of March
0800 hours
Weather improving
Lat. 42.78 Lon. 63.67 SW

For two days *The Dolphin* rested on a quiet lake-like ocean while we mended her rigging, sewed sails and tightened shrouds. We felt excited relief. The crew regaled and embellished our encounter with the bizarre warship over every meal and during every chore. Eben, however, did not share the rest of my crew's elation over our triumph and talked of little else but returning home. He had grown disillusioned with the sea. I could hardly blame him. Nothing in his schoolbooks prepared him for a clash with an iron warship.

My brother sat in the lifeboat hanging from the aft davits, staring at the swells with obvious trepidation. He long forgot the excitement of taking his first sea venture with me. And he had yet to see his precious sunset or sunrise at sea, only the deep black of night lighten to a filthy gray.

Alas, my brother lacked the spirit of adventure so indelibly a part of my soul. He is a good student and grasps modern seamanship quickly, but he prefers problems with tidy solutions. This run has taught him that the sea's angry moods and dark secrets are beyond any man's control, and he fears anything he could not predict with mathematical certainty. I suspect this heartless ocean frightened him terribly, yet he would admit nothing of the sort to me.

To defend himself against this strange and hostile world, he took a knife from the galley and made it a formidable weapon by weighting its handle and sharpening both sides of its blade to obsession. But I doubted he would find the courage to use it. No, my brother would be happy once again only when we put *The Dolphin* on a course back to Potters Bay.

Several unexplainable events about this journey trouble me deeply. I am convinced Myles is here with me, perhaps by my side this very moment. I can sense his world beyond the grave as though I am a part of it. To my utter frustration, however, I cannot speak to him. And what am I to make of the awful screaming that accosted me without substance or source? I cannot forget the looks from my crew when I heard the shrieks of children as their young souls crossed over to the world of the dead. The eyes of my comrades betrayed alarm for their safety as a result of my going mad.

Perhaps I have, and they are indeed in danger.

— A.F.

* * *

"We should return to the Bay and tell Uncle about the iron warship," Eben said for perhaps the twentieth time since the attack. He leaned over the rail to sharpen his knife on a whetstone, while I sat with my back propped against the bulwark, sketching Vanessa's likeness in the back of my ship's log. I could not capture her smile, only an expression of resigned sadness that reminded me of the afternoon she told me she was with child.

We were in the forest far from the Bay, walking hand in hand beneath a row of tall oaks. A perfect day. I could smell the autumn scent in her wavy auburn hair as we walked away the morning, neither saying a word. Then she stopped by a fallen tree, sat down and beckoned me to sit beside her.

Vanessa, her expression sad, her blue eyes downcast, said it quickly, letting it out like a desperate breath she could no longer hold. "I'm carrying your child."

The forest grew quiet. For a moment neither of us moved as my world came to a halt. She feared my reaction, feared that I might leave her. Nothing, of course, could be farther from what I felt. Her revelation had a powerful effect on me, intensifying my love for her.

I broke into a broad smile and took her hand. "I give you my word that we will be together always—a family."

"What if the warship is out there just beyond the horizon?" Eben said. "We should warn Uncle."

His voice roused me from my thoughts during the brief respite of this brilliant blue morning. I needed time to think—some peace to ponder the extraordinary events of the past two days.

"What if we're being watched at this moment?" he pressed, glowering at me. "How long are we going to just sit out here?"

"Until this ship is mended," I said, my tone short.

"When will that be?"

"Soon—perhaps we'll raise the mainsail by nightfall."

"What if we're attacked before then?"

"Then we'll fight again."

"What about Uncle?"

I closed the logbook with a snap. "Please, Ebby."

Eben ceased sharpening his blade. "You think she's dead, don't you?"

Do I look so grim? I shook my head. "I know she's alive and wishes me to find her. You must trust me on this." I paused, considering the limits of my candor with him. I supposed he deserved to know everything. "I haven't told you about my visions."

Eben looked at me, curious. "Visions?"

"I don't know how I come by them, or what they mean, but I dare not ignore them. They are as real as anything my eyes can see and my ears can hear. An entity not of this world is beckoning, leading me to..." I shrugged, "I don't know to what."

His skeptical eyes remained locked with mine, and I regretted broaching the subject. I couldn't blame his disbelief.

I redirected the subject. "What torments me most is I arranged for Vanessa to travel with Myles to Baltimore. When this dreadful business started, I felt the terrible emptiness of being alone again. My loneliness without her eats at me like a living thing. I need her, Ebby, not as a man needs a wife or a mistress, but as I need air to breathe. If harm comes to her—" I clenched my teeth against the rage that twisted my stomach into an unbearable knot.

"Boat off the port bow," Charles shouted.

Eben spun on his heels, the knife blade swishing as he turned.

I tossed the log book aside and jumped to the rail. "Where away?"

Charles, shading his eyes from the water's reflection, thrust a finger due east. "Yonder."

I squinted at a speck about three miles off our port beam. "How in heaven's glory did you spot her?"

The old man spat overboard. "Am I the only one who bothered to look?"

"Is it British?" asked Eben over my shoulder.

I unfastened the glass from my belt and leveled it at the speck. "Stand easy. It's not a warship." I could see arms waving, but from this distance, I couldn't discern if it was a man or a woman. "A longboat ... someone hailing us." I turned to the others with a rush of excitement. "Charles, raise our mains. Ebby, bring us about on a port tack for that boat."

The two men jumped to comply.

While my crew ran up canvas, my brother brought the schooner within easy reach of the boat. As we slipped alongside, the lone occupant—a slight man, middle-aged, wearing a plaid suit—threw us generous kisses with both hands. Williams tossed a rope to him, but the fellow could not summon the strength to climb. As he hung awkwardly against our side, Williams reached down and hauled him aboard with a quick pull of his hand.

The stranger's flushed face glowed with excitement. "*Grace a Dieu!*" he said, hugging Williams' large torso. His voice was high pitched and musical, yet masculine. I would describe him as a Frenchman approaching forty years of age, short, with a slim figure. His plaid suit was badly soiled, and a knotted bow tie hung loosely around his neck. His hair was dark and thin, and he sported a pencil mustache trimmed and waxed.

"*Monsieur le Capitaine?*" he asked me in a happy tone. I

extended my hand, but he reached past it and embraced me, resting his oily hair on my chest. He reeked of lime. "*Grace … Dieu! Grace … Dieu!*"

"Can you speak English?" I asked.

"*Excusez moi.*" He released me and said in a heavy French accent, "Yes, I can speak English very well. My name is Henri La Gallienne. I am delighted to be with you." He shook my hand with both of his.

"My name is Andrew Finsbury. You are aboard my ship, *The Dolphin.*"

"Aaaahhhh," he said, almost singing. He pirouetted as though dancing, his arms spread with full approval. "And what a *magnifique* boat you have. I will remember always how beautiful she looked when first I saw her." Then he grew still, his eyes growing dark and distressed. "I feared you would not see me and leave me out here to die."

"You can thank the eyes of that old hawk," I said, jerking a thumb at Charles. The Frenchman, his face brightening, saluted Charles in mock military fashion. Charles cleared his throat with a rasp and spat, missing the sea and decorating the rail with a rope of spittle.

"Are there others?" I asked the Frenchman.

Long lines of fatigue replaced his cheerful expression. "*Oui.* Three others. You must help them ... or they will die."

I leaned over the rail and saw blankets covering three objects on the bottom of the longboat. A putrid stench of decay drifting up from below made my stomach roll.

The little color in the Frenchman's face disappeared, and he grasped the rail for support. He stood rigid, chest heaving, sweat dripping down his pale features, and began to swoon. I made a quick grab for his arm. Williams helped me ease our visitor against a stack of canvas.

Eben gestured to our visitor's plaid suit. "On his way

to a social?"

I felt the Frenchman's rapid pulse. "He's a peculiar fellow, but who wouldn't be daft riding the North Atlantic in a lifeboat with corpses for company."

Eben, curious, glanced over the rail at the boat bobbing below. I joined him and felt an eeriness about the way it carried its cargo of death. I would swear I heard whispering from below, three distinct voices, spouting indistinct warnings up at me.

Charles slipped to my side. "Don't go down there. That boat is cursed. Sink it quickly before its restless spirits come aboard our ship and do us harm. Do it now."

Could he hear them too? "Get below and finish securing the hull," I said. Joseph also turned to look at me, his eyes wide with apprehension. "All of you get back to your repairs."

Charles took Joseph by the arm and led him away from the rail while filling his ear with whispers of ghosts.

I swung my legs over the rail.

"Andrew," Eben said, touching my arm, "listen to Charles and leave it."

I ignored him and climbed down. The longboat could carry a dozen men with supplies and oars. Every corner reeked of death—I couldn't escape it. I covered my mouth with a handkerchief and surveyed the strewn supplies, then directed my investigation to three bulging blankets with the name *Burlington* stitched into the fabric.

I drew back the blanket from the largest bundle and stared down at the leathered features of a corpse clad in a seaman's uniform. My mouth tightened. The sun had hastened decomposition. The dead man's dark, sunken eyes were rolled deep into his head, and his shrinking lips were frozen in a silent, agonized scream. His clawed hands still clutched a boat paddle, and he appeared ready to fight anyone who tried taking it from him.

Eben lowered himself into the boat and likewise covered his mouth to filter the stench. Shaking, he knelt beside me and inspected the corpse, then pointed to a black paste on the crown of its head. "His hair. There's something in his hair."

"Help me turn him over."

We lifted the corpse and dropped it face down in the bilge water like a piece of driftwood. Dried blood turned his hair into a dark paste. A large caliber bullet had shattered his skull, leaving a gaping cavity.

Eben drew back. "He's been murdered."

I covered the body and stumbled backward, tripping over a smaller bundle arranged neatly to one side of the boat. I positioned myself to block Eben's view before lifting the blanket. I stared in dismay at the corpse of a girl no more than six years old. Her flesh hadn't dried to the extent of the sailor's, suggesting she died only recently. The child's dress, sooty and burned, partially concealed her legs wrapped clumsily in gauze and blackened with dried blood. She held against her chest the remains of a kitten that appeared to have been dead for some time. She appeared gently asleep. Her innocent expression looked so peaceful I expected her to wake and reach for me.

I replaced the blanket over the child. There was little dignity for the corpses laying with rubbish on the bottom of a lost boat. How could this tragedy have been allowed to happen?

Eben pulled the blanket aside from the last bundle and stared for several moments. Finally, he dropped the blanket and turned away. "I—I think it's a man. The body is badly burned."

I let my mind sift through the many questions this boat posed. Were there other boats like this out there?

Other corpses?

"There's a little rice and hardtack left," Eben said. "La Gallienne must have eaten well. And what's this?" He felt through the contents of a small carton. "A medical kit, everything you might need ... but nothing has been touched. Burn dressing, bandages, sulfur..." Eben hurled the carton to the bottom of the boat and shouted, "Why didn't he treat these people?"

"They were already dead."

"Then why leave them in this deplorable state? Why didn't he have the decency to bury them at sea?"

I stood and grabbed his shoulder. "La Gallienne is no seaman. How would you behave if you shared a boat with corpses, perhaps family members, not knowing if today you would join them? To him, these people are still alive."

Eben, his eyes angry, said nothing more. In spite of the chilled air, trickles of sweat rolled down my temples as I stared at a group of holes in the boat's hull.

I knelt and ran my fingers over the bow's shattered wood. "Bullet holes. La Gallienne is fortunate these planks held together."

Eben began gathering the few remaining supplies.

I had seen enough. "Leave everything." I grabbed the rope and climbed aboard the schooner. Charles was waiting for us at the rail. "Fetch some wine."

Old Charles withdrew from his sea jacket a crude vial filled with a yellowish liquid and passed it to me.

I uncorked the flask and sniffed its contents. The strong vapors burned my nostrils.

"French wine," Charles said.

I waved the vial under the Frenchman's nose. He opened his eyes and gasped, *"Mon Dieu."*

"Drink this," I said, forcing the tip of the bottle between his lips.

The Frenchman opened his mouth slightly, swallowed several drops and then exploded with a coughing fit. When his coughing subsided, he managed, "That is very good. You are a generous host."

He snatched the bottle from me and took several swallows before expelling another deep cough. I pulled the bottle from him and passed it back to Charles. "How long were you adrift?"

The Frenchman stared at me as though in a daze, and then closed his eyes. "I suffered in hell for two days, *monsieur*. Our ship was attacked during a storm by men who held no value for human life. Countless good people were murdered. They destroyed our ship." When his eyes opened, they were full of rage. "Our merchant ship had no armaments. I am an accountant by trade and have not harmed a man in my life. But I have sworn to the souls of my lost family that I will hunt and kill the men who did this."

Exhausted, his eyes rolled back in his head and he fell against the canvas, again unconscious. A light slap on his face and a firm shake failed to revive him. Charles thrust his bottle at me, but I waved it away.

"Take him to my bunk," I said.

Williams and Charles lifted the Frenchman by his arms and carried him below.

I said to Eben, "Let him rest. But I want some answers by nightfall."

"What about the longboat?"

I leaned over the rail and stiffened. The blankets were moving as though the restless bodies beneath were struggling to rise. The sight terrified me.

Eben noted my distress and attempted to move to my side for a look. A quick hand pushed him back.

"I'm sinking this boat immediately."

THE *BURLINGTON*

1900 hours
Weather calm

We were underway on a course back to Potters Bay before Henri La Gallienne woke from his exhaustion some twelve hours after coming aboard. When I looked in on him in my cabin that evening, he showed fine spirits, having just finished a hearty dinner of boiled beef strips, bread and cheese. His face held some color, and he offered a smile to everyone.

"Another, please," said La Gallienne, passing his tin cup to Eben. My brother obliged the Frenchman with a second cup of Bordeaux from my trunk.

Old Charles, clad in a well-traveled steward's apron, stood over his small oil-burning stove, which he set up on my desk to ensure our guest had warm food and ample hot coffee. The Frenchman, however, reserved his hearty appetite for my red wine.

"A toast, *Messieurs*," he said, raising his cup. "To *The Dolphin* and her captain and crew. There is not a grander ship on all the seas."

La Gallienne, his eyes gleaming, indulged himself with several long swallows. Eben, Charles and I each found a cup and shared the toast with our guest.

"Henri," I said, easing onto the bunk beside him, "we're eager to know what happened to the *Burlington*. We saw her founder but were unable to render assistance. We found no survivors. Tell us."

The Frenchman's smile faded, and he aged ten years as I watched. The light from the cabin's lanterns etched deep lines on his face and made it look mask-like—the mask of an old and bitter man. He raised the cup to his lips and finished the wine in a single swallow. I refilled his cup, and he nodded his gratitude.

"*Capitaine*," he said, finally, "a fire broke out aboard the *Burlington*."

After another long swallow, he looked less disturbed and seemed ready to talk. "I was taking my wife and son to a new life in America, a voyage we planned for many years. Four days after leaving Portsmouth, lime stored below deck ignited and turned the ship into an unbearable hell. Thick smoke billowed everywhere, and I could not open my burning eyes."

I stared over my cup at the Frenchman as he rose and began pacing, agitated, distressed to relive the horror.

"The fire spread quickly, and I found a place for my wife and son above deck next to a small boat in the event we were ordered to leave the ship. All the men came forward to help throw the dangerous cargo into the sea. I had no choice but to leave my family and help where I could. But we labored in vain as the fire spread to every deck."

Charles interrupted with an apologetic cough. "Then the captain should be faulted for carrying dangerous cargo."

The Frenchman shook his head. "I do not believe *Capitaine* Alberts knew of the lime aboard."

Charles shot him a queer look. "The captain didn't

know the contents of his cargo hold?"

"The lime was disguised in wine casks," said La Gallienne, raising his cup. "*Capitaine* Alberts had been de-
ceived."

"Do you recall the name of the winery?" I pressed.

"I will never forget it. The casks were from the cellars
of Dom Garrone of France."

He finished his wine and then pointed for another
with a trembling finger. I emptied the bottle into his cup.

"Then we came under attack," he continued. "Please
forgive my memory ... everything happened very quickly.
Explosions rocked the ship—I cannot recall how many—
and injured men and women lay strewn across the deck,
screaming and calling for help. Dazed passengers searched
in vain for their families. I crawled to the rail and looked
out across the sea. What I saw by the fading daylight
nearly stopped my heart. The explosions came from
cannon fire from a large ship, an evil vessel as black as the
night.

"The ship's decks opened, and men came forth to at-
tach cables and chains to the *Burlington*. They meant to
tow her. Farther out to sea, I saw yet another monster ship
standing sentinel behind us. There were two of them. We
could not escape. Even now when I close my eyes, I see
those twin black devils towing us into the heart of the
storm and to our deaths."

La Gallienne, his face pale, sat down heavily on the
bunk and raised the trembling tin cup to his lips. But it
was empty. He spotted the empty bottle on my desk and
then gave me the sad, deprived look. I withdrew another
bottle from my trunk, removed the cork with my knife
and filled his cup. La Gallienne downed its contents in
two swallows, which brought some color back into his
cheeks.

He sat staring at his cup for a moment before continuing. "Pirates descended into the ship's hold and brought up many trunks, which they transferred to their vessel. Other pirates brandishing guns rounded up the passengers and selected several women—those who were to live—and herded them like goats to their ship. They also demanded that we surrender our children. They were looking for a child—a boy."

"A boy?" I interrupted, puzzled. "What boy?"

"I cannot say. Nor do I believe they found the young man they were seeking. The others suffered a terrible slaughter. The pirates shot the ship's crewmen on sight, including *Capitaine* Alberts. Those of us who remained— the older men and women and the very young—were shot or left to die with the ship.

"I knew then that God chose to save me. The spreading fire forced our attackers to abandon their work below deck, and everyone, even the pirates, ran to save themselves. There were flames everywhere. The smoke alone killed many.

"I will never know what became of my wife and son. I ran to the spot where I left them, but the place was a wall of flames. I could not pass. I prepared to jump overboard in a desperate effort to save myself. But I regained my senses when I saw two people attempting to lower one of the lifeboats. A seaman who managed to elude his captors shouted orders to an older man who could not manage the heavy ropes. A small girl I assumed was his family, cried at his side. She clutched a frightened kitten to her chest.

"I hurried to help and to have a place in their boat. What else could I do? I took the rope from the man, pretending to know how to lower such a boat. I mishandled the lines and caused the longboat to fall into the sea and almost sink. The sailor shouted at me, and I am certain he would have struck me down if the situation been less desperate. But this was not a time for reprimand. He had little choice but to climb over the rail and dive into the sea before the boat was lost. The sailor fought the difficult waves and managed to climb aboard the boat where he struggled to control its movements with a paddle.

"I jumped next, not knowing how I would survive. The cold water eagerly swept me under waves that were like mountains. I would have drowned had I not found a paddle near my face. I grabbed desperately for it. The seaman pulled me into the boat, and I felt grateful to be alive.

"I heard shouting above us—the fire had trapped the man and the girl. I will never forget their screams as the poor man grabbed the child and struggled to hold her above the flames. The sailor shouted for the man to jump. But the fire terrified him, and he could not bring himself to climb over the rail. He did, at last, throw the child to us. The seaman and I both jumped up at once to catch her. The sailor missed. I only caught the poor girl's arm, allowing her full weight to hit the bottom of our boat. Both her legs broke in the fall."

Eben, seated at my desk, turned away from us and I thought he would begin sobbing. Charles just shook his head.

"The screams of the older gentleman trapped above us filled the night," La Gallienne continued. "I wished to stop my ears as the fire consumed him. Finally, he fell over the rail and tumbled like a torch into the sea behind us. The noble sailor dove into the water and brought the man aboard our little craft. We laid him on the bottom of the boat, but the fire had ravaged him beyond our help.

The shock proved fatal. I heard his final moan, and then he grew still.

"What remained of the *Burlington* burned with great fury while it moved away from us. As if fate had not been cruel enough, the pirates discovered our escape. The sea around us splashed with bullets from men aboard one of the black ships. The sailor rowed with all his strength to put distance between the warships. I hid on the floor next to the poor woman. Eventually, the shooting stopped as the darkness and high waves cloaked our escape.

"When I raised my head later, the *Burlington* appeared as a distant flare on the dark sea. The sailor who saved my life sat grasping a paddle, his head bent forward between his knees. He had been unlucky. A bullet shattered his skull.

"I attended to the girl. Her legs were twisted, and I did not know what to do with the splintered ends of red-and-white bone sticking through her thighs. Her eyes told me of her pain and her terror, and she would not stop trembling. The child found comfort holding the cat, which she had crushed to death against her chest.

"I watched our burning ship grow ever dimmer. After a time, the light grew brighter and then vanished, leaving nothing but the black sea. I heard thunder, an explosion, *Messieurs*. I knew the ship was at last out of the hands of her tormentors.

"I prayed throughout the night. By morning, God saw fit to quiet the waves. But the poor girl suffered terribly until death took her innocent soul last night. I wept bitterly for her. I trusted the mercy of our Father, and today he delivered me safely into your hands. For that blessing, I will be forever grateful."

Henri La Gallienne sat staring at his partially filled cup of wine, while Eben sat with his head bowed, hiding a sagging face. Even the unflappable Charles, his face pale, appeared affected by the Frenchman's story.

"Henri," I said, breaking the cabin's somber silence, "tell me more about the trunks taken from the ship's hold."

The Frenchman waved away my request, wishing to forgo more questions.

"Please. We need to know every detail."

Eben touched my arm to spare La Gallienne further inquiry, but I shrugged off his hand.

The Frenchman looked timidly at me, and I saw a tear roll down his flushed cheek. His voice when he spoke came in sobs. "*Capitaine* Finsbury, I have told you everything. There is no more I can say."

I moved closer to him. "My fiancé was lost when a merchant brigantine very much like the *Burlington* was destroyed. Other ships have vanished as well. Her life and perhaps the lives of others depend on what you can tell me. I must know every detail."

The Frenchman wiped his eyes with the sleeve of his plaid jacket and nodded. "Of course … I will tell you whatever I can."

I poured our guest another cup of wine and started to fill my cup as well, but thought better of it. I set the bottle aside.

"Tell me more about those trunks."

"*Capitaine* Finsbury, the trunks were perhaps one meter long, and half that high and wide." He set down his cup, freeing both hands to show me the size. "They must have weighed considerably—two pirates were required to carry each trunk with effort. Their contents could not have been delicate, for the pirates cared little if the trunks were dropped or mishandled."

"Gold can take its share of bumps," I said.

The mention of gold brought an alert sparkle to everyone's eyes. Charles gave a short laugh. "You mean we might profit from this run?"

"It belongs to Her Majesty," I said.

"Then the motive is obvious," said Eben, excited. "They were after this gold."

I turned back to the Frenchman. "What can you tell me about the men who sank the *Burlington?*"

La Gallienne shook his head grimly. "They were disciplined like soldiers, and prepared for any event, even the fire."

"Because they set the fire," I said.

The others watched me curiously.

"These pirates concealed the lime in wine casks before the voyage began," I said. "They intended to disable the vessel before commandeering it. Their only blunder was timing—they allowed the ship to burn out of control before they could unload the last of the trunks."

"But who brought the lime aboard?" Eben asked.

"Perhaps one of the passengers, an agent working for these pirates." I pressed La Gallienne further. "Could you deduce the nationality of these men?"

The Frenchman shifted uncomfortably in his chair. "They were ruthless barbarians—men of no nation."

"Iron warships are not the sort of items pirates come by easily. Did they speak English?"

Tears gathered in La Gallienne's eyes, and he hid his face in his hands. "I am ashamed to say it."

"What?" I demanded.

"They ... were Frenchmen." He looked at me with eyes wide and red. "Men of my own country."

An awkward silence followed, broken only by the even creaking of the ship.

"I am afraid this incident will lead to a war between

our countries," he sobbed. "I do not wish to be a part of that."

"Henri," I said slowly, "the warship showed no flag." I squeezed his shoulder and tried to sound optimistic. "These men took great care to make the ship's sinking appear as a natural sea disaster—hardly a provocation for war. I am convinced that our enemy is a very private navy whose motive is profit, not war." I leaned forward and stared into La Gallienne's eyes. "I must know where they went. Can you remember anything that might help me?"

The Frenchman squirmed in his seat. "The pirates made no secret of it. I heard one of them utter a Spanish name. Lone ... Leone. When one of the pirates carried a woman passenger to his ship, he said to her, 'You and I will become great lovers before we reach Saint Lone.'"

"Sierra Leone," Charles corrected him.

La Gallienne slapped the mattress and sprang from the bunk. "Yes. Sierra Leone." The excitement in his voice grew. "The pirate said Sierra Leone!"

I looked at Charles. "You know this place?"

The old seaman nodded. "You'll need a map of Africa."

"Africa? Are you certain?"

"Quite. Sierra Leone is on the Grain Coast of Africa, above the Gulf of Guinea. Back in the fifties, we spent many nights anchored in the port of Freetown, hiding and waiting until it was safe to load slaves aboard our clipper."

As the old man spoke, I retrieved a satchel of charts from my trunk and flattened a map of Africa over the bunk. It took me a moment to find a region along the western coast marked Sierra Leone.

"What do you know about this place?" I asked the old mate.

Charles sat in the desk's chair and rocked it back

against the wall. "Doesn't have the class of The Bay, but it does have its share of good native whores." He grinned for the first time since La Gallienne began his story. "Freetown once was a British settlement run by Negroes freed by the slaving squadron. We called that damned region the white man's grave. The Lord in his wisdom saw fit to infest that part of the world with enough mosquitoes, malaria and yellow fever to prevent the likes of Europeans from settling there. If you fell sick in Africa, there were no hospitals, no doctors, no nurses. Within days of arriving, the younger men amongst us became acquainted with delirium, vomiting and dysentery. Still, we persisted in visiting for economic reasons until the territory fell under French rule."

"French rule," I noted. "That fits."

"Why in God's glory would you visit such a place?" Eben asked the old man.

Charles coughed up some phlegm and spat it into his apron. "When I was still a teen I sailed with Captain Philip McCord aboard the merchant clipper *The Brooks*. We put in at Freetown for supplies and whatever trading we could arrange with the British squadron. Captain McCord was the shrewdest bastard ever to sail a clipper. He could always find a good deal on 'blackfish oil.'"

Eben looked at him questioningly.

"That's what we called the Negroes," he explained. "And while the captain attended to his trading, the rest of us would be up to our peckers in African whores."

Charles smiled without humor. "McCord made a nice profit off any slaver who wanted to unload his cargo quickly. We made money in that port—a lot more when slaving became illegal, which raised prices and brought out the best slavers. McCord was the best."

"Could a warship dock unnoticed along that coastline?" I said, leading the old man back to my interest.

He smiled, rocking his chair back and forth. "No doubt. There are hundreds of abandoned prison castles and barracoons scattered up and down the Grain Coast. Any one of 'em would make a fine camp for your pirates. A slaver always took twice the number of human cargo he needed; he would lose half during the voyage. But the jungle's the worst of it—full of puff adders and mambas." He winked at Eben. "Ever see a mamba, boy? We called 'em 'three steps' 'cause after a bite that's how far you got before dropping dead. We always slept with our legs apart so's we weren't swallowed whole by a python—"

"What an ideal arrangement," I said, silencing Charles. "A navy of iron warships operating out of a port in Africa where the environment is unsuitable for the likes of Europeans. But who are these men?"

No one offered an answer.

I slapped the satchel hard against the mattress, causing the others to jump. "The Atlantic slave trade isn't dead—in fact, it's very much alive. Now it's white slavery, and they're taking the women and children." I thought of Vanessa, fair and beautiful, dressed in bright colors. If she had become an object of barter and trade—

The knot of rage in the bottom of my stomach tightened again.

Charles brought his hands together with a crack. "Chief, every good seaman should visit Africa at least once in his youth."

"I appreciate your support," I said, "but I can't ask you to go."

Charles scowled. "We've got to go. His story gives us our best chance of finding your lady. No one will expect the likes of us showing up in Freetown. I'm sure the others will want to go."

I looked at Eben. "What do you say?"

My brother lowered his eyes, trying to conceal his reservations about the idea. But he nodded, only for Vanessa's sake, I'm sure.

I turned to La Gallienne. "I can't take you back to England. At least not yet."

The Frenchman bobbed his head. "No one wants justice for what has happened more than I. I will go with you."

I stood with a swell of urgency. "Charles, tell the others I'm plotting a course to Africa." I turned to La Gallienne. "Henri, you may use my cabin tonight. I won't be needing a bunk."

FREETOWN

Ninth of April
0800 hours
Weather Clear & Hot

We reached the African coast at Cape Verde in eight days and sailed south, arriving at the port of Freetown in Sierra Leone in a fortnight. I will never forget my first impression of that quiet village. The place looked charming enough at a distance and offered few visible clues to its dark past. The gently sloping hills sweeping down to satin white beaches were draped in the richest green foliage and trimmed with quaint straw-roofed dwellings and villas. A cluster of fishing canoes gliding towards the fertile inshore waters completed a picture of naive serenity.

The Dolphin slipped past a band of canoes, attracting scowls from the black watermen visibly annoyed by the arrival of our larger vessel. Perhaps our presence meant bad luck for their sea harvest. I offered them a smart salute as we swept past them.

"Sailing vessels aren't much use to the natives down here," said Charles at my elbow. "Can't take them inland through the river brush."

My gaze found a European clipper anchored next to a

stone jetty, notably out of place among the smaller craft. "What do you make of that?" I asked, pointing.

The glare off the morning water narrowed Charles' eyes to thin slits. "Probably carrying tobacco. A clipper anchored here four decades ago meant black human cargo. Yet there she sits just like in the old days." He sported a grin. "Her crew's more'n likely ashore wallowing in sweet whores."

The village may have held a certain charm from a distance, but at close quarters I found little to admire. We anchored next to a stone jetty strewn with decaying fish culled from watermen catches. The dock stench nearly suffocated us. But the smell was the least of my concerns—a group of black fishermen with resentful stares gathered on the jetty to watch us moor. We were not welcome here. I thought it best not to leave *The Dolphin* unattended and ordered Williams and Joseph to stay aboard while Charles, Eben and I scouted the settlement.

"This place smells worse than anything Porter dragged up from the bottom," said Eben, squashing a bloated fish carcass with his boot as he stepped ashore. "How can anyone work here?"

"Forget the smell," Charles said. "Be mindful of the swindlers who make a living cheating new faces. Whatever happens, stay cheerful and walk with purpose." He slapped Eben's shoulder hard. "A wide-eyed and confused-looking boy will draw hustlers like sharks to a bloody goose's ass."

I fanned the heat from my face with a ludicrous straw hat Williams loaned me. "We'll stay together."

"What exactly are we looking for, Andrew?" Eben asked.

I covered my head with the hat, caring little how foolish it made me look. I welcomed its shade. "Anything that doesn't belong here."

We walked to the heart of the settlement by way of a clay road barely wide enough to allow a cart to pass. What once served as a resettlement base for Negro men, women and children freed by the Atlantic slaving squadron, lay in squalor. We found evidence of poverty everywhere, with residents outnumbering the wretched huts ten to one. Most troubling were the scores of children squatting in the roadside garbage, rummaging for anything that would keep them alive for one more day. I wondered how many of them would succumb to disease in short order.

We hadn't walked far when I sensed activity behind us and glanced over my shoulder. A group of leprous beggars had gathered about twenty paces back, their hunched and robed bodies hobbling after us most determinedly, desperate for anything we could give them.

Charles jabbed me with his elbow. "Our welcoming committee."

"What do we do?" Eben asked, his eyes large and his voice anxious.

I chanced another glance behind and stared, dumbfounded. These were no longer beggars. They bore the contorted faces of demons with white eyes and melting skin. The noise pouring from their elongated jaws was the wail of the dead. What was this madness of mine?

I turned and quickened my pace to stay well ahead of them. "Let's get on with it."

A derelict sitting on a low wall, notable as the first Caucasian we encountered this morning, could not contain his amusement as we passed and exploded a high-pitched giggle. I didn't like that dark, unsettled look in his eyes.

"Are you Her Majesty's escort?" he asked us, his speech British. When none of us responded, he blurted, "The queen is waiting for you at Excelsior."

I stared at him, puzzled. "What are you saying?"

"Listen, you quirk," Charles said, pushing in front of me. "You can do us a favor by pointing the way to the local militia."

He thrust a bony finger into Charles' face and hissed, "Excelsior."

I glanced back at the hobbling group of lepers. Gone were the demons—they were anxious beggars again.

"They want your balls," the fellow said, grinning at me. "The testicles of a foreigner will forever change a poor man's luck. Let me show you." He stood, unfastened his pants and dropped them to his ankles. The man was a eunuch. "You see what he bloody did to me? The beggar who took them is now a wealthy solicitor in Paris." He doubled over, racked with hysterical laughter. The poor man was hopelessly mad. Then his eyes grew pure white, and the skin on his face sagged as though the skin had detached from the bone. "Beware of his messengers."

I peered into the twin white orbs that had once been eyes and saw something stirring there, shadows of faces gazing back at me. An illusion? Charles and Eben saw none of this and pulled me onward.

We spent the morning scouting the settlement and found nothing to suggest that this region served as a haven for wealthy pirates with ironclads or otherwise. Wretched, rotting and unimpressive, Freetown was a maze of narrow, randomly intersecting alleys stuffed with a chaotic mix of donkey-drawn wagons, grass-roofed huts and a few produce carts. We found two card parlors and several bordellos. Nowhere did I see a hotel. We did, however, find a church that doubled as a telegraph station.

By noon the rising heat had evaporated the fluids from

our bodies along with the last of our hope.

"There's nothing here that could interest the civilized world," Charles said, wiping the sweat from his hair. "We're chasing our tails. What a waste."

La Gallienne's fascinating story a fortnight ago thus far yielded nothing. However, I wasn't ready to concede the futility of our visit here. I wanted to see more. We turned down a sunless street on our way back to the pier and passed a sailor—a white man dressed for a European merchant vessel—and watched him enter a two-story plaster building, the only brothel in town that advertised ale. A seaman from the clipper anchored at the pier, I wondered? I jerked Charles to a stop and pointed to the sign above the establishment's door: *Excelsior.*

Charles lifted his bushy eyebrows. "We've earned a pint before heading back."

Eben refused to join us. "This place frightens me," he said. "You're both daft. I'm going back to the schooner."

I pointed out the church with its telegraph service at the end of the thoroughfare. "I'm charging you with getting off a message to Uncle. Tell him our present whereabouts and the sinking of the *Burlington.*" I pressed twin pound notes into Eben's palm. "Tell him to expect another telegraph tomorrow."

My brother, impressed by his sudden wealth, ran off to carry out my instructions.

Charles and I followed the sailor into the brothel, marveling how the old structure still stood after decades of neglect in this raw climate. The first level was a common barroom, dark and cool and quiet, furnished with simple tables and chairs. The European sailor, three parts drunk already, shouted something in French on his way to the bar. Several black patrons, sedated under a haze of opium, were slumped at the bar, oblivious to the arrival of the clamorous jack. A few black men sat at the tables, content in their stupor.

I removed my straw hat, laid it on an unoccupied table by the door and followed Charles. A powerfully built Negro behind the bar picked his teeth with a nail while watching us approach. There were also women here—whores to relieve the patrons of whatever currency they had not handed over to the barman. Most of the women were black with thick, woolly hair and skin like oiled mahogany. I also noted an Asian, Caucasian and Latin among the lot, a fitting mix to entertain travelers from most ports.

Business must have been slow today, for we no sooner entered when two of the Negro women—resplendent in bright robes—approached us with broad smiles and eager eyes. To them, we represented two farthings each. The women exchanged mischievous grins. On cue, they unwrapped the tops of their outfits, allowing the fabric to drop to their hips, exposing nude torsos. They each cupped their voluminous breasts and offered them to us, like produce merchants with their fruits.

Charles, charmed by their vulgar display, gave each of them his most engaging grin, minus several teeth, while his eager eyes explored their every curve. The two half-nude women responded to his interest, each taking one of his arms in a mock tug of war.

Charles, grinning, said to me, "They always sense when a great lover enters a room."

I gave his shoulder a slap. "You mean they'll do anything for a farthing."

I stepped to the bar and slid next to the French sailor. He was making quite a scene, laughing loudly and passing a brandy bottle among the bar's women. When the bottle came back to him, he downed an impossibly long swallow and then let the liquor flow freely over his face while pretending to scrub himself with an imaginary brush—a mime bather. The women laughed and applauded him like children.

"What are you drinking?" asked the large barman. His speech sounded American.

I looked up into a pair of hard, dark eyes that were belligerently on guard. "You speak English." A statement rather than a question.

The barman's eyes narrowed while he scrutinized me. "Your daddy taught you to be real observant." His tone was angry, mocking, his words clipped unsociably short.

I spotted the casks behind the bar. Each had the name of a winery stamped on its side: *Dom Garrone.* I recalled La Gallienne's mention of similarly labeled kegs filled with lime aboard the *Burlington*. I did my best to hide my keen interest. "I'll have an ale." I jerked a thumb at Charles. "And one for my friend, too. Draw one for yourself, if you're thirsty."

"I'm always thirsty," he said in that mocking tone. The barman returned with two ales, took my pound-sterling note and never returned. This would be the most expensive brew I ever tasted.

I turned my attention to the sailor, a balding man with a wart on his left eyelid. He paused in his merriment long enough to cast a glance at me.

I raised my stein to him and toasted, "To the taste of ale so far from home." I drained off half my brew, disappointingly flat.

The seaman's face grew dark. *"Pourquoi tu m'embêtes?"* he demanded, discharging a gust of stale rum into my face.

I again raised my stein to the seaman. "My name is Finsbury, a fellow sailor who wishes to buy you a drink."

Charles offered an awkward translation while using his free hand to point out the seaman's near-empty bottle. The sailor's suspicious gaze shifted from Charles to me. Finally, his stone expression evaporated into a sly smile. He thrust the remainder of his bottle at me.

Obliging, I swirled the dark liquid, raised the bottle to my lips and took a cautious sip. I noted a foul trace of disinfectant in the brew, suggesting it had been doctored to extend its life. The women watched in silence, awaiting my reaction. I hid my disgust under a forced grin and chased the rot with the remainder of my ale. The sailor burped, unimpressed. The whores giggled teasingly.

Charles snatched the bottle from me, let out a lively hoot and downed the last swallow. His face contorted and he exploded a life-saving cough, spraying the bottom of one of his companion's robe. "Damn piss."

The woman reared back in anger, her breasts bouncing, and stared unbelievingly at the hem of her outfit decorated with Charles' spittle. The sailor's head flew back and out came a piercing shriek of laughter. The women drew up the fabric over their breasts and stomped off in tandem across the bordello. Charles bolted after them, shouting apologies between fits of coughing. He bounded up a staircase at the far end of the room and vanished.

The sailor turned to an Asian woman in his party. He reached beneath her sheer top and scooped out a drooping white globe of a breast. She giggled deliciously. He pulled her into his arms and ran his hand down the back of her dress, stopping to squeeze her lean bottom. She let out a pealing laugh. The sailor uttered his approval.

"He is a merchant seaman from the clipper ship *The Raven*," came a low, feminine voice with a distinct Spanish accent.

I turned and looked down into the luminous brown

eyes of a woman dressed in a white robe, standing apart from the sailor's party. I found her instantly attractive. I assumed she was Latin by her almond complexion, elegant nose and dark eyes that seemed to peer deep into my soul. Her feet were bare, and she wore her black hair pulled back and braided into a crown. A look of sadness marred her exotic beauty.

She lowered her eyes. "My name is Gabrielle."

"Tell me you don't work in this hell hole."

She turned her head as though ashamed and said nothing.

"Forgive me," I said, regretting my question. I glanced at the barman, who made no secret of watching my every move, and then at the sailor, who held the Asian woman locked in a steamy embrace.

"Do not harass the sailor," Gabrielle warned me. "His ship is anchored here only long enough to collect water and load its cargo. Then it will leave for South America."

"Why are you telling me this?" I asked.

She forced a smile—such a beautiful face—and said, "You are not like the others who come here. I see loneliness in your heart. You have lost someone very dear to you?"

I felt the barman's eyes boring into the back of my neck and, as we talked, he positioned himself so as not to miss a word. I touched her chin. "You can read me very well."

"Come." She took my hand and gave it a gentle tug. "I wish to show you something."

Gabrielle led me across the barroom and up a flight of steps to the second level of the brothel. I went with her readily. She knocked twice on the door at the top of the stairway. A short, fat black man smoking a cigarette cracked open the door and locked his suspicious eyes on me. The oppressive scent of heavy perfume laced with burnt hashish drifted through the opened doorway. Gabrielle placed her right hand over her heart and, bowing slightly, intoned, *"Salaamu 'aleikum."*

The doorman bowed respectfully and allowed us to proceed down a dim hallway. I paused by the first door and heard someone crying within, a woman, her voice pained and desperate. Gabrielle pulled me away, and we continued down the hallway. I did not care for this place. I feared a sordid madman consumed with liquor would stagger from one of these rooms and find perverse pleasure in slicing my throat. Where was Charles? I imagined him bound to a chair with his throat open from ear to ear.

"Charles?" I called.

Gabrielle placed a finger on my lips. "You must be quiet."

She led me to another door and knocked once before entering. The room's lone window was boarded, rendering the place a permanent night. A willowy old woman of Spanish descent dressed in black sat at a small table in the center of the musty room. The table's candle, planted in the neck of an ancient wine bottle, provided just enough light to see several colorful cards laid out before her. The old woman did not look up as we entered, and, in fact, she appeared asleep. Gabrielle directed me to a chair opposite her. I obliged and sat, never taking my eyes off the woman.

Gabrielle placed her hands upon the woman's frail shoulders and said to her, "Mamma, this man has a kind heart and has come a long way. His soul is in pain. Please help him."

The withered woman raised her head and revealed eyes that were two white globes without irises or pupils. She lowered her head again and extended a bony hand from the sleeve of her black gown.

"She must touch you," Gabrielle said.

I took the woman's hand, cold and callused and firm. The woman fidgeted, as though my touch caused her discomfort. Her breathing became deep and labored, her look tormented, and I regretted that I somehow caused her pain. A tear spilled from the corner of one of her sightless eyes and, nodding, she let out short gasps as though struggling to breathe. Something frightened her. Me?

Gabrielle squeezed the woman's shoulders. "Tell him what you see, mamma."

"You have brought him here," she said to me, her voice strained and coarse. "The boy whose spirit has haunted me all these years, taking refuge in my dreams— you have brought him here at last."

The room felt cold. I looked at Gabrielle for an explanation, but her eyes remained fixed on the candle. I recalled La Gallienne's story—the pirates were searching for a boy. What boy?

"You have begun a great journey," the old woman said to me. "I see … I see … black canyons and crimson water … deep forests with trees as tall as mountains…" Her breathing became more labored, her fear building. "Evil places … hungry places … and very dangerous. It is the only way, the only path. You must protect the boy … see that he finishes his journey … fulfills his destiny." Tears flowed down her cheeks' deep grooves and collected in a tenuous reservoir under her nose.

"What about my Vanessa?" I asked. "I must find her."

The old woman shook her head, her expression drawn. "She has led you here, and now her purpose is finished. You cannot help her."

Cannot help her? She spewed rubbish. I shouted at Gabrielle, "I will *not* abandon her."

Gabrielle did not move. She kept her eyes fixed on the candle, avoiding my gaze.

"His minions are everywhere," the old woman warned. "He set a trap for you. His soldiers are stronger than you, but not as smart. He intends to imprison you, keep your body in chains until it's old and useless and can do him no harm. Don't let him seize you. Be swifter than his minions, more clever than he."

"Who?" I asked, reining back my temper. "Where can I find this man?"

She shook her head. "He is no man. He is a beast—a demon. Beware of his messengers of life and death."

Here it was again—"messengers"—obviously the raving of unstable minds. I managed a snort of disdain. My skeptical grin faded when my eyes fell upon the candle, its glow highlighting the hollows of the old woman's face. The flame fluttered as though caught in a draft, yet no breeze could enter this boarded room. I saw movement within the flame. And faces—vivid faces. I sat mesmerized and allowed the image to fill my eyes until I saw a garden, the same splendid place where I saw Myles sitting with a child. He came again, walking to greet me. With him were my brother and the rest of my crew. I looked at the old woman and said slowly, "Where do these images come from?"

She directed her opalescent eyes at me. "From a place where a man no longer needs a vessel of flesh and blood."

"I don't understand."

"It is the world of the dead."

What sort of ruse had I fallen for? I stumbled backward, spilling my chair in a bid to be rid of her. My growing unease, coupled with the strange visions, sent a tremor through me. I wanted to be rid of this place, be rid of these people.

I returned to the hallway and marched down the corridor. *"Charles."*

I heard a groan from behind the last door followed by irregular gasping. I froze at the thought of Charles dying. The groan came again, much louder—Charles' voice.

I jammed my boot against the door, splitting the fixture down the middle. Another kicked smashed the planks inward. I stood at the edge of the gloom as a waft of heavy perfume swept passed me. Several figures on a bed made no attempt to move. Perhaps they couldn't move. Perhaps they were already dead. Two long strides took me to the side of the bed where I stared down at a maze of tangled extremities, three people intertwined. In the center of the heap lay Charles, unabashedly naked, with two women nestled under each of his arms.

Charles grinned stupidly up at me. "Ahoy, Chief."

The women's legs were wrapped around his, holding him prone in a position that allowed them free reign over his erect mast. The women giggled playfully.

Before Charles could speak, one of the women silenced him with her abundant lips, while the other slid her huge breasts down his bleached body on her way to his loins. Charles' breathing grew heavy, and I knew they were about to finish him.

I returned to the hallway and joined Gabrielle waiting for me.

"You do not have much time." Her voice dropped to a whisper. "The men of this place serve the captain of *The Raven*. It is an evil ship. The fishermen dare not go near it."

As soon as she uttered the name of the ship, I felt it—a chill along my neck and spine, an aura of dread I couldn't explain.

"The ship will leave today for the Island of the Devil in French Guiana," she said. "It will never return."

I felt another shudder of dread. Something she said unsettled me profoundly.

Charles, his face flushed, dashed into the hallway while pulling on his shirt. He gave up on the row of buttons and stuffed his opened shirt into his trousers. "Sorry, Chief. I had to unload my ballast."

The old man gave Gabrielle an awkward grin of greeting while forcing on a boot with a stomp. His face went pale when the door at the end of the hallway opened with a crash. I whirled. There, filling the doorway, stood the huge barman, leading a handful of desperate-looking men. I saw a trace of sinister amusement in the barman's eyes, likely the result of seeing a flash of terror in mine. He shoved the doorman aside with his bear-size paw and stormed down the hallway with the men at his heels.

"What have we gotten ourselves into?" Charles asked.

Gabrielle gave my arm a firm tug. "This way."

She led us through a doorway at the opposite end of the hallway and closed it behind us. With a rattle of chains, Gabrielle threaded a shackle through a ringbolt. I grabbed the chain from her and secured it with an effective overhand knot.

We heard pounding and shouting from the other side of the door. I looked at Gabrielle mutely. The door was sturdy, made of oak planks, but it wouldn't hold up against this determined bunch. In a moment they would break through.

"The large man who owns this place is my father," she said. "He forbids me to step outside."

"Today you will make an exception." I turned and almost fell headlong down a flight of steps. Charles grabbed the top of my trousers and hauled me back onto the landing.

"You must be careful," Gabrielle warned.

We clattered down the dim staircase, Gabrielle in the lead, our hands braced on the wall's chipped plaster. Modest light from a tiny skylight showed the way. The steps squeaked and protested under our feet—the stairway was as neglected and dangerous as the brothel it served. An overpowering malodor of decay drifted up from below.

At the bottom stood another door, bolted, much thicker and stronger than the one up top. An opened padlock hung loosely in its ring. I glanced back at the steps and saw two figures squatting in the shadows underneath.

Gabrielle threw back the bolt and opened the door, allowing sunlight and fresh air to pour over us like a clean stream. An army of walnut-size roaches scampered away from our feet. The service entrance opened into an alley behind the brothel where several children were picking through the refuse piled there. With the added light, I saw why the steps reeked so terribly. Two corpses sat propped against the wall—white men beaten to death, grinning back at us with broken smiles in their shattered skulls.

The pounding above gave way to the sound of wood splitting. We looked up, startled, and watched the planks give way under the force of several well-placed kicks.

Gabrielle beckoned me away from the steps. "Quickly. You must leave this place."

The door at the top of the steps exploded in a shower of splinters, unleashing a row of dark, vicious men. They stormed down the steps after us in single file, screaming and howling like wild dogs. I caught a blurred glimpse of them as I ran into the alley, passing Gabrielle struggling with the padlock.

"Leave it," I called back to her. "There's no way to lock

it except inside."

"And so I shall."

"What?"

She closed the door in my face, and I heard the rasp of the bolt driving home followed by the snap of the padlock.

"Gabrielle?"

I heard angry shouting on the other side of the planks coupled with what sounded like wood pounding wood. I swallowed hard. What had she done? I brought my fist down hard on the door.

"Gabrielle … *Gabrielle!*"

Only an unsettling silence now. I stepped back, listened and stared at the door in shocked incomprehension. What would they do to Gabrielle for helping us?

Charles pulled my arm. "Let's go, Chief. They'll come round looking for us."

I pushed him away. "We can't leave her."

"Are you suggesting we go back inside to fetch her?"

I knew, of course, that we couldn't. She was beyond our help now. Gabrielle—her face would forever remain in my memory. Who was she and why did she risk her life to help me? What power did her mother possess that allowed her useless eyes to see the unknowable? And what did her strange instructions mean?

Charles gave my arm another firm tug. I stifled a swelling rage for the men who ran this hellhole and moved down the alley in quick strides with Charles at my heels.

"To hell with this place," I said.

"What's your plan, Chief?" he called after me.

"She wanted me to have a look at *The Raven*. And so I will."

CAPTAIN MARART

My misgivings about the well-traveled clipper refused to take any definite shape. She appeared weary with worn planks, three bent masts and paint peeling down her hull in long sheets. I could barely read the faded letters R-A-V-E on her bow.

Charles shaded the sun from his eyes with a raised hand. "Her captain will never let us board."

"Wait for me aboard *The Dolphin* and be alert for trouble. Tell the others what we found this morning." I could not stifle a grin. "Tell them about your latest African adventure."

Charles said nothing. I left him and approached several seamen on the pier loading wooden crates into a net to be hoisted aboard. They were dressed in blue trousers and sea shirts similar to those worn by the jack we met in the bordello.

I said to no one in particular, "Who is your captain?"

One of the seamen scowled and waved me away. *"Je dois vite finir mes travaux."*

"Their captain's name is Jules Marart," came a deep voice with a heavy French accent from above. I stepped back and, shielding my eyes from the sun, saw the outline of a huge man leaning over the rail of the clipper.

"My name is Andrew Finsbury. I am the merchant captain of that ship." I waved in the general direction of my schooner. "I need a word with Captain Marart."

"You are having a word with him," bellowed the figure.

"May I come aboard so we can have a word in private?"

"These men speak no English. We have privacy."

"One of your crew," I said slowly, creating a lie I hoped would give me access to his ship, "a balding sailor with a wart on his right eyelid was arrested along with my first mate after a fight in a bordello."

The captain shrugged. "He will learn manners when I leave him in this hole to rot."

I already disliked this man. The intolerable sun bore down on me, and I had very little patience left. "I can have both men freed directly, but you must give me a letter claiming custody of your man." When the captain did not respond, I made the deal irresistible by adding, "I will pay both fines."

"You wish to pay for the freedom of my man?" he asked.

"I want my first mate freed from jail. We cannot leave without him."

A lengthy silence followed while the captain considered my offer. Finally, he waved me aboard and disappeared from the rail. I hurried up the gangplank to the ship's main deck, while the captain studied me from the gangway. Captain Marart was an imposing figure, sinister to behold. His massive torso, grizzled black hair and unkempt beard gave him the appearance of a wild boar, and his massive limbs suggested unnatural strength. His face looked oddly familiar. He had the disgusting habit of scratching and picking at his nostrils with fingernails longer and more offensive than any I had ever seen.

The Raven was a spacious vessel with tall, thick masts and immense backstays with classic skysails. Only *The Dolphin* could overtake her under full sail. The moment I stepped onto the deck, I felt an aura of evil radiating up through the planks and a feeling of foreboding that warned me not to relax my guard.

"Do hurry, Englishman," he snapped. "I have no time for this."

Two seamen with carbines escorted me across the deck, while Captain Marart followed. The fetid odor of excrement and decay drifting up from the bowels of the ship made my stomach tighten. There were chains with cuffs bolted to the bulwarks port and starboard—shackles for men. I shuddered to think of my Vanessa chained to such a foul ship. A cry—or more aptly a shriek of human anguish—poured from the hatchway, interspersed with what sounded like flogging. I moved towards the gratings to investigate, but the seamen with carbines blocked my path.

I glanced back at the captain. Marart, scratching his nostril, ignored my curiosity.

The seamen ushered me into the captain's cabin, a dark room that reeked of sweat. Marart ordered the pair of sailors to stand guard outside and then closed the door behind him, shutting us in his gloomy quarters.

"Great idea drawing the shades," I lied. "Keeps the midday heat out."

Marart wasn't interested in conversation. Without a word, he tore a page from the back of a logbook, and then rummaged through the rubbish on his desk until he found a quill pen, blotting paper and, with some difficulty, a bottle of ink. He lowered his considerable bulk into a chair at a table too large for the cramped cabin while scratching the persistent itch from his nostril. The closed door made the room insufferably hot. The heat combined with the awful smell of decay that permeated every corner of the ship sent a wave of nausea through me. Sweat rolled down my back in a continuous stream.

There came voices outside the cabin's door. Before the captain could move his formidable hulk, an elderly man wearing a white apron spattered with blood intruded into our meeting. His wrinkled face was ashen gray, and his hair consisted of several wispy white patches. He appeared visibly upset about something.

"I cannot stop the infection—" he blurted, before spotting me standing in the shadows. He fell silent and looked questioningly at the captain.

Marart gestured to me. "This is *Monsieur*…" The captain scratched his nostrils, unable to recall my name.

"Andrew Finsbury," I said, stepping forward, offering a hand to him.

The man extended a trembling hand that glistened with grease. "The ship's surgeon, Dr. Dane."

We gripped hands without a word, while he kept his suspicious eyes locked on mine. The doctor was anything but a model of health. A frail figure, Dane's drooping shoulders gave the impression of decrepitude, and his mouth hosted an uneven set of gray, broken teeth embedded in purple gums. When he released his grip, a fetid odor laced with disinfectant wafted from my hand.

Marart said to the doctor, "He has come for a letter claiming custody for one of my men who, he tells me, is in jail."

The doctor nodded, but obviously not at ease with my presence.

"Dysentery problems on board, Dr. Dane?" I asked.

The doctor's jaw dropped, displaying those awful

teeth. I looked skeptically at the captain.

"There is nothing wrong with my crew," Marart growled. His coal-like eyes glared at me from beneath brows furrowed into a thick, unbroken line. "If you insist on prying into my business, I will end this meeting in a manner you will regret."

I drew out a chair from under the table and sat down across from the doctor. "I apologize, Captain. I know something about medicine—a lot about ship hygiene— and I am not keen on taking a dangerous organism back to my ship."

Marart slammed his mallet-like fist onto the table with a crash, and I was surprised the planks held together. "You accuse me of keeping my ship unclean. I will put you in irons."

I returned Marart's cold stare and said slowly, "If there is an infection spreading through your ship, and I know its source, perhaps I can offer a remedy."

The veins in Marart's neck stood out like a network of branches.

I leaned across the table and said to the captain in a tone of concern I hoped would make us allies, "Allow me a look at the men below. My experience with ship epidemics may be useful to you."

With speed I would never expect of a man his size, Marart sprang from his chair and towered over me, his ugly face ridden with murderous intent. He drew a pistol from under his waistband and jammed its business end against my forehead.

"This game of yours is over," he growled. "Your man can stay in this hellhole for eternity, as will my crewman." Marart clicked back the hammer of the revolver with his fat thumb.

I did my best to appear unfazed. "My crew is waiting

for me at the authorities. If I am not back directly, they will send word to my uncle, Admiral Joshua Finsbury."

Marart's head flew back and out poured a howl of laughter that reminded me of a shrieking bear. "And when he arrives, you will be dead, and I will have long left this hole." Then his voice grew low and threatening. "I have killed many men who meddled in my business, men far more resourceful than you."

Dr. Dane laid a hand on the captain's arm. "No one in the settlement knows medicine."

Marart considered Dane for several long seconds. Finally, he withdrew his pistol and eased back the hammer. I let out an audible sigh.

"If our paths cross again, *Monsieur* Finsbury," Marart sneered, "I will kill you without hesitation. Do you understand me?"

I nodded, unable to think of a single retort that might ease the room's tension.

Marart tucked the revolver into his pants and allowed his abundant gut to swallow the weapon. I wondered if he would never find it again. He opened the cabin door, flooding the gloomy quarters with fresh air and sunlight. The two seamen stood beyond the transom, holding their carbines ready.

"These men will escort you from my ship."

"Thank you, Captain Marart. A most enlightening visit."

I sprinted out on deck with the two seamen at my heels. I headed straight for the gangway where I met the jack from the bordello coming aboard with the help of a fellow sailor. He blinked at me uncomprehending, too drunk even to speak. I bid him a nod of recognition. In unison, the two seamen gave me a cruel poke with their carbine muzzles, forcing me down the gangway.

"Most enlightening indeed." I dashed down to the dock and headed straight for *The Dolphin*.

Thus far, the answers to this ugly business eluded me. But I knew that I had come close to the truth. Perhaps too close.

BARRACOONS

I climbed aboard *The Dolphin* and snatched the water flask from my brother.

"You cost me a week's gross," Charles said, frowning. "I wagered you'd never get on board."

After several healthy swallows, I poured the flask's water over my hands to wash away Dr. Dane's medicinal smell. "*The Raven* is a slave ship. And she's infected. Captain Marart almost killed me when I asked to see his cargo. I'd hoped his kind of criminal died off years ago with the slave trade."

Williams pointed over my shoulder. "She's goin'."

We watched *The Raven* sprouted canvas and move away from the pier to begin her flight to the vast sanctuary of the open sea.

Charles shook his head. "We'll not see her again."

I appealed to the old seaman. "I need to find Marart's base. I need to know the location of every slave camp in this territory."

Charles pointed northward. "In the old days, most camps were hidden in the bush along the Sierra Leone River, about six miles up the coast. We would land a boat in the shoreline thicket and load slaves from the factory a short run inland."

"What about lions?" Eben asked.

"Indeed," Charles said, "but beware of the leopard. They're the bold sons of bitches who lie waiting for us inside our tents. I remember one night—"

"Right," I said. "I want a look. Charles, go to that telegraph station in town. I'm charging you with getting off another cable to Admiral Joshua Finsbury. Tell him we're sailing to French Guiana in South America."

Charles felt through his pants until he found a shred of paper on which to note my instructions.

"And when you finish, purchase anything fresh you can find that will see us across the Atlantic. Take La Gallienne with you." The men exchanged puzzled glances at my talk of a trans-Atlantic voyage. "The rest of you will come with me to scout this river. We'll take the longboat." No one moved. The day was half over, and we were running out of time. *"Now."*

The men shook their stupid stares and scattered to complete my orders.

Williams and I uncovered the longboat, fixed the keel and fastened the rudder in place, and then lowered it into the water. Joseph gathered a few supplies, while Eben rolled several blankets for cushions and set them on the two benches. I stuffed a rucksack of personal items under my seat and signaled the others that we were ready.

"If we get back early," Joseph said, climbing down into the boat, "how 'bout we spend the night in town."

"We're leaving tonight," I said, and then gestured to the mast.

Joseph gave me a sulking look and unfolded and raised the sail, while Williams put up the jib and spinnaker.

Charles called down to me from the rail. I glanced up as he tossed me his personal flask of "French wine" and offered a salute. "Beware of the crocodiles," he said. "They killed too many to count. We cut open one croc's belly and found the rings of a dozen men inside."

I waved him my thanks.

The coastal breeze filled the sail and pushed our boat away from the ship. A half hour passed ... an hour ... an excruciatingly long spell under the afternoon sun, and in all that time we saw only a solid wall of jungle along the coast. Six miles from Freetown, just as Charles said, the coastline opened into a large river estuary with a splendid volcanic configuration. A dense jungle blanketed both banks.

I guided our boat into the river.

"What the devil is that?" asked Eben, pointing to the left bank.

I moved our boat closer. A black film covered the water along the shore.

"Oil," I said.

"From a steamer?" Williams asked.

"They didn't bother to cover their tracks," Eben observed.

As we approached the bank, the jungle revealed one of its secrets: a narrow channel cutting inland—an ideal site for a warship to anchor and offload prisoners.

Eben pointed down-river at a patch of shoulder-high cane grass. "We can put in there."

"Too overgrown. Let's stay on the water as long as we can."

The top of our mast barely cleared the twisted vines marking the entrance to the channel. A dense, dark jungle lay beyond.

"Rocks," Williams warned, pointing.

My attention returned to the water ahead in time to steer the boat clear of a cluster of boulders breaking the surface. I kept a tight hand on the tiller.

"Use the paddles," I said.

Williams and Joseph folded the main-sail and jib. Then they dipped paddles into the still water and used them to push us away from the tangle of roots that sprouted from both banks and formed a dense web under our keel. The channel narrowed and spun to the left. The air became oppressively heavy as the jungle tightened around us, inviting a mass of insects that formed a swirling curtain around our boat. The four of us sat rigid, listening, and peering into the gloom beneath the overhanging branches.

Joseph shifted in his seat to look at me. "I don't fancy getting lost in this place. We'll suffocate in here."

Eben and Williams watched me carefully, also doubting the sanity of continuing along such an inhospitable stream. I could well understand their apprehensions; a pervasive evil marked every twisted stump in this swamp. Nevertheless, I refused to give up this route.

"Row," I said.

Eben cried out, "What the bloody hell...?"

I screwed my neck around and saw an insect the size of a man's fist making a peculiar flapping sound near his ear. He was unaware of another large insect—a strange, rat-like thing with scaly wings and long, stringy legs—clinging to the back of his shirt. I swatted the creature on his shirt with the back of my hand. The thing gripped Eben's shirt more firmly, defending its territory with a sharp, stinger-like beak. My brother let out a shriek and nearly jumped overboard. He ripped off his shirt in a panic and flung it into the channel along with its living cargo.

"Keep them off of me," he yelled, standing naked to the waist.

We all enjoyed a hearty laugh.

"Clearin' ahead," Williams announced, pointing.

As we rounded the bend, the sun, effectively blocked, began to filter through the overhanging branches. When we reached the clearing, our boat grounded, and the four of us disembarked, dragging the boat onto the muddy bank. Despite the remoteness of this beach, impressions of several small boats and countless fresh footprints were etched into the mud.

"There were people here recently," I said, examining the tracks.

"By t'night the tide will've washed away everythin'," Williams noted.

I returned to the boat, retrieved my rucksack and re-moved a matched pair of Tranter rod-ejector revolvers and a German Mauser. The others gathered around for an eager inspection of my modest firearms collection. I gave Williams and Joseph each a revolver and passed the Mauser to Eben. "I cleaned and loaded them last night. Be certain what you point them at."

Eben tucked the Mauser into his trousers next to his sheathed galley knife, while Williams and Joseph each found a secure spot for their pistol.

"No wandering off on your own," I said. "We'll break into pairs if necessary."

I led the way inland along a trail of thick, clinging sod strewn with abandoned crates and other rubbish from earlier travelers. Williams found a branch and used it to probe the underbrush for snakes before walking through. We hadn't seen a lion or a leopard yet, nor did we wish to.

The trail widened into a clay road rutted with deep wagon tracks, which ended at a high wall of mature baobab trees. Beyond the trees lay an encampment. An aroma of roasting meat clung to the hot and humid air, reminding me of a summer picnic.

I removed my pistol, waved the others back and peered through the brush. What I saw was astonishing. In the open field beyond, eight ramshackle barracoons—stable-like structures that once housed black slaves awaiting trans-Atlantic passage—stood in a neat row. The encampment resembled a military compound with enough barracoons to house a garrison. There were no signs of inhabitants save for a lone column of smoke beyond the farthest building—the source, undoubtedly, of the aromatic roast.

"I's heard of these prisons," Williams whispered behind me, "but I's never seen one."

"Let's go."

"I'm coming too," Eben said, scratching a sunburned and peeling nose.

"No," I said. "You and Joseph stay here and watch. Keep well hidden until we return."

Williams and I waded through the grass into the clearing and proceeded across the compound. We first encountered a solidly built bungalow with several chimneys, notably out of place among the other sagging structures. I signaled Williams to stand guard outside while I investigated. The bungalow's door opened easily. Holding my pistol ready, I passed inside. The room housed cutters, lathes, a foundry, chains and winches—a metal shop for making extensive repairs to a steam vessel, I surmised. Glowing foundry coals, adding to the room's oppressive heat, indicated that the shop had been used today.

I withdrew.

The second structure was an old barracoon. I leaned against the warped door, wrenched it open and edged inside. The light from a single, high window illuminated the shack's dismal interior. The stench of excrement permeated every corner. Countless rows of chains with leg irons fastened every few links covered the floor. The chains were oiled, not the rusted scraps suggested by the building's age and condition.

Williams followed me inside and gazed at the chains, incredulous to this monument of human disgrace. "'If'n I didn't knows better, I say this here's a stable."

I waved him outside, and we continued our search. As we passed each barracoon, Williams remained outside looking around uneasily, while I entered. Each time I emerged shaking my head in disgust.

A child screamed. Williams and I exchanged anxious glances. I signaled him to remain quiet, and we moved quickly, silently, past the remaining barracoons. As we neared the last structure, I heard children beyond laughing and squealing. I flattened against the wall and ventured a peek into the clearing behind. Four children—three boys and a girl—were gathered around a roasting pig hanging over a pit of burning coals. They were picking apart the carcass with their fingers and devouring what may have been their first meal in days. The children were all under ten years of age and dressed in European clothing reduced to rags. Were these poor children aboard The *Burlington*, I wondered? I returned the revolver to my waistband and motioned Williams to follow.

With the appearance of two strangers, the children grew quiet and just stared at us, startled, as though we caught them stealing food. Two of them began to cry.

"I don't like this," I said to Williams. "These children are worth money on the slave market. Why leave them here alone?"

"Maybe they's been hidin'."

A slight boy, the youngest, edged towards me, carrying a glistening piece of meat in both hands. He stood at my feet, his eyes downcast, and offered me the food. I knelt down and raised the boy's chin. He had large blue eyes.

A tear rolled down his cheek. "Please don't beat me like they did me mum," he implored. His speech was British.

I wiped away his tear with my thumb. "I won't hurt you. No one will, I promise. We've come to take you and your friends home. Would you like that?"

The boy's large eyes grew wider. He dropped his piece of meat into the dirt and grabbed me around the neck with both arms. I felt a rush of compassion.

He broke away from me and ran to tell the others. "We're going home! We're going home!"

The other children's frightened expressions brightened with smiles, and they danced around Williams and me, laughing and throwing their food at each other. I couldn't help laughing with them. As I watched them play, a thought occurred to me: the boy had seen his mother assaulted. Perhaps he had seen other women as well. Had he seen Vanessa?

I caught the boy by his arm as he raced by. "Lad, I need to know where the men took your mother."

He pointed to the jungle behind us. "Ask them. They shuffled off through those bushes when they saw you coming." Then he turned and pointed to the barracoon. "I think some are in there. They'll let us go, won't they?"

I felt a sudden chill and drew my revolver. "Williams," I hissed.

Williams stood at the center of the children's game, laughing and hooting with them. His face grew rigid when he saw my revolver out. I tried to grab two of the children closest to me, but they persisted in their merriment, avoiding my grasp as though I were part of their game.

"Get them down," I yelled to Williams.

The little girl ran to me with a beautiful tropical flower

she carried as a gift to me. I will always remember how innocent she looked, how grateful she appeared that I would take her home. Suddenly her head flew apart. I barely recall hearing gunshots—like a distant echo in a dream—while staring at her exotic bloom at my feet.

A ripping noise filled the air and bullets plowed into the ground around me, throwing up stinging bursts of clay. The remaining children shrieked and scattered. A tremendous force struck my chest, ramming the air from my lungs and hurling me backward to the ground. Several moments passed before I realized that Williams had tackled me out of the line of fire.

He cried in a frantic voice, "What's they doin'? Why is they shootin'?"

"Stay down," I shouted, holding my aching ribs.

Williams withdrew the revolver, spun onto his stomach and pointed it at the barracoon's sole window, one of the sources of gunfire. Screaming like a savage, he fired his pistol until it clicked empty. A thud from inside the structure suggested that someone had fallen heavily onto the wooden floor.

A man dressed in a merchant seaman's uniform and armed with a rifle squatted just outside the doorway. The seaman jockeyed the rifle between his hands and pointed it at me.

Williams leaped up and stormed the sailor.

"Williams, for God's—"

Before the jack could fire, Williams grabbed the sailor's head and jerked it back with his powerful hands. The sailor wheeled round and fell face down in the dirt, his head partially torn from his body.

Two more men, each carrying rifles, trudged through the underbrush between the barracoons. I pointed my revolver at the two and fired until it, too, clicked empty.

After a brief struggle, their flailing arms and legs fell still. Still, they stood upright, supported by a web of vines that held them.

I heard shouting and gunfire from the opposite edge of the compound where we had left Eben and Joseph. How many other sailors were there? I started to rise, but a shot from the barracoon's window sent a hot streak across my cheek.

"*Damn.*" My hand flew to my face but found no blood.

I sprang for the barrack, keeping low, my eyes fixed on the entrance. I lunged through the doorway. A seaman lay on his back among the chains; one of Williams' shots had put a bullet through his eye. But I saw something far more disturbing. The flesh on his face was white and drawn, his features shrunken. If I didn't know better, I would swear this man died days ago. A disease?

Another sailor sat on the floor next to him clumsily reloading a rifle cradled in his lap. I rushed him. Still seated, he swung his weapon in a wide arch, grazing my shoulder and knocking me to the floor. He lunged at me, his rifle upraised like a club. His face, too, bore the sallow look of the dead. I grabbed his ankle and brought him down with a crash. A hiss escaped from his throat. I dove onto his back and struck him hard on the side of his head with both hands locked in a fist. He hissed again. Although I had taken off part of his ear, there was no trace of blood.

I mashed his face against the floor and jammed my knee solidly into the middle of his back. He jerked, kicked and flailed his arms, trying to maneuver from under me. I grabbed a length of chain, wrapped it around his neck and pulled it taut. His skin felt cold and dry.

I grabbed the seaman's straw-like hair and yanked back his head. "Where have you bastards taken the prisoners?"

"Aaahhhgggggggg…" The ghastly wail coming from his throat wasn't human.

I shook him furiously by the hair. "Are they aboard *The Raven?* Answer me or I'll break your bloody neck. I'm looking for one woman."

"Aahhh … aaahhhhgggggggg…"

I tightened the chain. "Tell me why you killed the children."

His tongue lashed out, snake-like, a dry and shriveled appendage that bounced off the floor planks like the tail of a trapped rat.

Overtaken with rage, I jammed my knee against the base of his spine and pulled back his head till there came a dry snap. His body jerked with convulsive spasms. I rolled off him, shaking. His head, twisted around unnaturally, afforded his glassy eyes a helpless look at me. However, his corpse would not lay still. It continued to wiggle and twist, struggling to rise, but could not summon the coordination now that its spine had been severed at the neck. What was this horror?

I staggered outside, dazed. An eerie silence overtook the camp. The smell of gunfire mixed with burnt pork permeated the heavy, humid air. Three of the children lay still, strewn across the clearing as though asleep for an afternoon's nap. I found Williams sitting against the side of the barracoon, sobbing bitterly over a blood-soaked bundle in his lap. I was too numbed by this unspeakable massacre to summon any emotion, even outrage. The anger, I knew, would come later.

I went to Williams. He held in his arms the little boy who only moments earlier danced so happy when I promised to take him home. The boy trembled uncontrollably, his frightened eyes fixed on mine, his bloodied chest rising and falling in short, shallow gasps. He alone had survived this massacre.

"He done nobody no harm," Williams sobbed.

I gripped Williams' shoulder and shared his grief.

Williams looked up at me, his eyes glistening with hope. "He might make it if'n we gets him to the village fast."

I nodded. Williams stood and gathered the boy close to his chest. Without a word, we raced across the camp until we came to the bodies of three more sailors half buried in the tall grass at the edge of the compound. Their heads had been crushed by powerful blows—yet, like the others, I saw no blood. Still, they refused to die, their pale corpses twisting and struggling to rise.

"There's evil here," Williams said, "powerful and deadly."

Eben, crouching in the brush, stood up when he saw us approaching. His face was pale, and I feared he would swoon. I doubted he was even aware that he held his makeshift galley knife in his hand ready to plunge it somewhere. Williams brushed past him and disappeared down the trail to our boat with the boy in his arms.

Eben looked at me, his eyes misty. "Jesus, Andrew. How could this happen?"

I could offer him no explanation. "Are you alright?"

"Yes ... yes ... I'm ..."

I saw Joseph propped against a tree, a dark stain running the length of his trousers.

"He ... took a bullet," said Eben, following me to Joseph, bleeding badly from a wound above his right knee.

Joseph let out a throaty sigh. "Bloody bastards are an abomination."

Quickly, meticulously, I searched his leg for an exit wound. But I found only a single hole. "I'll have to dig for it. Let's get you back to *The Dolphin*."

I pulled off my shirt, tore it into long strips and applied a tourniquet above the wound. Joseph clenched his teeth against the pain.

"Hold still," I said. "You will die if I don't stop the bleeding."

Joseph rolled his head around, his eyes shut tight. "Bloody hell ... bloody damn it all to hell."

"What happened?"

"They knew we were hiding here," Eben said. "They knew everything. They came on to us steady, firing their rifles into the brush, trying to get us to run into the open."

Joseph gestured to the bodies and huffed, "Our guns didn't stop them. I got close enough to bash their bloody heads with that rock. I told your brother not to get near them. 'Fraid I got clipped for my troubles—" He screamed when I tightened the tourniquet. "B—burns like all bloody hell—" Joseph's voice trailed off and his head fell backward.

"He's gone into shock," I said.

Eben and I each grabbed an arm and, moving swiftly, carried Joseph down the path to our boat. What remained of the day's sunlight was quickly fading.

BETRAYAL

Sweat-soaked and shaken, we laid Joseph on the bottom of the boat and pushed off into the swamp-like channel. Williams sat in the rear, the boy tucked in his arms. Dusk had descended, sealing us under a thick blanket of gloom. Images were replaced by a cacophony of sounds—chirps, screeches and howls from an unseen chorus of jungle denizens. An occasional roar of a leopard augmented the clamor. We cast frequent and apprehensive glances astern but, save for the jungle's vociferous creatures, we were quite alone.

Joseph's eyes were shut tight from the pain. I retrieved Charles' flask from my rucksack and held it under his nose.

He grimaced and muttered, "What the bloody hell is that?"

"The finest scotch in all of Africa."

"Bloody liar," he gasped.

I lifted Joseph's head and offered him the mouth of the flask. He allowed himself a cautious swallow, coughed, shut his eyes and took two more tentative sips.

"Damn you," he hissed, then looked up at me apologetically. "I'm all right, Captain. Really." He propped himself up on his elbows. "Give me a paddle."

"Stay on your back until we get that leg looked after properly." I winked and added, "I know a good doctor in Yarmouth."

Joseph fidgeted in protest and drove his leg against the side planks. He winced in agony and fell back wearily onto the bottom boards, resigned to the seriousness of his wound.

With the help of the current, I paddled our boat through the channel, and soon we were clear of the mouth of the Sierra Leone River, sailing south to Freetown. The sky held the last of a glorious sunset. The vast golden-red canvas of sky surrendered to a wash of lavender, mauve and deep purple. Wisps of color-shaded clouds streaked the horizon and framed silhouetted gulls gliding inland for the night. Nature's apology for the horror of man.

Eben, sitting in the stern next to Williams, was oblivious to the heavenly display. Williams cradled the boy in his arms, his eyes fixed and unseeing on the sea.

"How is he?" I asked.

He clutched the bundle close to his chest. "He stopped breathin' before we shoved off."

* * *

We reached the settlement just before midnight. The dark waterfront stood uninviting and treacherous, the piers black and deserted. The citizens of Freetown hadn't seen fit to light the docks for strangers. To compound the problem, no one aboard *The Dolphin* left a lantern burning as a beacon. In fact, I saw no sign of the rest of my crew.

"I could have missed the pier in the dark," I said, putting our boat next to the schooner. "Where's our navigation light? If Charles passed out…"

Eben jumped onto the dock, and I threw him a mooring line. I knelt beside Joseph and touched his leg, causing him to stir and mutter incoherently. He had grown delirious, his breathing shallow. I said to Williams, "Stay with him while I find something for a stretcher."

Williams nodded and placed the boy's body gently on the dock. We would bury him later.

I hauled myself up onto the dock and peered down the walkway. The schooner stood dark and quiet. I climbed over the rail and scanned the deserted deck while Eben watched the dock. "Charles?"

There came no reply to break the eerie quiet or any movement on or about the vessel.

I moved to the companionway, which afforded me a view down into my cabin. A soft light burned below, enough to illuminate a solitary figure seated at my desk. I recognized La Gallienne, dressed in a tailored white suit with a red-striped shirt, a red silk tie and polished white shoes—a complete change into splendid attire. How was this possible? He had helped himself to a bottle of Bordeaux from my trunk, too engrossed in his drink to notice me.

I descended the steps. "What are you doing in my quarters? Where are the others?"

La Gallienne whirled.

"Stay where you are," came a deep, thick voice from the cabin's shadows.

I froze. A mountain of a man with a grizzled black beard sat up on my cot, pointing a revolver at my chest. Captain Jules Marart smiled sardonically. "Do not attempt to leave this compartment or I will kill you. I want you alive for a few minutes more."

I looked accusingly at La Gallienne. "Why did you let this man aboard?"

The little Frenchman shrugged and took another swallow of my wine.

I swept the glass out of his hand. "I want some answers."

Captain Marart lifted his hulk from the bunk, replaced the revolver in his waistband and stood menacingly before me. I stared at brute in sudden recognition. I had seen him before—the vision in the hold of Porter's steamer when I touched Myles' corpse. Marart took my Vanessa.

I seized the front of his coat, but as hard as I tried, I could not shake this mountain of a man. I heard a distinct click behind me. I turned and stared down the barrel of a rifle pointed at my head. The weapon's owner, the balding seaman with a wart over his right eye, offered me a grin as he descended the remaining steps of the companionway. The sailor I met in the bordello awaited the order to discharge a bullet into my brain.

Marart grabbed both my hands and squeezed them in his powerful grip, threatening to crush the bones. "I despise your touch."

I summoned all my strength to break his hold, but I couldn't match the unnatural strength of this beast.

"You are a fool," he barked, squeezing my hands still tighter with his massive paws.

I dropped to my knees in agony.

"I do not think he understands," La Gallienne giggled.

Marart shook my arms. "You spoke to a woman in the bordello. I want to know what she told you. Tell me everything or I will tear your arms from your shoulders."

"My fiancée," I gasped, "she disappeared a fortnight ago aboard the *Timonium*..."

"I am not interested in your lady."

Marart pulled me up by my hands and hurled me across the cabin. I landed heavily on my desk, crushing it and scattering charts, books and papers. I could not open my hands. La Gallienne scored a blow of his own with a kick to my side with his pointed shoe.

I looked up at him, uncomprehending. "Why are you helping this pig after I saved your life?"

The Frenchman looked at Marart, and the two, grinning, shared some private amusement. Marart plucked me from the floor and slammed me against the wall.

"Henri is in my employ," he said.

La Gallienne discarded his slouched posture and stood proudly erect and arrogant. Those sad, gentle eyes of his were gone, replaced by a ferret-like gaze that revealed a cunning and devious mind.

"Those poor people aboard the lifeboat," I gasped, "you murdered them just to deceive me?"

"They are not important," Marart said. "Your ship should have sunk with The *Burlington*. But you survived that night and damaged one of our warships, a small victory you will regret. Henri's simple disguise allowed him to learn a great deal about you while leading you here to me. I would have killed you in my quarters had my ship's surgeon not interfered."

I couldn't take my eyes off La Gallienne. I no longer knew him. "You never were aboard The *Burlington*, were you?"

La Gallienne giggled maliciously. "Of course I was. As one of the ship's passengers, I ignited the lime I brought aboard disguised in wine casts. I selected those who died with the ship and those few who were brought here. You see, I have been buying and selling slaves since I was fourteen years old."

"Bastard—"

"There is one more item I neglected to tell you," La Gallienne offered. "I sailed as a passenger aboard the *Timonium* as well. Captain Myles Edwards was a most cordial host. He even gave me the logbook that describes his ship's final hours. Most interesting reading."

I broke Marart's grip in a rage and dove on La Gallienne, bringing him down onto the floor. I drove my knee into the little man's groin and slammed his head against the floor, hoping my numbed hands still possessed enough strength left to crush his skull. He squealed and squirmed beneath me like a stuck pig.

Marart's massive hand grabbed my hair, lifted me off the little man and flung me against the cabin wall with enough force to split the planks. He formed an enormous club with his fist and rammed it into my stomach. I felt a rib snap. I struggled to free myself, prompting Marart to deliver several hard slaps to my mouth until I tasted blood.

With a snarl, he grabbed my neck and flattened me against the wall, his thick fingers closing around my throat. Through the diffusion of pain, I stared at the steps leading to the upper deck. The jack with the rifle had gone, probably off patrolling the deck. Despite my rib, I still could move faster than this mass of a man. As my breath returned, I stared at the companionway, hypnotized by the idea of escaping up these steps if given a chance.

I forced a smile. "Your men in the jungle ... we killed them all. A small repayment for murdering children."

Marart emitted a throaty chuckle. "Those men were already dead. As were the children."

He delivered another hammer-like blow to my stomach. I doubled over and my knees buckled. Marart swung my sagging body like a sack against the companionway.

My one chance. Summoning the last of my flagging strength, I scrambled up the narrow steps and pushed open the hatch. Marart grabbed at my heels.

"I will tear off your legs," he bellowed after me.

I fell out onto the deck. Marart grabbed the edge of the opening and pulled himself up the companionway. I placed my full weight on the hatch and slammed it down onto his hand. His shrieked like a wild boar.

Dazed, I inhaled great lungfuls of humid night air, while giving my eyes precious seconds to adjust to the darkness. Before I could move, a rifle butt struck my forehead. I flew backward onto the deck under a grand shower of crimson stars, certain my head had separated from my body. Through the blur, I could barely distinguish the outline of a sailor standing over me, ready to smash my face with the butt of a rifle.

"Don't kill him," Marart hollered. "I want him."

A strong hand clutched the front of my shirt and dragged me along the deck. I was too insensible to resist.

"You will sleep with your friend tonight," Marart said.

I lifted my head and, with great difficulty, struggled to focus my eyes. I saw Eben sitting beside the open hatch to the schooner's hold, his hands and feet bound with chain. Two seamen with rifles stood over him. Williams, also bound with chains, lie beside him, senseless, probably the result of resisting.

"Not these friends," said Marart, lifting me up over the hatchway. "Down there."

I groped for the ladder, but my fingers found nothing. He flung me like a piece of cargo into the ship's hold where I landed hard on a stack of tarpaulin. The pain in every bone and muscle rendered me senseless.

Marart waved a lantern over the hatchway. "It is good to sleep with friends. Yes?"

His light afforded me a sight that will ever remain in my nightmares. I stared into the grisly visage of Old Charles, his throat open from ear to ear. I lay in a gruesome pool of his warm blood. My ship had become a slaughterhouse. Charles returned my horrified gaze with a glazed stare of contempt as if accusing me of his murder. I could hear his voice spewing incoherent reprimands at me.

Marart's deep laughter hammered me from above as darkness enveloped me.

But I did not black out. Instead, I found myself falling through a cold, starless night.

DARK ICE

I plummeted at an impossible speed. The wind, bitter cold, flogged me like a whip with razor edges, desperate to tear apart my soul. I reached for a handhold, something to break my fall, but I felt only the thick wind rushing past. Below me lay a vast, black ocean.

I could do nothing but watch the dark sea rush up to greet me. It didn't take long. I hit the water with a bone-shattering smash and plunged into a churning sea. The water felt frightfully cold, and the shock of the impact left me senseless.

My head broke the waves in a swirl of foam, and the bitter winds of a raging storm hammered me. What was this nightmare?

"Do your worst," I shouted into the night. "I am not afraid."

Abruptly, the violent winds quieted, the high swells sank into the sea, and the distant thunder echoed and faded, leaving behind an eerie calm. What power did I hold over the storm? I thought of heat in an attempt to will away the awful cold. The sea felt immediately warmer. Its warmth against the cold air produced a rapid fog that clung to the sea like a shimmering ice field. I had indeed gone mad.

A persistent bell pierced the night. I trod water and listened. Then I saw something, a shadow moving through the fog, hiding, revealed, then hiding again—the silhouette of a two-masted vessel.

Something within me—another sense I could not explain—reached out and touched it. I sensed some familiar feelings, a few vague images, but nothing recognizable. But more important, I did not detect an evil presence. Reassurance enough.

I shouted through cupped hands, "Over here. Over here!"

The bell stopped ringing. In the quiet that followed, I heard the slap of waves against a wooden hull and the creak of masts straining against wind-filled sails. Odd. I felt no wind to drive a sailing vessel.

The shroud of fog parted and uncloaked the ship in all her glory—sheets of billowed canvas suspended from two lofty masts, an arrowy hull ... *The Dolphin.*

I began laughing. "Come to me, my proud lady."

The Dolphin pivoted gracefully, circled me once and glided to a stop with her ladder an arm's length from me. Whoever handled her was a seasoned captain.

I climbed aboard. Her decks were littered with tools we used to make emergency repairs.

There came a sudden jolt, and the schooner resumed its quick glide over the water. I ran to the helm and found no one there. Yet the tiller moved on its own, guiding my vessel with grace and speed through these dark waters. My elation turned to apprehension. I felt a force— dominant and decisive—moving the ship as though we were a toy in a stream. Where was it taking me?

The bell ringing resumed. I whirled. My heart skipped a beat. There stood old Charles yanking the fog bell. His skin was as pale as flour, and a gash across his throat from ear to ear served as a brutal reminder of his murder. His eyes were dark and sunken, and he looked quite dead.

I stepped to him, tentative, and pulled his stiff arm away from the bell cord. The ringing stopped.

He tried to speak to me, but his breath hissed from the throat wound, producing a gargled croak. He covered the wound with his hand. "I … I …"

Our minds met, and I heard a shameful string of curses. Charles squeezed his throat until I heard something snap into place. He smiled and wheezed, "I figured I might find you in these waters."

"Where am I? Why are you here?"

Charles pulled the collar of his sea jacket around his throat wound for warmth. "You wanted out of the water, so your ship pulled you out. You looked like you could use some company, so I rushed to join you."

"But where are we?"

"Really? You don't know, do ya?"

"This place seems very real, but how could it be?"

He grinned. "Welcome to the dead, Chief."

Dead!? "That's … not possible."

"Get over it. You died on the twenty-third day of April."

"Two weeks hence. There's still time to change—"

"It's in the past. The passage of time here isn't what you remember. It doesn't exist. You died, and now you're here with me."

I let out a sigh of regret. "You're dead because of me."

"Don't fret over it, Chief," Charles said. "I've seen too many bitter men swallowed up by this land, all because of misplaced guilt they couldn't shake. You're calling the same for yourself." Charles let out a huff. "Besides, the choice was mine. I lived a long and full life. 'Twas my destiny to sail with you to Africa and be buried at sea. I have no regrets. Besides, this place is far more interesting than the Bay."

"But I feel whole and alive."

"You still think you have a body of flesh and blood," he said. "But don't be fooled; it's an illusion. When you figure out that you no longer have a body, you'll crave one again. If your desire grows strong enough, you'll enter a womb where you will be reborn of the flesh to finish what you started on Earth."

Reincarnation. Again, I rejected the notion that I stood here as anything but a living human being.

"Don't succumb," he warned. "We've waited a long time for your arrival here, and we desperately need your help."

"We?"

Charles, his dark eyes narrowing, spotted something in the fog off our starboard bow. The dark night prohibited visibility beyond the length of the ship, yet I heard the rush of a larger vessel approaching.

Charles huffed, "Damn ... I never thought he'd try this."

"What is it?"

With a startling jolt, *The Dolphin* suddenly, viciously, changed directions and began racing through the mounting waves.

Charles jumped to the helm, wrapped his bony fingers around the tiller and pushed. But the rudder wouldn't yield. I joined him and threw my own weight against the tiller to change our course. However, even our combined efforts could not wrestle control of the ship from the unseen hand that held her.

"It's no good," said Charles, wiping his pale brow. "He's got us."

"Who?" I demanded.

Out of the gloom of these haunted waters came the laughter of someone possessed, a long, deep cackle that roared through the heavens and dissipated into the night like thunder. I forced back the bile in my throat. I knew that laughter too well—it belonged to Captain Jules Marart.

I grabbed Charles with hands as white as his dead flesh. "How is it possible?"

He placed a cold hand on mine. "This is his world too."

The obscene laughter came again, the thick, night air throbbing with it, harsh, threatening and evil.

"Where is he taking us?"

A sudden crash against our hull hurled us both to the deck. The ship struck another obstruction, then another. Tools not stowed flew past us. I jerked upright, vigilant. The ship lunged forward, giving our hull a severe beating. I gripped the tiller for support, pulled myself up and stared soberly ahead. We were in shallow water, rapidly approaching a dark island crowned with jagged peaks.

"Drop anchor," I ordered.

"We'd be wasting our time," Charles said.

The ugly island rushed towards us. Huge rocks jutted from the surf, some pointed, all of them dangerous. Nowhere did I see a suitable spot to put in, even if we could negotiate a proper landing. A horrific collision was imminent.

Another tremor shook the schooner as her keel grated on the bottom. But even the severe drag did not slow her.

"She's going," Charles yelled.

"*Jump,*" I shouted.

I scrambled over the rail and jumped into the surf. Charles followed likewise.

I watched my ship rise from the water, spin sideways

and strike one boulder after another as it hurtled to the beach. The impact ripped the planks from her keel but did not slow the schooner. With a grinding, shattering and ripping of wood, *The Dolphin* swept up onto the rocks that battered her to splinters. My heart sank. What little remained of my prized ship flew across the beach, leaving behind a sad trail of torn canvas, spars and twisted timber. I cannot describe my pain at seeing her destroyed.

We waded ashore among the wreckage. A cold, ripping wind greeted our arrival, driving splinters of ice into our faces. The strange island appeared to be made of ice—black ice.

I wrapped my arms around my chest but felt no warmth. I tried to will away the cold, but the effort seemed to make matters worse.

"Don't think about the cold," Charles warned, reading my mind.

How could I not think about it? I found nothing here to warm my thoughts, only mountains of ice and this unearthly wind. Worse, I sensed trouble. Where and in what form it would strike, I couldn't determine. I knew by the way Charles scanned the terrain, watching and listening, that he felt it too. Did Marart intend this island to be our eternal prison? Is that why he brought us here?

"Inland?" I shouted over the ripping wind.

Charles tried to spit but could not summon the spittle from his throat. "No ... down the beach."

I agreed, anything to keep moving and warm ourselves.

We began our journey around the island. The driving ice with needle tips hammered all feeling from my face. I shook so violently from the cold that I feared I might collapse in convulsions.

We covered several miles of rock-strewn beach, and in

all that distance nothing of our surroundings changed. The unnatural cold turned the surf's once foamy waves into grotesque ice sculptures.

The wind grew ever stronger the farther we trekked. Eventually, we reached the opposite side of the island where the wind and cold had grown brutally severe.

We staggered closer to the source of the horrid wind and, I assumed, the answers to why we had been brought here. Charles' arm went out, pointing. "There."

Something loomed ahead, something huge. I squinted against the wind. As we drew nearer, it became clear. Before us, blocking the beach, lay a wrecked clipper ship.

The Raven.

The ship lay supine, clouded in mist, its towering hulk half buried beneath the ice. Huge icicles dripping from her countless backstays formed gruesome rows of teeth. The cruel wind seemed to originate from the ship. A violent spirit howled across her decks, a turbulence so appalling that it threatened to pluck us from the beach and hurl us over the superstructure. I dropped to my knees and looked away.

It took a moment for my eyes to clear of frost, and a moment more before my mind could comprehend what I saw behind me. Charles stood utterly still, encased within a pillar of ice like a porcelain figurine. I tried to reach him with my mind but felt only darkness and cold. He was gone.

Behind his frozen shell, I observed the outline of a figure approaching, a large shadow in the swirling snow. Then, Marart's deep laughter replaced the howling wind. At first, I could see only a pair of eyes or rather twin orbs of fire. As he drew near, I saw his terrible, bear-like face. The world of the dead stripped him of the last countenance of humanity, revealing him as a loathsome animal.

I barely could see his face hidden behind long, thick and matted hair. His icy beard parted to reveal a gloating grin.

"Your friend is not welcome here," he said. "It is just you and I."

My spirit sank. Marart had mastered the dark powers of this world, while I knew nothing. I scrambled to my feet and skirted the length of the clipper, searching for a way around it. I was trapped. Several planks in the ship's bow beneath the water line were splintered and missing, leaving a gaping hole large enough for a man to squeeze through. Behind me, the sound of footsteps scraping on ice drew closer. I had little choice but to flee inside the ship.

Grunting and twisting, I forced my way through the hole and slid down the ice-encrusted wall to the lowest point in the ship's hold. I looked warily around. *The Raven's* dark hold consisted of shadows embedded within deeper shadows. Each breath of frigid air made my lungs ache.

A sudden gust of wind strong enough to rock the ship poured into the hold. I shielded my eyes and saw Marart's wicked face peering in at me through the gaping hole. "We will journey together, just you and I," he laughed and then vanished.

My skin prickled when I heard ice cracking. There came a roar as the ship righted itself and crawled into the sea. I scrambled for a secure handhold. Frigid water surged through the shattered hull and froze instantly, forming a plug. The icy walls shook as the vessel struggled to maintain equilibrium. Finally, the ship began rolling evenly on her journey out to sea.

I was imprisoned aboard *The Raven*.

THE RAVEN

T he sounds of crying roused me back to my senses. Then nothing. No creaking masts, no slapping waves against the hull. Nothing.

The crying came again, a disembodied voice, neither male nor female. The back of my neck bristled.

Then I saw something—or someone. Momentary flashes of lightning from a porthole caught a face across the hold staring at me. I rose to my feet, my eyes wide and unblinking. The face never changed expression.

As I approached the wall, the enigma became clear to me—the sunken face belonged to a man buried beneath a wall of ice. I cleared away the frost like a windowpane in winter and saw that his wrists and legs were bound with shackles. I rubbed the frost from the ice beside him. Another contorted face appeared, its mouth open in a silent wail. I cleared the frost from the ice on the floor beneath me. More faces. More men. All of them bound with chains. Here, imprisoned within the ice, lay Marart's cargo of flesh. He had taken them to hell with him in his cursed ship.

The strange sobbing came again. Louder. Could one of these poor souls be conscious? I stifled a growing unease and followed the sound to the bottom of the companionway. The sobbing came from between decks. I could see nothing beyond the top step. I tried to purge my mind of fear, but as hard as I tried, I could not rid myself of the blurred and murky vision of those faces buried beneath the ice.

I wrapped my fingers around the rope rail and mounted the first ice-encrusted steps. As I moved from one step to the next, my mind scanned the corridor beyond the companionway. Several voices whispered to me at once, unearthly murmurs of dead men spouting unintelligible warnings. As I continued, another voice within my mind shouted at me to turn and flee. But where could I run?

I moved off the top step and stared down the darkened corridor, allowing my eyes to adjust. This time I heard a moan—not a reaction to pain, but a response to pleasure. Curious. Who or what was it?

I started down the corridor, the brittle ice cracking beneath my boots. With each step, the moaning grew louder, closer. I stopped before a door, Marart's cabin. The voice came from within—a woman.

A sudden wind blew open the door with a crash as if demanding me to enter. I stared across the threshold and tensed. On a pedestal of ice that had been a bed lay a woman, naked. I gasped when I recognized her—my own Vanessa.

I was too dumbfounded to move. Then, with her most flirtatious smile, she summoned me closer with an enthusiastic wave of her hand. A strong desire stirred deep within me, seizing my entire being. Not even in my youth did I feel such lust. I moved to her side, my vision obstructed by the steam produced by my rapid breathing, my eyes riveted to her supple flesh and her eager, beckoning hands. Despite the cold, I began to sweat. I knelt beside her, my desire for her growing ever stronger. Although I do not remember undressing, I too stood naked. Prompted by my strong lust, I quickly mounted her. We began furious lovemaking.

Vanessa began to writhe in agony, struggling to free herself from me. What happened? Only a moment before she positioned herself to achieve maximum satisfaction.

"No," she screamed at me. "Fight him. *Don't let him do this.*"

But I could not slow the rhythm of my thrusts. Despite her protests and warnings, a force within me I couldn't comprehend compelled me to finish. I buried my head between her breasts and increased the speed as I neared climax.

With each push, a strong force swept through me. My heart banged loudly in my ears. The room grew hot and close, and sweat poured over my skin. My head felt like an iron weight. I rubbed a weary hand over my face and stared astonished at a thick and stringy substance dripping from my fingers. I looked down. The viscous goo oozed down my entire body, leaving a trail into Vanessa's womb.

Vanessa's body shrank and shriveled beneath me until nothing remained. My head dropped backwards, and I began to swoon, the cabin walls spinning around me.

I saw someone standing over me. My eyes grew as I stared up into the beast-like face of Marart, wearing a bloated smile of contempt and conquest. He summoned me here for this. But what was happening to me?

I watched, powerless, as a bubble of light enveloped me and filled with the honey-like substance. Stringy red lines weaved an intricate network of blood vessels around me. Marart retreated, distancing himself, yet he continued watching me. What was he doing?

I looked at my hands, a pair of featureless stumps, and watched in horror as they melted into my body. Like

Vanessa, I too was shrinking. I hadn't the strength to cry out.

• • •

Summer. I was a boy sitting on the dock, lazily watching ships sail by. Children laughed and shouted as they played a game on a white beach.

Ships, children, beaches.

My body vanished, my memories fading. Fight, damn it. *Fight to hold onto what little mind you have left.* I slid deeper into oblivion. Images, sounds, smells. Very little remained.

• • •

Blue.

I was an infant immersed in blue water. Blue. Only blue. *Fight him.* But I couldn't stop the metamorphosis erasing my memories and, with it, all that I was.

• • •

I could still pray.

Lord, please leave me my memories. I cannot bear to give up what I once was. Allow me strength. I need more time...

The malevolent room turned black, and then nothing.

• • •

But God heard me.

He showed His mercy by making me aware that I was

suffocating. Someone began shaking me violently, desperately tearing apart the embryonic shell that imprisoned me. I hadn't the strength to assist. A pair of strong, determined hands reached through the thick pool, grabbed me by my arms and pulled me out into the cold night air.

I could breathe again. The brisk wind tasted of salt. I heard waves rushing past a wooden hull and, for a moment, I imagined lying on the deck of my own ship, rolling between great swells. These same strong hands laid me on the floorboards and continued shaking me. Sensations returned. My stomach ached as though I had been lanced by a spear.

Memory seeped back—Myles, Charles, *The Raven*. And then I recalled Marart's conceited look of triumph while Vanessa struggled beneath me. The image made my head throb, and I rolled onto my side and retched. Finished, I turned onto my back and breathed deeply. I wanted to lie quietly and sleep. But those persistent hands kept shaking me.

I rubbed a weak hand over my face to clear away the scum and forced open my eyes. Several painful moments passed before I could focus them on the figure kneeling over me—Eben, looking fairer and more handsome than I had ever seen him.

He grabbed my shoulders, his eyes full of concern. I saw in his face a strong sense of purpose, and I knew from his urgent manner that something must be terribly wrong.

"Andrew, you must stay awake."

A steady rain helped clear the gum from my eyes, and I rolled my head to the side and squinted. I lay on the frozen deck of *The Raven*, staring out at a dark sea. Beside me sat the residual of the shell from which Eben had just pulled me.

"Ebby..." I could barely summon the strength to

speak. "Where did you...?"

He helped me into a sitting position. "Can you move your legs?"

"I think so ... I'm so cold..."

He shielded my body with his from the icy spray shooting over the bulwark. "You entered her womb. If the transference completed, you would have been reborn."

I couldn't comprehend his strange explanation. "What about Vanessa?"

"She's alive. Marart lured you into her womb where a soul has yet to bond with the fetus. If he succeeded, you would have been reborn as the offspring of your own seed where you could do him no harm. You would have become your own son—flesh of your flesh."

I looked at the melting shell beside me and said bitterly, "Now my child is dead."

"No. The embryo is whole. He cannot do it physical harm here."

I felt a swell of anger that turned to an anchor pressing the bottom of my stomach. I dropped onto my back. I wanted to retreat to the refuge of unconsciousness.

Eben grabbed the front of my shirt and yanked me up. "Stay awake."

My head pounded. I tried to push him away. "Leave me alone—"

"*Stay awake.*"

MIDDLE PASSAGE

I tried to cry out but could not utter a sound. Nor could I open my eyes. My throat burned terribly and, after much effort, I managed a feeble groan.

"Thank God." Eben's voice. "I didn't think you would ever wake."

What little air I could draw tasted foul and corrupt. Through the fog of my confusion, I heard the scream of a man overcome with agony and despair. There were other sounds as well—the constant, strangling moans of men racked by physical and mental torment. Where was I? Surely still in hell. I forced open my gummed eyelids and strained to focus on a dark form leaning over me. A full minute passed before I could make out Eben's curls of hair scattered above a flushed and anxious face.

I raised myself onto my elbows and felt dizzy at once. Eben pushed me back onto hard floorboards.

"Don't try to move. You've been unconscious for two days."

"Two days—?"

"You were delirious, raving till you had no voice left." His voice threatened to break into sobs. "I thought you would leave me here alone."

I lifted my head. "Where are we—?"

"In the hold of *The Raven*, bound for French Guiana. Word is there are seven-hundred prisoners aboard. But no one's sure. No one has left this compartment since we put out to sea."

"Vanessa?"

He shook his head. "No one has seen a woman aboard."

I choked on the pain in my throat. "Water..."

"They won't serve today's swill till evening. But I've saved some water."

Eben lifted my head to bring my lips to a tin cup. I sipped the brown liquid until the burning in my throat subsided somewhat. "Something is happening to me, Ebby. I see horrid things. I no longer know if I'm alive or if I'm dead."

Eben eased my head back onto the floor and began dabbing my face with a wet rag. "The captain wants you alive. The ship's surgeon checks on you regularly. I didn't let him touch you. His medicine will kill you."

I closed my eyes and let the memories flow back—the ironclad warship, the massacre of children, La Gallienne. Then Charles' pale and withered face appeared from the gloom of my fogged mind, grinning at me from his macabre world beyond the grave. A profound sense of loss engulfed me. My eyes welled with tears. He was a good man and, despite what his corpse told me, it shamed me deeply to have led him to his death.

I opened my eyes with a start. "He can't be dead ... tell me it's all a nightmare...."

"Charles was buried with *The Dolphin*. Marart towed the schooner out to sea and sunk her."

I rammed my fist against the floorboards. "This can't be happening."

"Williams is chained in the compartment above us.

The jacks roughed him up a bit, but he's fit."

"Joseph?"

Eben let out a sigh. "Joseph is dying. The bastards refuse to treat his leg."

"Help me up."

"You can't go anywhere."

"Damn it, help me up."

Eben wrestled me into a sitting position with my back propped against the wall. The top of my head touched the low ceiling—we scarcely had enough room to sit upright. My wrists and legs were bound with shackles, and my clothing had become hopeless rags of sweat and stains. My joints protested every movement when I reached up and touched coagulated blood on my forehead that covered a deep gash. I coughed and regretted it—a sharp pain in my chest dug at my vitals like a busy pickaxe. I needed to take care of that rib.

I gazed across our detestable quarters, a hole unimaginable in the most ghastly prison. A sick, yellow glow from a pair of lanterns illuminated a field of haggard men all bound in chains. Captain Marart was indeed a seasoned slaver. He made the most of his cargo space by wedging together chained men as a scholar would fill a narrow shelf with too many volumes. A coffin would give each of us more space. To compound our misery, we rendered the hold's intolerably stale air noxious by the vapors excreted from our bodies. How long before we all succumbed in this hellhole?

"What day is this?" I asked.

"The eleventh day of April."

Thirteen days. I have thirteen more days to live.

Eben lifted his shirt to reveal the sharpened galley knife half hidden in his waistband. "I managed to get this on board."

I rocked my head from side to side. "They'll kill you if they find it."

Eben tucked the knife under his waistband.

A scream cut through the fog in my brain—my eyes strained to focus on its source. Against the far wall, a man in a bloody apron knelt over a prisoner, cursing and working with an iron probe. I recognized *The Raven's* surgeon, Dr. Dane.

The prisoner gave an agonizing sigh then slumped in a dead heap beneath the surgeon's trembling hands.

"He's gone," the doctor said to an indifferent guard.

Dane wiped the bloody probe on the dead man's clothing and sat back beneath the low ceiling, exhausted. The doctor wore the withered look of a man who came to realize his life's work yielded nothing of value to anyone, least of all to himself. His weary eyes scanned the rows of chained men, assessing the futility of his enormous task of keeping Marart's cargo alive. His beaten expression brightened when he spotted me sitting up against the far wall.

"*Mon Dieu.* The merchant seaman is awake."

Dane handed the probe to his assistant, grabbed a black satchel and crawled over the rows of men to reach me. He pushed past Eben, squeezed next to me and offered a quick prognosis: "Awake and coherent. That is good. That is very good. To be awake, one first must be alive." He let out a cackle of laughter that made my head throb. Frowning, he inspected the gash on my forehead. "From a fall?"

"Get away from me."

He felt my head with his bloody hands. "No fever. That is good. I won't have to cut." He said to the guard, "Take him topside."

The midshipman singled out a key from a large ring and, with a rattle of chains, removed the clamps from my ankles and wrists.

I grabbed my brother's arm. "Him too."

"Just you," the doctor said.

"Go while you have the chance," Eben said. "I can take care of myself." His words were hollow and unconvincing.

The sailor swung my arm over his shoulder and, wrestling me away from the wall, proceeded to drag me across the appalling field of shackled men. I prayed that Vanessa had not been chained aboard this or any other ship—a slave for the amusement of a ship's officer. I shook my head and forced the unconscionable thought from my mind.

The open air above deck proved a potent elixir, and I drew in deep breaths, filling my lungs with fresh sea air. With each breath, I clenched my teeth against the stabbing pain of my cracked rib.

The morning sun's reflection off the shallow waves bore painfully into my eyes while the sailor, stumbling and slipping, dragged me across the deck. We passed a row of naked corpses heaped by the bulwark awaiting disposal overboard. Although my eyes could not focus properly, I could see clearly enough that the corpses were mutilated. Their hearts had been cut out and their ears, eyes and testicles removed. Several were decapitated. I squeezed my eyes shut and shook my head. A hallucination?

Dane, ignoring the macabre sight, led the way into a dark cabin—Marart's quarters. The seaman followed and lowered me into a chair. What I saw made me shudder. A glowing cauldron filled with iron probes sat on the blood-soaked floor surrounded by burning candles. In the center of the cauldron sat what appeared to be a charred human brain. My anxious eyes darted from one corner to another. There were other smaller urns scattered about filled with a grisly stew of blood, human hair and dismembered human parts. A bloody machete lay beside the bunk. It became clear to me now; the row of corpses on deck had been no delusion. The men chained below were unwilling participants in a madman's satanic rite.

The sailor withdrew and left Dane and me alone, or so I thought. Marart stepped from the shadows and approached, appraising me in silence. The cauldron's glow cast a crimson flush over his dark features, illuminating a drawn expression of defeat, oddly out of sorts on the face of a man so fierce. A profusion of sweat dripped from his face, and his breathing was short and shallow. Something terrible happened, something Marart couldn't defeat.

Responding to an unspoken cue, Dane removed the lantern from the table and, holding the light above my head, inspected my face and hair as though looking for lice. He even inspected the palms of my hands.

Satisfied, the doctor affirmed, "He's clean."

I grimaced. "Clean? Hardly. Just put me down as one more case of dysentery."

The captain's eyes constricted into twin black beads. "I would not concern myself with an outbreak of flux. Belial is impatient and needs more troops. It unleashed this disease on my ship to summon a garrison of soldiers to his lair. I should dump the lot of you overboard in spite."

Marart had changed. Two days ago he was a man who feared nothing and was to be feared. Now, something frightened him. What?

I winced and clutched the table as another wave of pain shot through my chest. "What sort of epidemic have you started, Marart? Syphilis? Or perhaps malaria from your God-forsaken Africa?"

Dane leaned forward and said to me, "You said you knew something of medicine."

"My father served as a surgeon in Her Majesty's Navy."

The doctor considered my remark, and then said slowly, "What do you know of a highly contagious disease that produces red pustules and causes the skin to rapidly mortify?"

A cold hand ran down my spine. "Smallpox."

Marart did not move.

Dane, noticeably shaken, said, "I have seen many diseases aboard ships—dysentery, Guinea worms, yellow fever, even leprosy forces us to dispose of profitable cargo. Now I must deal with an unmanageable disease contracted in Europe. How do I stop it? Tell me what you know, or we all are doomed."

"When I was a young man of sixteen, I sailed aboard my uncle's vessel *The Nightingale*. We lost half our crew and passengers to smallpox before reaching port in Baltimore. I'll never forget the way the disease destroys a man. Those infected left tracks of their flesh and blood over the decks as they walked." I added quietly, "I lost my parents on that hellish voyage." I looked at the doctor. "I need a drink."

Dane shook away his vacant stare, withdrew a bottle of dark liquid from an open desk drawer and thrust it before me.

I scowled. "I'm dehydrated. I need water."

Dane fetched me a water flask from a table beside the bunk. I uncorked it and swallowed half its contents.

Marart snatched the bottle of dark liquid Dane first offered me. "The doctor says you might be of use to him in this matter. That is the reason you are still alive."

Alive.? I stopped sipping from the water flask to ask, "How far has it spread?"

"Seventeen cases," Dane said. "But I have yet to inspect the lower hold."

I dropped the empty water flask on the floor beside me. "The number will double each day."

Marart indulged himself with a long swallow from the dark bottle and let out a disgusting belch. "I do not trust you. I have prepared another way to deal with this problem." His ferret eyes shot to Dane. "Is that not so?"

The doctor offered a feeble nod, exhibiting anything but confidence.

I did not bother to conceal my disgust. "There is no way to treat smallpox. Its contraction can only be prevented through inoculation of a mild strain. I've had two such inoculations in my lifetime. What about you, Captain?"

"I do not need inoculations." Marart removed an iron probe from the cauldron and watched a slender cord of smoke from its glowing tip spiral towards the ceiling. "There are methods to rid ships of disease."

I shifted uncomfortably in the chair. "You cannot treat smallpox by cauterizing the wounds. It's hopeless. Soon you will command a ship of corpses."

Marart thrust the tip of the glowing rod dangerously near my eyes. "They will all be better off dead. Those who survive this voyage will perform hard labor duties for the remainder of their short lives."

Marart thrust the rod back into the cauldron, producing an angry flurry of sparks. "There is no longer a profit in slaving. The risks far outweigh any rewards. Now the power I summon to protect this ship grows ever weaker. But I do as I am told."

"Who is giving you orders?"

Marart ignored my question. He opened the door to the cabin, barked an order in French to a pair of guards, then returned to the table and lowered his bulk into a chair. Finally, the seamen returned, dragging a pathetic figure into the room. The sailors withdrew in haste, hiding their disgust behind crudely fashioned masks of wet rags.

Marart gestured to the heap on the floor. "He brought this scourge aboard. I am holding you responsible."

I rose unsteadily to my feet, took the lantern from Dane and held the light over the man on the floor. I winced.

Joseph.

His frightened blue eyes, dulled with agony, told me that he knew of his imminent death. Sacks of red puss, many of them weeping, covered his cadaverous face, and those ridiculous chains cuffed to his wrists had worn away the flesh, revealing the repugnant sinew within. A strong odor of gangrene emanated from his neglected leg wound, the entry point of the disease, no doubt. Despite his suffering, Joseph's twisted lips gave me the smallest smile of greeting.

The room blurred. I fell back into the chair and gripped its arms to prevent my spilling onto the floor next to Joseph. I rolled my head to look at Dane. "In the name of God, why didn't you treat his leg?"

He looked away, ignoring me.

Marart motioned the doctor and ordered, "Proceed."

Dane removed a glowing probe from the cauldron with trembling hands and stepped over the heap that had once been Joseph.

I gasped. "For the love of God—"

Before I could move, Dane touched the probe's glowing tip to one of the bleeding sacks on Joseph's face, producing a momentary spark of burnt flesh. Joseph let out a horrid shriek.

I jumped from my chair. *"Damn you."*

Dane drew back like a frightened dog, holding the smoldering probe before him defensively like a sword.

I dropped to my knees and grasped my shipmate's

shoulder. "Joseph ... forgive me."

"Captain," he said to me, his chest heaving. "I can see her ... quite clear ... she's come for me..." His lips twisted into a smile, and I saw a bright look in his bulging eyes. "She's ... beautiful ... so beautiful—"

With the last word still on his lips, his life came to a merciful end, his agony ended. His vacant eyes stared at me with quiet resignation. I asked God to have mercy on the soul of my friend who suffered so terribly before his death.

I swept around and said to Marart, "At last he's out of your reach."

"He will do as I command." Marart closed his eyes and bowed his head. When he again opened and lifted his eyes, I saw only blackness. He thrust a fist over Joseph and boomed an order in a strange, ugly tongue.

Joseph's muscles began spasming, giving his ravaged body a strange illusion of life. His sallow eyes opened, and he sat bolt upright. I reeled in horror. Marart's severe expression grew intense while he continued spouting his cryptic commands. Joseph's jaw opened and out poured a ghastly sound, a wail of the dead. I held my ears to block the terrible noise.

"Stop this," I shouted. *"STOP THIS."*

Marart grew rigid and, grunting, grabbed the edge of the table with a trembling hand. He looked deathly ill. His eyes rolled back into his head, and his enormous body fell onto the table with a crash, reducing the oaken fixture to splinters.

Joseph's animated corpse slumped back onto the floor and fell silent.

Marart began groaning. Every few seconds his hands would twitch spasmodically like a sleeping man experiencing a bad dream. His sweat-covered features appeared bloated and crimson. Dane crawled from the corner and examined Marart, raising an eyelid, feeling his skin and counting his pulse.

"What evil did I just witness?" I managed.

Dane didn't answer my question. Instead, he said, "He is burning with fever." He went to the window, tore off the ragged drapes, soaked the material with water and began wiping Marart's face.

The thought of Dane nursing this animal like a mother appalled me. I pulled the blanket from the bunk and covered Joseph's remains. I grabbed the glowing poker and stood over Marart. "Move aside."

"What are you doing?" Dane demanded.

I raised the probe over my head. "I said move aside."

Marart let out several deep coughs and opened his eyes, his cheeks puffing. He stared up at me and slurred, "Your woman … is with child…"

I lowered the probe and stared.

Marart leered wickedly up at me. "I have seen your son."

"Where is she?"

He grinned. "Far away…"

"You wish to kill him," Dane said. "But he alone knows the whereabouts of your lady."

Marart pulled himself into a sitting position and, his eyes glazed, muttered an order to Dane in French. I glanced at the doctor for a translation, but he ignored me, his gaze riveted on his captain.

I threw the probe into the corner. "What did he say?"

Dane shook his head. "The fever robs him of reason. Put him to his bunk."

With great difficulty, I helped Dane pull Marart from the debris of the broken table, dragged him across the room and rolled his colossal hulk onto the bunk. He ranted incoherently.

"I must know where he's taken her," I said.

Dane wiped his hands on the soaked drapes. "The captain is surrendering to the spirits of darkness who, he says, have come for his soul. He wants this ship sunk."

Sunk? He can't be serious."

Dane placed a skeletal hand on my shoulder and ushered me away from the bunk. "Do you know why Marart never faced smallpox aboard his ship? His loyalty to a powerful demon makes this ship impervious to attacks of any kind. But this voyage is different. Everything is changing. It is the end of all we once knew. Marart will sink this ship, of that I am sure, and then his soul will again rule the underworld."

"I've seen that awful world, and I know for a fact that he will be there soon. I don't wish to join him." I loomed over the captain lying in his sweat, his beard full of froth. "This is madness. We must return to Freetown."

Dane shook his head, a ripple of anxiety passing over his face. "If we return to Africa with a slave ship ridden with smallpox, the French militia would hang the captain and his crew."

"We are facing two-thousand miles of open sea with an unmanageable epidemic," I said. "One way or another, we will all die if this ship doesn't turn back."

"I cannot imagine the suffering this disease will cause," the doctor said. "Perhaps the captain is right. Perhaps it is better if we end this horror now."

"And let seven-hundred innocent men die because of a madman's raving?" I pushed Dane aside and moved to the bunk. "Marart, listen to me. We can save this ship ... save your precious cargo—"

Marart grabbed my shirt into his enormous fist and pulled me close. "Burn this ship," he said, discharging a gush of breath that reeked like an open sewer. "Do it now—"

The captain's grip loosened, and he fell back onto the mattress. Delirious, he continued uttering a string of unintelligible French.

I wrestled the captain's fingers from my shirt. "Who is the ship's first officer?" I asked Dane. "And will he follow Marart's orders to sink this ship?"

"Lieutenant Barbier is a coward," Dane said. "He will not give his life to scuttle this ship."

"Then let's break the news to Barbier that he's now in command of *The Raven*. And with all due haste."

LIEUTENANT BARBIER

That evening, *The Raven's* new commander, a slight seaman named Barbier, summoned his fellow slavers to a meeting in the galley. I attended on Dane's order.

"We are facing a grave problem, gentlemen," Barbier said as I took a seat beside the doctor. "I need not tell you that if Marart regains control of this ship we are all dead men."

The others nodded and muttered their unease.

Barbier was an unassuming man, barely thirty, with a scheming, pallid face and darting eyes that betrayed his many uncertainties. His lack of experience in commanding a slave ship, or any vessel at all, was readily apparent. But at least I saw something in his eyes that affirmed that, unlike Marart, he was not a vicious murderer. He strolled around the galley with his hands clasped behind his back, keeping his head low, contemplating the facts as they were presented.

Finally, he turned to Dane and asked, "What have you done with the infected corpse?"

Dane stood and responded in a quiet voice, "After making a positive identification of smallpox, I disposed of it into the sea."

Barbier fingered his lips pensively. "And what about the other prisoners? How far has this disease spread?"

Dane shrugged. "I cannot say. There has yet to be a full inspection of the cargo."

Barbier considered the remark, his eyebrow raised. He didn't know how to deal with an emergency of this magnitude and seized this opportunity to issue at least one order in confidence. "Then do so at once. But I must warn you all that I will not alter our present course to Guiana. Regardless of what you find below, we will finish this voyage." Barbier lowered his eyes. "And may Satan spare our lives."

. . .

Despite the grimness of our situation, I had good reason for hope. For the moment, the ship's crew no longer regarded me a prisoner and, because of my experience with medicine—however limited—expected me to render whatever assistance the doctor required. Prisoner or crew, we all shared the same fate. I intended to play my role to the fullest to gain freedom for my imprisoned countrymen.

My first business after leaving the meeting was finding modest medical attention for my ribs and a change of attire, both of which I found in Dane's quarters. Foraging through his supplies, I unraveled a spool of fabric and tightened a strip around my bruised chest. Next, I helped myself to an odd-fitting pair of trousers and the doctor's best shirt and then explored his medicine chest. His crucial duties distracted him from noting my rummaging. His medical chest held the usual remedies for scratches and fever, but nothing here would treat an epidemic. I sniffed the contents of an unlabeled bottle and recognized the pungent odor of rubbing alcohol—the one item of Dane's of any real value. I corked the bottle and tucked it beneath my waistband.

We then undertook the grotesque chore of inspecting prisoners. I led a group of Dane and four seamen into the hold to begin a systematic inspection of each man, searching for symptoms. Despite our best efforts to ventilate the cargo area, the decks below still reeked intolerably of human vapor.

I made my way to the compartment forward of the mast where Eben lay chained. He sat up as I approached, surprised to see me leading a ship's detail.

"I didn't think you were coming back," he said, his voice shaky. "What's happening?"

"I'm getting you out of here now," I said.

He noticed the other seamen raising lanterns over each prisoner in turn and examining the face and arms. "What is it, Andrew? What are these men looking for?"

"Smallpox. I watched Joseph succumb."

Eben just looked at me, recalling the disease that made him an orphan before he had any real recollection of our parents. He sank back against the floorboards. "Then it's hopeless."

I pulled the bottle of alcohol from my waistband. "Keep this with you. Rinse your hands now, and each time you come in contact with anyone. When in doubt, rinse." I examined his face and arms and found no trace of the disease. I prayed that the inoculation he received six years earlier would protect him.

Eben uncorked the bottle and sniffed its contents, but the stench in the hold masked its signature medicinal odor. He corked the bottle and tucked it under his legs, then drew close to me and whispered, "We're not going to make it, are we, Andrew?"

I could well understand his apprehension. No one could last long in this hellhole, smallpox or no. He and the others were vulnerable to any number of lethal influences, if not disease, then melancholy—a man imprisoned in this manner with no hope could simply lose the will to live.

"You've been inoculated," I reassure him.

"But what if it's no longer effective?"

I had no answer for him. I directed my attention to the prisoner on his left, a mere skeleton with brown-yellow skin hanging off his bones like empty bags. I examined the poor chap and found no trace of the disease; nonetheless, from the looks of him, he most likely would be dead of one malady or another by morning. The men down the row appeared little better off.

"There you are," called Dane, crawling to me beneath the low ceiling. "I've found three cases aft."

"Take them topside before they infect the others." I gestured to Eben. "And have this man released at once. He is a student of medicine."

Dane nodded, turned, and headed aft to find a seaman who could unshackle my brother.

"Marart is delirious," I told Eben. "The good news is this vessel is now in the hands of men who are concerned with saving lives—primarily their own. I'll attempt to convince them that the way to deal with this crisis is to get everyone topside. At least they will have air to breathe." I decided not to tell him about Marart's gruesome rituals.

He offered me a weak smile.

I gave Eben's hand a reassuring shake, while my own doubts churned inside me. "We'll talk more topside."

I hurried to join Dane.

* * *

In all, our inspection that evening revealed twenty-seven infected men—appalling numbers, and we took little comfort from the fact that the epidemic hadn't spread as far as initially feared. As Barbier prepared to retire for the night, Dane and I intruded into his cabin with the news.

"Still too many," Barbier said after hearing our report. Sitting on the edge of the bunk, he removed his boots and, with great agitation, hurled them one at a time into the corner with a crash. "Doctor, I order you to use laudanum to rid us of this threat. Give a dose to every stricken man and put their corpses over the side as quickly as possible."

"Are you ordering me to poison these men?" Dane asked.

"Have you another solution?" Barbier snapped. "Laudanum is quick, and it will simplify your task. Begin at once before the number grows larger than twenty-seven." Barbier swung his feet up onto the bunk.

I stepped to the edge of the bunk and towered over him. "It won't work, Barbier. Once smallpox is contracted, it takes days for symptoms to appear. For every case we've found, there may be dozens infected who have yet to show signs."

Barbier stared up at me, unnerved. "And what makes you an authority?"

"I've witnessed this disease spreading through a ship. You can poison twenty-seven men tonight if you like, and fifty more tomorrow when they begin showing symptoms. And when your supply of laudanum is exhausted, you can keep tossing screaming men overboard until the decks are empty. But be prepared to join them."

Barbier rubbed his head into the pillow but found no

comfort. "What then do you suggest?"

"Allow Dr. Dane to set up a hospital in the forecastle where we can isolate those stricken men from the others. Once they are quarantined, the risk of further contamination will be greatly reduced."

Barbier slapped the mattress with a quick, agitated snap. "That's not good enough." He looked severely at Dane. "Have you anything at all to treat these men, doctor?"

Dane stood with his mouth agape, obviously unable to handle a medical emergency of any kind.

Barbier gave the bunk another slap. "You see. We are singularly fortunate to have a supply of laudanum aboard."

"For the love of God, man," I said. "At least give these men a chance to fight the disease with their body's natural defenses. Otherwise, you'll deliver no cargo at all to Guiana. Will your employer forgive that sort of incompetence?"

Barbier considered me carefully and then looked at Dane. "Do you agree with all this?"

Dane offered a feeble nod.

Barbier let out a long, weary sigh, pulled the blanket around him and settled in for the night. "I am tired. Let me know of your progress in the morning."

As we turned to leave, he added, "You have three days to show me results. Less if Marart wakes."

* * *

We transferred the twenty-seven infected men to the forecastle and gave them to the care of a handful of prisoners who had been inoculated for smallpox in Europe. Among them was Eben, who proved himself an exceptional nurse. We also managed to find Williams and had him released for cleanup duties. Our hospital was nothing more than a small room dimmed by shutters where the sick lay sweltering, naked and screaming in agony. Buckets overflowed with excretion and bile faster than we could empty them, and we depleted our supply of blankets the first morning.

Despite our best efforts to contain the disease, our sick list grew to forty by morning. By the end of the second day, the hospital Dane and I set up could no longer accept patients. Our plan seemed hopeless; worse, none of these men were in any condition to mutiny.

Determined to stem the loss of life, I convinced Dane to organize a detail to undertake the horrid task of hoisting bodies from the hold and disposing them into the sea. The living desperately needed more space below to breathe. Those assigned to this duty were soaked with rum in a crude attempt to protect them from a myriad of infectious organisms. Admittedly crude, this method nevertheless seemed to work.

That night I spotted Williams wallowing in the steam and the mire between decks, helping purge the dead from the hold.

"Williams, are you OK?"

He jerked upright and, seeing me, gave a hoot of joy. "I feared I'd find your ass in this heap. Instead there you stand, wavin' like you owns this here ship."

I leaped down the companionway and caught him by the shoulders. Despite his miserable duties, he appeared in good health and spirits. "Thank God you're all right."

"It'll take more'n a germ to get old Williams to sit down and die. Looks like you came awful close, though. Somebody stepped all over your face."

"I've felt worse."

He wiped a moist eye with one of his heavy gloves. "I seen your baby brother working sick duty in the fo'castle. Praise God. But I's yet to find Joseph anywheres."

"He was among the first to show the symptoms. We buried him at sea."

Williams let out a sigh of regret and, shaking his head, said, "Maybe he wasn't the best man who ever served a Cap'n. But he didn't deserve to go that way. Nosir."

I grabbed his arm and gave it a reassuring shake. "Keep your wits about you. We'll regroup later and plan our return to England."

He allowed himself a smile. "Aye, Cap'n. Jus' keep me out of them chains."

By the third day, we could not distinguish the healthy from the sick. Four of the ship's crew developed symptoms and were forced to lay with the infected prisoners. Sailor or prisoner, the disease did not discriminate. Twenty-nine men had perished. Our plan proved an utter failure.

If matters already were intolerable, at dusk on the third day, I noted intermittent limb spasms of some of the corpses hoisted above deck. I went about my chores uneasy, fearful that Marart was awake and issuing orders. I did not wait long for the inevitable summons to his cabin. Dane stepped into the forecastle and said, "He wants us."

We entered the captain's cabin and found the ship's four officers, including Barbier, gathered around the bunk, arguing loudly. Hearing Marart shout orders again sent a tremor of dread through me.

All eyes turned to us as we entered. Marart, his breathing labored, stared at me while the officers ushered us to his bunk. He let out a shriek of rage. "You brought a curse aboard my ship." His hand flew out, reaching for me. I recoiled beyond his reach. "I should have killed you when we first met."

Dane pushed Marart back onto the mattress. "We have isolated those afflicted. There is a chance, a good chance, you can deliver your cargo to Guiana as planned."

Marart broke the doctor's hold and began thrashing his arms. "I gave an order. Why did you ignore it?" None of the officers responded. "I will hang all of you."

Exhausted, Marart sank back into the drenched mattress, his breathing short and labored. Still, no one dared move. Finally, Dane ventured forward and touched Marart's forearm.

"Fever," he whispered to me. "It is very bad."

I moved to the bunk and grabbed Marart's wrist. His pulse was dangerously rapid, his eyes red and swollen. I inspected his arm and found several crimson blisters.

I dropped his wrist. "Smallpox."

The officers recoiled.

Marart wrestled the sheets away and, propping himself on one elbow, pointed a trembling finger at Barbier. "Burn this ship now," he ordered, spitting yellow foam over his black beard.

Barbier did not move.

"You are refusing?" Marart hissed.

Barbier croaked, "I will not scuttle this ship—"

Marart grabbed at the desk beside his bunk. Before anyone could move, he produced a revolver from a half-opened drawer, pointed it at Barbier and fired. A blast roared through the cabin. The unfortunate lieutenant reached for his left eye and toppled backward with a shriek. The bullet produced a ghastly socket where his left eye had been, releasing a stream of brain matter. After a moment, the seaman's limbs ceased twitching.

When the blast subsided, I heard only the captain's labored breathing. He pointed the pistol at the officer standing over Barbier's corpse and discharged three rapid shots. The officer uttered a gargled gasp and dropped headlong into the arms of the two remaining officers, who stared in disbelief at the blood spewing from the wounds on their comrade's back.

Marart's deep-set eyes scanned the room. Sweat poured from his bushy beard while he looked at each of us in turn, searching for another target. He spotted me. I dove to the floor as he brought the pistol to bear and fired. A single bullet hissed over my head before the gun clicked empty.

I sprang forward with both hands locked in a single fist and delivered a solid blow to the side of Marart's head. The captain crumbled against the mattress. The two surviving officers sprang forward to subdue him. Dane found a piece of rope and passed it to the officers, who secured Marart's hands behind his back.

"You are mentally and physically unfit to command this ship," I said to Marart. "By the authority of International Maritime Law, I relieve you of command."

Marart's dark eyes glared at me like a fierce animal captured in the wild. "You are a madman to talk of mutiny aboard my ship. I will have your soul."

One of the officers intervened with a wave of his hand. "This ship is now under my command. I have no intentions of letting it become my coffin."

I knew this man as the ship's quartermaster, an English seaman named Francis Moore. His coarse, black hair draped over his shoulders framed a mocking grin that displayed a broken row of teeth. The boatswain at his side, burly with no obvious intelligence, returned my stare with a look of contempt.

I bowed slightly and offered no challenge.

Moore turned to the doctor, lifted an intimidating eyebrow and said, "You are responsible for the health of those aboard this ship. And so far you've proven yourself worthless. Show me results, or I swear I'll hang you myself. Am I clear?"

Dane bowed his head and nodded.

Moore gestured to the corpses on the floor. "I am also putting you in charge of the dead. Dispose of all corpses quickly before Marart uses them to destroy this ship." He thrust a finger at me. "And put this man back in chains below."

Moore and the other officer turned to leave. "This man will remain as my assistant," Dane said.

Moore stopped in the doorway and shot the doctor a penetrating gaze. "Very well. I will grant you this one favor. Pray that it gets your results. Otherwise, both of you are dead men."

Moore clasped his hands behind his back and led his only surviving officer out into the night.

THE GREY SEA

The heaps of corpses on deck created an intolerable sight, and we worked through the night disposing of bodies to make room above deck for the living. Overcome with exhaustion, I eased into a corner of the hospital recently vacated by a dead man and fell into a deep sleep. Just before daylight, a rough hand on my shoulder woke me with a start. Startled, I glanced up into Dane's anxious face.

"Come with me."

Shaking the sleep from my mind, I followed Dane out of the forecastle and across the deck. We entered Marart's cabin unannounced, leaving the door open behind us. The room lay wrecked with overturned furniture. Dane walked to the bunk and raised a lantern over Marart's corpse for me to see.

He had been murdered.

Marart's eyes, wide and ghastly, were bulging from his head and his thick tongue oozed out over his beard like an obese leech. His corpse leered up with a mad smile as though he were laughing at me. A rope, tightened with a steel poker, had been wrapped garrote-style around his neck. He had torn free of the bonds, and his long, sharp fingernails were broken and bloody. The disarray of sheets and the overturned desk beside the bed suggested that his killers had a difficult time with their task.

"I'll be damned," I said, basking in a great wave of relief.

Dane lowered the lantern. "Moore did this with the help of several strong seamen."

"I commend them."

Dane's expression reflected his confusion. "But why kill him? He would have died soon enough of disease."

"As long as Marart lived, his order to burn this ship with the help of his demons may very well have succeeded. Obviously, the crew wasn't willing to wait and take that risk."

I unwrapped the rope from around the corpse's neck and flung it under the bunk, then righted the overturned desk.

The doctor watched me, puzzled. "Why bother with that?"

"Spread the word that Marart died of smallpox. Otherwise, you and I will be suspected, and Moore might hang us quickly to divert suspicion from himself."

Dane raised his eyebrows in agreement and helped me arrange the sheets naturally around the corpse.

"How is your patient this morning?" came a voice from the doorway.

Dane and I whirled. Moore, flanked by two seamen, gave us his ugly, broken smile while touching several deep scratches on his cheek.

"You know very well, Moore," Dane snapped.

I waved the doctor silent and stepped away from the bunk. "I regret that the captain succumbed to the disease during the night. God rest his soul."

I wanted to leave the cabin, but Moore extended his arm, blocking my way.

"I haven't excused you."

"With your permission," I said, "I will dispose of the corpse."

Moore considered me for several long moments. Finally, his lips stretched into a devious smile. "Yes." He withdrew, allowing me room to pass, adding, "And do so quickly."

I proceeded to the forecastle with Dane at my heels. On our way, we encountered a group of sailors and prisoners huddled by the rail, pointing out to sea. Among them stood Williams.

When he saw me, my friend thrust a finger seaward. "Looks like we gots an escort."

I looked where he indicated. There, not half a mile off our starboard quarter, sat two large, black vessels—ironclad warships. I stared, fascinated to see them clearly by the light of day. They weren't the ferocious sea beasts we imagined under the cloak of night—the daylight stripped them of their otherworldly qualities. I now understood their need for stealth and darkness; with guns so close to the waterline, they would have limited range. Still, the pair were formidable instruments of destruction and death, each carrying thirty guns, most likely twenty-four pounders.

"The warships will stay with us until mid-journey," Dane explained. "Then they will travel on ahead. Until then, we are safe from predators."

I left the others by the rail and entered the packed hospital where I found my brother arguing with a patient. Seeing me, Eben broke away and said, "He wants special treatment."

Henri La Gallienne turned to look at me. His red eyes protruded from their sockets, pleading for someone to rid him of the disease ravaging his body. We stood facing each other like duelers, neither saying a word.

When he realized no one would help him, La Gallienne wavered, eyes upturned, face glistening with sweat, and then collapsed in a heap next to several stricken men. Dane and I lifted the little Frenchman onto a table we used for examinations. I unbuttoned his shirt to expose a bare and sweaty chest. There were red blisters everywhere.

La Gallienne stirred and grabbed my arm. "I … I must not lose my flesh." He could barely talk.

I pried his bony fingers from my arm. "There's nothing we can do for you."

His outstretched arm fell limp. "He promised me...."

"Who promised you what?"

"Marart. He promised I would not lose the flesh. We made a bargain."

"Marart is dead. Whatever deal you struck with him died with him."

La Gallienne's face turned a shade paler. "Then you must help me. You must rid me of this scourge."

I leaned over the little Frenchman. "Tell me everything you know about the *Timonium*. Tell me what became of its surviving passengers."

His eyes darted about, uncertain.

I grabbed him by his lapel and dragged him off the table until we were nose to nose. "Listen to me, you pathetic wretch … give me some answers, or by God I'll drop you into the sea right now."

"*Monsieur*, p-please," La Gallienne stuttered, his protruding eyes locked on mine. "We took many women that night. I … I did not note their names."

I shook him severely. "You know very well who I'm looking for."

"Yes, but I do not know her fate."

I shook him again. "But you know something."

He whimpered, "S-some of the women were taken to Africa with the children, some to South America to be sold, some were kept for the officers. A man, a powerful man, took your woman for himself."

"Who?"

"A general. He commands all."

La Gallienne watched me carefully. Seeing that I may have believed him, he said, "I have told you all I know. Now you owe me your best treatment."

Disgusted, I pushed him roughly back onto the table. "I'm going to enjoy watching your miserable carcass die on this ship."

"*Swine,*" he hollered after me. "You and I will meet again in hell. I promise you."

I left the forecastle for some fresh air.

· · ·

I saw La Gallienne for the last time on the morning of the seventh day of *The Raven's* epidemic. Fewer and fewer bodies were hoisted from below, signaling that Death had been satisfied. But not before the disease had reduced seven-hundred men to two-hundred walking corpses.

On my way to the forecastle, I spotted a familiar pair of pointed shoes jutting from beneath a stained tarpaulin. Kneeling, I drew back the cover and stared at the body of Henri La Gallienne. The disease's blisters had destroyed his face almost beyond recognition. But I knew those sunken marble eyes that reflected a fear of smallpox that finally claimed him.

I once again heard La Gallienne's desperate curse: 'You and I will meet again in hell.' His laughter drifted away on the wind that pushed the ship westward, leaving behind an empty stillness.

I stood and backed against the ship's bulwark to allow two prisoners from the burial detail to hoist the body onto the rail and dump it overboard like the rubbish it was. I watched his body vanish under a large swell, gone forever. What would a minister say about the life of La Gallienne? That he caused the suffering and deaths of an untold number of women and children? And possibly of Vanessa? He did not deserve a eulogy.

I began walking the long decks, reflecting on events, reassessing my life, my purpose, my sanity. Eventually, I understood that I was guilty of selfishness and worse—my desperation to find Vanessa caused the deaths of good people who trusted their lives to me. And possibly mine as well. With these thoughts came a voice that said Vanessa would never again be part of my life.

Her angelic face, always with a warm smile for me, radiated before my eyes with excruciating clarity until it faded into the gray sea.

LANDFALL

Vanessa and I were alone in my shop where we planned to spend the night together. Darkness fell, and the sounds of the Bay faded for the night. While she drew the shades, I lit several candles so that I could see her clearly. Then, with a smile, she settled down upon my unmade bunk and brushed a hand across the furrowed sheets.

Without a trace of modesty, Vanessa slid out of her green dress and removed her undergarments, folding each item neatly on the floor beside the bunk. She pushed her heavenly silken hair behind her shoulders and settled back comfortably onto small mound she made from pillows. She looked so beautiful. Her seductive grin made my heart pound, and she beckoned me with a mischievous hook of her finger.

I shook my stupid stare and, laughing, shed my clothing. I lay down beside her. She rolled on top of me, and we held and kissed each other like new lovers. I cannot begin to describe the wondrous sensations she summoned with her gentle caressing and touching.

I suddenly felt weary. A great wave of fatigue descended upon me.

Although I mentioned nothing, she sensed my exhaustion and said to me, "Close your eyes."

When I continued to stare up at her, confused and frustrated, she ran a hand over my forehead and, with a brush of her fingers, pushed my eyes closed. "And sleep," she said. "You carry on your shoulders the weight of several lifetimes, and now you must sleep. This will make you strong."

• • •

Twenty-Second of April, 1894

"Land ho!"

My eyes opened with a start. The air in the room felt heavy and humid. I rolled off Dr. Dane's bunk and made my way topside, dragging my feet and rubbing the stiffness from my arms, all the while recalling my dream with Vanessa. What did it mean?

Nine days ago we buried the last diseased corpse in the sea. If Charles were correct, my death would occur tomorrow.

The midshipman kept shouting from the masthead, "Land ho!"

Captain Moore appeared on deck, stuffing his open shirt into a pair of tight trousers. "Where away?"

"Off the lee bow," the midshipman called, pointing.

"How far?"

"Ten kilometers."

A crowd of prisoners and sailors formed on deck to see. There was a charge of excitement among the men, an undercurrent of anticipation. The sailors rushed about, barking orders, trying to restrain the prisoners climbing out the hatchway.

After consulting his nautical charts, Moore slapped his first mate's shoulder and conceded with unabashed pride, "We have come home."

As word spread, a collective cheer resounded from the

emaciated men who celebrated the sight of land, even if it was a penal colony. I made my way to the rail and surveyed the wild coastline on the horizon. My jaw tightened. The lush, steamy jungle brought back too many bitter memories of Africa and the slain children.

By noon, *The Raven* entered the broad mouth of a river, and I envisioned our ship sliding down the throat of a colossal sea monster that would swallow us forever. The distant banks were lush green, diffused by the mist blanketing the tropical river like a morning fog. My dislike for this land mounted with each passing mile. I had been naive to tell the others that we would be free men at the end of this voyage. But now, staring at the jungle beyond the steamy river, I realized that the region itself served as the bars of a prison. A trek through this wilderness, even for fit men with equipment and guides, would be suicide.

The seamen arranged the prisoners in rows of two facing the gangplank. I sat on the rail, watching, wondering what would become of us, when Moore, flanked by two armed guards, seized my arm.

"You will join the others," he said. "Regardless of the circumstances, my commander would not understand a prisoner enjoying special privileges aboard this ship." The guards escorted me back to the other prisoners, thus stripping me of my duties as *The Raven's* assistant surgeon.

The afternoon air felt thick and hot, and we waited in agony under the scorching sun while the ship docked. Moore pushed his long hair beneath a large captain's hat that once belonged to Marart. I noted unease in his eyes as though he feared the man who chartered this voyage. Who, I wondered? He inspected the rows of ravaged men he managed to deliver alive. When he came to me, he stopped, removed the huge hat and fanned himself with it. The sun quickly became too hot, and he replaced the hat, indifferent to how foolish it made him look.

"I should like to know," he said to me, "if the accommodations of a French prison are preferable to a slave ship ridden with disease?"

I looked at him severely. "No."

"Of course not," he said, breaking into his broken smile. "You prefer freedom in hell to a prison in paradise. Am I right?" His smile vanished. "*The Raven* completed her mission, and now I will carry out my orders. May God help you." Without finishing his inspection, Moore led an entourage of petty officers including Dr. Dane down the gangplank.

The prisoners were already swooning from the heat when the guards ordered us to disembark. We shuffled double file down the gangplank and lined up along the dock for another inspection. A group of native children stood at the end of the pier, laughing and pointing at us. Beyond them lay their quiet little village of mud huts.

The guards divided us into lots of twenty and marched us off along the beach. Williams, walking behind me, muttered just loud enough for me to hear, "They's gonna brand us with a cattle iron, that's what they's gonna do."

One of our guards, a stocky man with a voice like a steel chisel, struck Williams to his knees with the butt of a carbine.

"No talking."

Our group stopped. Williams touched the back of his head and stared at the blood painting the tips of his fingers. He directed a bewildered gaze at the soldier who struck him.

The guard raised his carbine. "Take your place."

Williams rose unsteadily to his feet.

We resumed our march through a thin patch of jungle and entered a high-walled compound resembling a common marketplace. Guards with rifles were everywhere. Black women with large hats watched us through doorways.

"Eyes forward," the guard warned.

We were shepherded into a stone building, a single large room without furnishings, and given to the care of two desperate-looking men, unshaven and clad in filthy trousers. The wretched pair ordered us to strip. Those who refused were beaten with wooden clubs. The two watched me with twisted smiles while I surrendered the tailored shirt and trousers I had taken from Dane's wardrobe and stood naked before them.

The two characters went to work, running their filthy hands over each of our bodies, feeling muscles and examining testicles in their search for disease. They were particularly keen to probe our rectums. After this humiliating inspection, they passed out bundles of grey uniforms. We were not given shoes. The prison garbs transformed us into the most desperate looking criminals.

"These trousers are filthy," Eben complained, waving them at me.

"Ssssssss," Williams whispered. "They'll club you with guns."

"Put them on and do exactly as you're told," I said.

One of the men fixed my brother with a malicious smile. "You wish to march naked by my side?"

Eben hurriedly dressed. I saw him secure his knife under his prison clothes.

A sergeant entered the barracks. "This way."

Outside, we were lined up and presented to a pair of officers dressed in white uniforms and black boots, who inspected us as though we were livestock. We were sorted and assigned to smaller groups. Eben and I were ordered to join a group of older men, while Williams joined a group of hefty types, most likely to be sold into slavery. The thought of him no longer a free man after agreeing to help find Vanessa crushed me. Williams gave me a nod as the guards led him away. I felt vulnerable with him no longer at my side.

Our group of nine men, strung together with chains and shackles, plodded back to the pier. Next to *The Raven* sat an old steam tub with the name *Demoiselle de Grâce* in faded letters on her rusted hull. She looked tired and worn, much like the men she had been enlisted to transport. We shuffled single file up the gangplank and into the tub's hold. The interior felt unbearably hot. We squeezed into a rusty cage with a single porthole, while a pair of guards, indifferent and arrogant, patrolled the passageway outside. Soon the engines were churning roughly, pushing the tub out to sea.

When the guards left the corridor, an older gentleman from our group, a man with pure white hair and deep features, said to me, "We have just left the penal colony of St. Laurent at the mouth of the Maroni River." All eyes shifted to this man who, despite his haggard appearance, spoke with eloquence and authority. "They are taking us to an island set aside for political prisoners, where the sea will be our prison walls and the sharks our guards. Executions are routine."

"How do you know this colony?" I asked him.

He said tiredly, "I am, or I should say was, a professor of criminology at Cambridge. I was traveling to Maryland for a year of research when our ship was attacked and sunk. My wife burned to death in that terrible disaster. God knows why I am still alive. I assume they will hold me until the University pays a ransom."

"What else do you know about these islands?" I asked. "How do we escape?"

He let out a sigh. "Even if we could reach the mainland, the climate and diseases would not allow the likes of Europeans to survive long in these jungles. We are singularly fortunate to be going to the Salvation Islands, though. They are reasonably free of the disease-carrying insects that killed most of the mainland's original settlers."

There followed a lengthy silence, broken when Eben said, "But why? We've committed no crime against France."

There came an outburst of agreement from the other men. The guards appeared, their carbines braced in the firing position. Under the threat of execution, we were forbidden to utter another word for the remainder of our short voyage.

Eventually, the ship's engines cut to a crawl, and there came a blast from the steam whistle. The Cambridge professor stood up to the porthole.

"We've arrived," he said. "Most fascinating."

Others pushed for a glimpse out the porthole. When I had my chance to view our new home, I saw three lush islands with unusual contours and colors. A thick, green jungle draped each rounded peak—a primitive world, isolating its inhabitants from the rest of humanity.

As our little tub anchored, the guards lined us up on deck facing the gangway. I saw a harbor area beyond the docks with heavy equipment—an industrial-class shipyard. The two iron warships were docked under scaffolding for maintenance and repairs.

"This island is called Royale," the Cambridge professor whispered from behind me. "Here we will find the prison's administration building, the church—"

"You will not speak unless ordered to give information," roared the sergeant of the guards. "Who does not understand this?" The sergeant removed a revolver from his holster, cocked the hammer and looked directly at the professor.

No one uttered another word.

HELL'S WARDEN

Our little party, flanked by four guards, filed onto the beach and followed the sergeant up a steep, twisted path, bordered on both sides by a thick tangle of jungle.

At the top of the island, we marched into a squat stone building with the words *Administration du Port* posted above its door. The sergeant led the way into a stone foyer, up several steps and into a room staffed with assorted military types who appeared to be occupied with administrative duties. The sergeant put up a hand, bringing our group to a halt. Across from us sat a distinguished-looking administrator who could not be bothered to look up from the neat stack of papers on his desk. He had been wounded recently. A layer of bandages covered his left eye and half his forehead.

A stout, florid-faced gentleman, dressed in a suit two sizes too small, waddled forward and peered questioningly at us over his reading spectacles. In practiced English, he said, "Listen to me carefully and do as instructed. Each of you will give your name, nationality and previous occupation. I do not want to hear anything other than those three facts and in that order. Those of you who do not cooperate will face a firing squad. There will be no exceptions, no clemency."

He glanced myopically over his glasses, searching our faces for signs of contempt. Finding nothing but vacant stares, he opened a ledger book and said, "We will proceed from left to right."

As each of us stepped forward to give information about ourselves, the man scribbled notes in his book with the speed of a court stenographer. The interrogation identified among our group two naval officers, the university professor, a chemist, an architect, a lawyer of criminal law and a Catholic priest.

When I gave my name and occupation, the dignified gentleman, who had been sitting undistracted at his desk, looked up from his papers and brought the interrogation to a halt with a wave of his hand.

"Aaahhhh, so you are Andrew Finsbury." His voice resonated with the quality of a trained baritone.

He stood, stepped around the desk and appraised me with his good eye. He had the bearing of a military man, with white hair impeccably trimmed and coiffed, and a weathered but princely face. I would even call him striking for his age, save for those bloated bandages covering his left eye. Oblivious to the brutal heat of the island, he wore a tailored gray suit made of silk. I would declare him in his late-fifties, impressive in every way. What was his business in this hellhole?

After studying me for several long moments, he broke into a smile I would come to loathe. "I have been looking forward to our meeting, Mr. Finsbury."

He spoke perfect English, save for an occasional word he pronounced with a slight French accent. He beamed when he saw Eben and stepped forward for a closer look. "The resemblance tells me the young man at your side is your brother, Ebenezer. Very interesting. Welcome to my islands. I trust you enjoyed your journey here." Smiling, he withdrew an elegantly carved pipe from his coat pocket and began scraping the bowl with a golden reamer.

"Have we met before?" I asked.

"Heavens no," he huffed. "I know of your uncle, Admiral Joshua Finsbury. He and I never met socially, but I had the thrill of battling his fleet on the Black Sea during the war. Do you know why I remember him so well?"

I shook my head.

"Because he commanded the only warship my armada failed to sink." His good eye sparkled with pride as he peered into his past. "Your uncle taught me a great deal about naval firepower and the vulnerability of wooden warships."

He knocked his pipe on the edge of the desk and then blew noisily into the stem to clear any lingering debris. "I am known on this island as Albert Bonnet, but my given name is Philippe Rudler. I have several official titles, but you need only know I am governor of this colony."

I recalled Uncle speaking of an admiral named Rudler in the French navy. Although a brilliant naval strategist, the man Uncle spoke of had been convicted of piracy and war atrocities and, as I recall, executed in France some years ago. How could this be the same man?

"Are you Admiral Rudler of France?"

He laughed with surprise. "Quite right, Mr. Finsbury. No one has addressed me as Admiral for—" He paused in mild disbelief. "Has it been ten years?"

"An admiral executed for piracy," I said. "A dark, undignified end to a brilliant career. Nevertheless, congratulations on your resurrection."

Rudler's smile faded. He sat on the edge of his desk and tamped his pipe with tobacco.

"I am not ashamed of my past, Mr. Finsbury. My country sent me to war. But my commanders did not appreciate the efficiency with which I carried out my duties. They did not understand that in war, there is no mercy, only calculated destruction. The weak die. They sentenced me to death over a single incident of no importance to the war effort. Obviously, I arranged for them to execute the wrong man. I took refuge in this God-forsaken colony and continued my work here unhampered by intrusive bureaucracy."

I forced a smile. "So you've made these islands a model of penal reform?"

He did not acknowledge my sarcasm. "Here I have been able to finish what in France I could barely start. I have designed and built a new generation of warships with unmatched firepower and maneuverability. Unlike steam, their unique electric propulsion system allows my vessels to hunt their prey without making a sound."

"Electric," I said, impressed. "I would very much like to see that."

"Perhaps you will have that chance." Rudler stepped to a window and thrust his pipe at the desolate rock-like island across the channel. "The Island of the Devil. It is from these islands that I launched my modest fleet four months ago—two warships that have no equal in the world. They have been more effective than I dared dream. With them, I have accumulated great wealth thanks in part to your Majesty's gold, placed in your Uncle's care. I will use them to begin a war—an expensive war. Already your country is preparing for confrontation on a global scale." He faced me again. "I look forward to the day when the world recognizes what I have accomplished here."

"I'm aware of your warships. One of your ironclads almost destroyed my ship."

"Steel vessels," he corrected me. "My vessels have impenetrable steel hulls."

I bowed slightly, acknowledging my error.

"My only mistake was putting unmeshed glass in the conning tower." Rudler's smile faded and his face set like stone, his eye locked with mine. "You see, I have been on the dangerous end of your guns." He gestured to his wounded face. "I commanded the vessel that attacked your schooner. I stood in the conning tower, relaying instructions to the pilot, when one of your shots shattered several portholes and turned the small compartment into a nightmare of carpenter nails. The pilot died instantly. A lucky shot for you, I am sure."

I felt the color draining from my face. "A pirate should expect a strong defense..."

"I am a soldier," he flared. "And this is war—global war." Rudler gave a small sigh, almost of regret. "Perhaps I have grossly overestimated you." He pointed the stem of his pipe at me. "A woman, someone close to you, tried to convince me that I should fear you. The conviction of her warnings tempted me to believe her, or at least to look forward to meeting you. I now realize that my apprehension wasn't justified. You are nothing."

My heart soared, and I did everything in my power to contain my excitement. "Vanessa is alive?"

Rudler laughed. "Yes, she is alive and under my personal care. And such a lovely woman. I can assure you that I have fully explored the depths of her charm and her ability to please."

I roared and swung the short length of chain between my wrists, struggling to use it as a weapon. At the same time, four guards moved in to restrain me.

Rudler gave a throaty chuckle. "You Englishmen act quite the fools when your emotions are aroused." Then his eyes took on a dark, sinister look. "I can promise you will never leave these islands."

The stout note taker coughed apologetically. Rudler acknowledged him with a nod.

"The tribunal is waiting." Rudler buttoned his jacket and said to the sergeant of the guards, "Take them below until they are called."

As the guards herded us away, Rudler pointed to me. "Not him. He will be the first."

TRIBUNAL

"The prisoner will not speak unless addressed by this court," said a gruff voice, well tuned to giving orders. "This tribunal is in order."

Two guards shoved me before a long table at which sat three officers, reigning over the tribunal like Baghdad regents. Rudler stood behind them, gazing out a latticed window with an air of feigned disinterest.

For several long minutes, the three military judges studied me, whispered among themselves and consulted papers laid out before them. Finally, the officer seated in the middle—a general—leaned back in his chair and locked his fingers behind his head. He spoke in a hard and cold voice.

"The accused will tell the court his name and nationality."

The general's khaki uniform resembled those worn by the French Camel Corps, yet he spoke English like an Englishman. He was an older man, past the traditional retiring age, with a high, bald forehead and a grizzled mustache. The rows of colorful ribbons decorating his coat suggested a war hero.

"My name is Andrew Finsbury."

"British?"

"Yes."

"Tell the court why you docked in Sierra Leone?"

"I'm a scholar of West African religions. I had hoped to study voodooism."

The general slapped the table hard with the flat of his hand. "You are on trial for your life. This court will not tolerate insubordination. The punishment for giving false testimony is death."

He leaned forward and repeated in a low, cold tone, "What did you hope to find in Sierra Leone?"

"I answered your question."

The general looked astonished, then enraged. Rudler turned from the window to glare at me.

"Forgive me," I said. "Voodooism, sir."

"You dare mock me?" the general hissed. "You are accused of scouting our operation while in the service of the British Navy. I have evidence you attacked one of our warships on a routine patrol of the North Atlantic. You also are accused of organizing a mutiny aboard the merchant ship *The Raven* while on a supply run from Africa, an action which resulted in substantial loss of lives. Do you have anything to say that will lead this court to believe you are not the man responsible for these crimes?"

These charges astonished me. How could I respond to this farce of a court? I held no illusions that my trial would be fair; regardless of my defense, the judges had already dug my grave.

The general stood and gave me a severe look. "Guilty or no?"

"I've committed no crime."

The general hit the table hard with his fist, causing the men on either side of him to flinch. He rounded the table and, as he approached me, I saw that his face and neck were pockmarked with powder-burn scars.

"Do you deny attacking one of our warships?" he said.

"We were the ones attacked—"

The general swung his fist, and I dropped to my knees, stunned by the blow to my jaw. He added a solid kick to my stomach with his heavy boot.

"Get up," he shouted, cradling his fist. Several pairs of hands yanked me to my feet. "You are indeed the man we seek."

I wavered drunkenly before him. "No."

"The same man who attempted to commandeer *The Raven*."

"No."

"You disregarded Captain Marart's orders and incited his crew to mutiny. It is all written here in his log book."

I could feel the blood churning in my head. "Marart was a madman. When Captain Moore assumed command, he allowed us to do what we could to save the ship from a deadly epidemic of smallpox. No one was in any state to mutiny."

"Moore paid for his insubordination," the general said. "He will remain hanging by his neck from the yard-arm of *The Raven* for seven days."

"Barbarians—"

The general swung his fist at my head a second time. I raised my arms and absorbed the blow on my metal wrist cuffs. The general withdrew his hand in anguish. Two guards grabbed my arms and bent them back, nearly breaking them off at the shoulders. Another yanked my head back by my hair, immobilizing me. The general pounded my stomach with vicious blows until his forehead broke out in sweat.

"Do you deny spying for the British Navy?" he huffed, clenching and unclenching his fist.

The blow left me doubled over, unable to produce any

sound except a lame sucking noise in the back of my throat.

When I did not answer, the general turned to his colleagues and announced his verdict: "I find the accused guilty of espionage, punishable by death."

Rudler could no longer contain his amusement behind a passive grin and began laughing loudly. He stepped before the table, wiping a tear from his eye. "Not so quickly. I am enjoying this far too much."

"Sir, our case ledger is long," the general said.

"Nevertheless, this court will hear one witness." He signaled the soldier standing next to the door. "Bring her."

The guard stepped into the corridor and returned with a woman. Though she looked pale and withdrawn, there was no mistaking her uncommon beauty. I cannot describe the intensity of emotions I felt upon seeing her again.

I pulled my stooped frame to its full height and whispered, "Vanessa."

She looked at me, uncomprehending. She didn't recognize me at first, and then she brought a hand to her mouth to stifle a gasp of surprise. We just stood there, reading in each other's faces the agony of our separation, the horror of captivity, to reveal in one moment all the longing we held in our hearts since we were last together.

"You have come for me," she said.

Her eyes dropped to the chains on my wrists and ankles, and I saw her hopeful expression melt into despair. My heart sank. She believed I would come as her savior, but I could not help her.

"Let her go," I said. "I'll do whatever you ask, but let her go."

Rudler approached Vanessa, his gaze making no secret of his lust for my lady. He gathered her flowing hair into his hand, caressing it. "You told me his uncle's fleet would attack these islands. I must know if there is any truth to that threat."

Vanessa returned his cold stare with a defiant gaze.

Rudler ran his fingers through her long, silken hair, then yanked her head back with a snap, forcing her to look into his good eye. "You will tell me."

Terror spoiled the beauty of her eyes, but her voice when she spoke was firm and controlled. "His uncle will find you here and see that you hang."

Rudler spun to look at me. "For two days a British armada has been amassing warships in the Caribbean. Tell me their intentions, or you will watch this woman die."

Uncle? Here? I did my best to hide my surprise. "Her Majesty believes the missing ships foundered in winter storms. I sailed against my uncle's wishes."

Disgusted, Rudler released his hold of Vanessa's hair. "I do not believe you. I promise that you will watch your brother and your woman die."

"They are innocent. Kill me, but I beg you to spare them."

He thrust a finger at me. "You will be my prisoner on this island for as long as I can keep you alive. I promise I will do everything to assure that you live a long life here."

Vanessa squirmed in the arms of the guard. "Let go of me!"

Rudler turned to her and, touching her chin, said, "You are indeed beautiful. I will miss you." He again grabbed her hair and began kissing her mouth like a famished man.

Vanessa wrestled an arm free and dug her fingernails into the warden's face just below his good eye deep enough to draw blood. Rudler staggered back, stunned. A slender trickle of blood flowed down his cheek.

Vanessa gave him a smile of satisfaction. "Admiral Finsbury will sink these islands of yours."

"Whore." With a brush of his hand, Rudler struck Vanessa's face with a hard blow. Her head rolled, and I feared he had broken her neck. There came a slight groan. I could see blood beneath the veil of hair that hid her face.

"What kind of monster does this to a woman?" I roared.

Rudler touched his cheek and examined his bloodied fingertips. He instructed the members of the tribunal, "Inform Diable that I want the equipment ready by morning. We will have a full day." Then he looked at me and said, "I never feared you—it is your brother who threatens what I will finish here. And I thank you for bringing him here to me from halfway around the world. Tomorrow I will finally be rid of him."

He made no sense. "You're making a terrible mistake. He is a boy and of no threat to you at all."

"Tomorrow you will bear witness to an interesting experiment involving your brother and your lady. I cannot promise that it will be painless for them." He signaled the guards with a wave. "Take him over to the unit."

Two guards bundled me out the door, and I whirled for another look at Vanessa. Her head stirred.

As they dragged me down the corridor, my mind spun with questions. Most troubling was Rudler's fear of my brother. Why?

I had one more day to find out.

ISLAND OF THE DEVIL

The soldiers transferred me by boat to the *Isle du Diable*, a mountain of rock a half mile north of Royale. Du Diable, a desolate island almost barren of vegetation, was the bleakest of prisons. With its sheer cliffs overlooking shark-infested waters, one's very soul would be forever imprisoned here.

We landed on a shallow beach, where the soldiers doubled my wrist and leg shackles and hustled me to the top of the island. They took me inside a concrete building with no windows, and we descended a dark stone staircase with the aid of a single lantern. The damp air stank of excretion and the sound of dripping water echoed below us.

We entered a corridor with walls lit with harsh incandescent lights—a by-product of Rudler's shipyard generators, I assumed. The guards handled me roughly down a passageway lined with wooden doors. A scruffy jailer with too much hair opened a heavy oak door and beckoned me inside with a hooked finger. I stepped into the cell and, shuddering, stood staring at the darkness. The floor below my bare feet felt damp and slippery with moss. The door banged shut behind me, followed by the rasp of a bolt.

"Sleep fit," the jailer laughed. "I'll be wakin' ya early."

The guards' retreating jeers echoed down the passageway as they left me alone in my lurid cell.

By the thin band of light leaking under the door, I inspected every inch of my quarters looking for a way out. The examination took seconds. My cell, a meager six-feet long, had no bench on which to sit or lay. Thoughts of escaping vanished.

"Andrew?" called a timid voice from across the corridor.

I jumped against the door. "Ebby … are you all right?"

"The jailer said I'm going to die tomorrow. It's not true, is it?"

I never heard him sound so frightened. I wished I could see him. "Uncle will be here," I told him in a half whisper. "Rudler needs us alive to bargain."

"It's not fair," Eben said. "They will guillotine us, won't they?"

"Put that thought out of your mind. It's not going to happen."

"I've studied anatomy," he said. "The central nervous system can't be blown out like a candle. It takes time for consciousness to fade. I'm certain my trunkless head will hear everyone cheering after the blade falls."

"Ebby—"

"As my dying eyes look up at the fallen blade, I'll understand very well what's happened to me."

"Think of Uncle. He'll be here."

"We'll be nothing but bones by the time he arrives." I heard him sobbing. After another long silence, he asked, "What will happen after I die? What do you believe, Andrew? Tell me."

Eben's voice was choked with fear, and I had little to offer to comfort him. Death—at least for me—haunts my waking hours with the cruelest of nightmares. But I would tell Eben none of this. I would lie to him again, as I had done every time he sought my assurance throughout our journey here together.

"I believe it's different for each of us," I said, "like a dream."

"So, there is something after this life, something beautiful. Isn't that true, Andrew?"

"Yes ... of course. We can never fulfill our destinies in such a short lifetime. We will live many times." I looked at my wrist and leg shackles and didn't realize my hands were shaking.

"I want to be back home with Uncle...." I could hear Eben trembling in his chains and sobbing.

I had failed him miserably. *I'm so sorry, Ebby.*

The strip of light under the door dimmed and sputtered as though something was diverting power. There came a loud crack, and the corridor plunged into darkness. Eben broke into uncontrollable sobbing.

"You need to understand everything I'm going to tell you, mate."

I whirled at the sound of Myles' voice but saw only blackness. "For the love of God, Myles," I said breathlessly, "help us."

"Help you, mate? I came to seek your help."

As my eyes adjusted, I saw a vague shadow of a man a shade blacker than the cell's smothering darkness. I reached forward but touched nothing. Could Eben hear him? "I can't see you?"

"I'm standing before you," he said. "I cannot stay long for reasons I won't even begin to explain. But you must come with me. I will tell you all that you are capable of knowing."

"What do you want from me?"

"The warden intends to keep you chained to these

walls till he finishes his business on Earth. That will take decades. We must finish him now before he gets his way."

"But there's no way out of here."

"You don't need that frail shell you call a body," Myles said. "Trust me on that point."

"I only care about the lives of my brother and Vanessa. How can I save them?"

"Eben's fate is already decided, as is Vanessa's," he said. "We've tricked Rudler. He's spent a decade searching for the boy he feared would defeat him. He murdered untold numbers of innocent children in that search. He now knows that Eben is that boy, and he will kill him. He doesn't realize that Eben is only a threat to him dead. It's all been arranged. We tricked him."

"I cannot let them die."

My friend's shadow movements became agitated. I could sense his impatience. "You don't have a choice," he said. "You can do nothing here. You can only help Vanessa once you've been liberated."

The room began to spin. I eased myself into a sitting position with my back propped against the stone wall, my hands over my ears. I wanted this conversation to end.

"He will shackle you to this wall. He intends to amputate your arms so you cannot do yourself in. You must come … with … me… nowwwwww…."

An unearthly noise, hostile and terrifying, drowned out his fading voice. My head shot up. I was no longer in a cell. Another migration to the otherworld left me sitting in a slight clearing surrounded by a grove of birch trees. My wrist and ankle shackles were gone. High above me, immense dark clouds rolled across the heavens as a great, ugly storm approached.

"Follow me," Myles urged. *"Quickly."*

I stood quickly but could not see him. "Where?"

"Go."

The grim clouds turned the sky into a dark, moonless night. A chill ran through me when Myles' voice called from within forest beyond the tree line. I looked desperately about, searching for some anchor on reality, but I saw nothing but rows of dark trees that had grown unusually tall.

Myles called my name again from a distance. I spun, trying to gain a bearing on his voice. Closing my mind to the doubts and fears that lingered there, I bolted into the forest, searching for him among the underbrush. I stopped to listen but heard no sound at all. No rush of wind, no leafy rustle, no voices. Nor could I see anything beyond the forest's deep shadows.

I was lost and quite alone.

THE FOREST

An unearthly noise blared from the forest. I spun, terrified. The sound, a bizarre high-pitched whine layered with cackles and hisses, was nothing like I had ever heard before. A bird cry, perhaps? No species I could recall.

I stood staring at the deep shadows, listening. The sound came again, nearer. My hand leaped to my waistband for a revolver but found nothing with which to defend myself.

I heard something stir in the underbrush. Not the sound of wind rustling leaves, for the forest lacked such mundane noise. But rather stealth—someone or something was stalking me. Then, over my shoulder, I spotted movement in the murk. Another bush fluttered ahead, then another to my right.

"Myles?" My voice echoed away hollowly and died.

A pair of eyes, bright and crimson, watched me from a deep shadow cast by an enormous tree. The eyes belonged to a creature much larger than a man. Fear as I had never known seized me, and I thought I would swoon. I forced myself to keep moving, hoping to find my way back to— what? My cell? My boots sank with every step. The under- growth—a mulch-like blanket of moss, leaves and needles—gave the ground a strange, sinking feeling as though I were treading on a living thing that meant to swallow me.

Something burst through the brush behind me. I turned in time to see a large animal disappear into the bracken, swallowed by the gloom.

I wanted to run far away from this frightening place. But where to go?

I hurried into a gully, the cruel branches and thorns grabbing and scratching me like talons. I stopped and listened, my eyes continually moving.

As I began to move on, the voice of an elderly gentleman called down to me: "Wait, Englishman. I must speak with you."

I spun and looked upward. A dark figure, a mere shadow against the tangled trees, stood atop the ridge above me. The shadow stood twice the size of a man. Its glowing amber eyes resembled a mourner holding a pair of candles at an unholy wake.

I ignored the voice and ran down the gorge away from this horror when something in my path brought me to a wavering halt. A vicious creature stood before me, fangs dripping, claws extended. Clad in grotesque armor, it resembled a lion standing erect on powerful hind legs—a warrior beast. Its crimson eyes were like a pair of glowing coals, born of evil.

I could not summon the slightest sound from my throat.

With a roar, the beast's paw, twice the size of a bear's, swept down and ripped into my neck and shoulder. The blow hurled me against the trunk of a large tree where I collapsed in a heap. My shoulder felt ablaze, my face numb. Stunned, I rubbed a hand over my bloodied face. Harm could still befall me here in a real, physical sense.

The beast clamped my chest into its vice-like paw and lifted my body into the air, squeezing my insides together and forcing blood into my ringing ears. An agonizing cry erupted from my throat. Delirious with panic, I scratched and pounded its enormous arm, refusing to surrender, but I was powerless against its incalculable strength.

The beast tucked me under its arm and bolted through the forest, stomping down small trees in its path. The foliage became a blur. I squirmed and twisted; the beast's grip on me tightened.

We came to a clearing on the shores of a lake, and a waft of malodorous air that reeked of rotting fish accosted me. The heavens glowed a deep crimson as though the sky were ablaze, its blood-like hue casting a foreboding glow over the forest. On the lake's opposite shore lay a barren landscape with a single mountain peak. Was this the hell Dante described?

The beast carried me down to the water's edge. I stared at the water and formed a plan. I was an excellent swimmer. Given an opportunity, I would use the lake as an avenue of escape.

We came upon another group of beasts huddled together near the water, also wearing armor, feeding on fresh slaughter. They gestured to each other while making that high-pitched whine with cackles and hisses—a demonic conversation. An arsenal of primitive armaments—swords, spears, clubs, and axes—jutted from the black mud. Several slept on their backs snoring loudly.

They had been feasting, celebrating a kill. Scraps of human bones and other butchered parts lay strewn about their grisly party. One beast displayed a deadly set of fangs as it devoured the flesh from the bone of a human leg. Another tore open the chest of a fresh corpse with its claws and then ate its heart and lungs, ravenous.

As we approached, the other creatures scrambled for their weapons and formed a tight circle around us, baring fangs. There was no mistaking their lusty looks of hunger—I would be their next meal. With a hiss of metal, the beast that held me unsheathed its cutlass. Holding me high over its head, it swung the sword in the air in a primitive ritual before the slaughter, just missing my head with each sweep. The others drew in closer, whining noisily and raising their peculiar assortment of arms at me. I watched them, detached, like a blurred dream.

What happened next is not entirely clear to me. The beast holding me grew rigid, its claws crushing me, and let out a howl louder than any steam whistle. Its claw opened. I dropped onto the mud and rolled clear as the beast toppled onto the beach, barely missing my legs. I raised myself onto an elbow and saw a homemade knife jutting from the armor between the fallen beast's shoulders. I recognized Eben's dagger, the one he had fashioned from a galley utensil and always carried with him after our clash with Rudler's warship. How could this be?

The other warriors fanned out, scrambling for battle, raising their weapons against the unseen attacker. Before I could move, one of the beasts, all fangs and armor, stepped over me with a double-bladed ax raised over its head. I rolled towards the lake as its blade whistled downward. I felt the sting of its edge cutting a groove along the flesh above my left hip. I staggered to my feet, splashed through the scummed surf and dove headlong into the lake's shallows. Two of the most vicious beasts bolted after me, screeching obscenely.

I scrambled farther out into the lake, whipping the water into a fine froth, then dove beneath the surface. The water was as thick as oil. I sank into a black abyss until I felt the soft squash of mud beneath my feet. I stood on the lakebed in total darkness, listening to absolute silence, waiting for something to happen. Nothing did.

When I realized I needed air, I had no time to surface. Panic swelled inside me as my chest muscles went into spasms. My lungs involuntarily heaved and the brackish water imploded into my chest. The awful sensation of drowning followed. Strangely, I did not black out and, in a moment, all discomfort passed.

Bewildered, I trudged to the opposite shore, feeling my way along the murky bottom, the last threads of my sanity straining to snap. I touched a slender piece of wood. Thinking it would be useful in digging through the muck, I steadied myself and wrenched it free. But it wasn't wood—I held in my hands a human rib cage. I recoiled in surprise, lost my balance and spilled sideways onto the viscous lakebed. Bones lay strewn everywhere. I crawled through the field of human debris until I reached the shore on the far side of the lake.

I surveyed the beach before me. Skeletons, skulls and bone fragments covered the beach. I also noted the remains of a wrecked ship—a three-masted brigantine that resembled the *Timonium*. Beyond the wreck stood a black mountain, its jagged peak reaching for the scarlet sky, giving a severe warning to all who dared land here. I saw no sign of the beasts.

I waded ashore and collapsed amid the rubble. I felt ill. I turned my head and expelled a great gush of green water from my lungs. My shirt, oily and shredded, stuck to me like a second skin. I reeked of dead fish.

I felt for the gashes on my arm. My heart stopped when I discovered I had no left arm at all! I sprang to my feet and stared at the stump below my shoulder. I watched, incredulous, as my left arm materialized, whole and without scars. I clenched and unclenched my fist to assure I possessed all coordination and control. I did.

Someone nearby began to laugh. I dropped to the ground and rolled. Did I really hear something, or had the voice come from within my mind? I couldn't be sure.

I waited. The laughter came again.

"Who are you?" I called.

No answer, but the voice continued to chuckle, teasing me, suppressing the urge to burst into laughter. Finally, the voice said, "Sorry, mate, but your expression while searching for your missing arm was a hoot."

"Myles?"

A part of my mind touched him, and I felt the presence of my friend. Without using his voice, I heard him say: "No one said this would be a holiday, mate."

I jumped up and searched the beach for him but found only bones. "Show yourself."

"That won't be easy," he said. "I'm stuck."

In the shallows I spotted a hand jutting above the reeds, waving. I dashed into the surf to help my friend and recoiled in horror at the sight of the thing with which I had been conversing. The corroded carcass of a man, mostly bones with the slimmest layer of white flesh covering its upper torso, extended a shriveled hand to me and said, "Be a pal, mate, and pull me out of this muck."

I recognized the same awful corpse I saw beneath the tarpaulin in the hold of Porter's steamer. I backed away. "Good God—"

"Stow it," he snapped, his voice sharp. "Help me."

The carcass struggled to stand but lacked the muscles to wrench its bones free of the mud. Its shriveled features contorted in frustration. "Bloody dammit."

I could do nothing but stare dumbfounded at the animated corpse.

"If you're just going to stand there gaping," it snapped,

"I'll leave you to fend for yourself."

Again, the husk of a man offered me his hand. Reluctant, I reached forward and touched it. The fingers felt cold and stiff, like a stone. My lips tightened as the corpse grabbed my hand and, with my support, kicked and pulled itself free of the mud. The thing stood upright before me.

The spoiled face undeniably belonged to Myles Edwards the ghastly way he looked after Captain Porter snatched his bloated body from the sea. I hated to look at it.

Using eyes that were two dark holes, the cadaver gazed across the wreck-strewn beach as though it still possessed all its faculties. It took in a deep breath to fill its useless lungs and then placed a bony hand on my shoulder.

I pulled away. "You look ... appalling—"

"My soul is whole, mate. You just refuse to see it. If you wish to remember me at my worst, so be it—for now. I understand and will take no offense. But you'll soon learn to see the truth."

I stared at the corpse, frustrated by my apparent failure to transcend my Earth-borne biases. Despite his dreadful appearance, my friend behaved amicably as he had in life.

"Myles," I said, "my earthly body is still alive."

"Wishful thinking," Myles said. "The bonds to life often get tangled during the transition."

From a distance came the chilling whine of the feline beasts. We both turned to see a contingent of warriors rounding the lake, charging through the surf and waving their weapons.

"Guardians," Myles said.

"What?"

"Belial's minions. Dreadful things ... the lowest life forms in this world. It's their purpose to keep you here, to put your soul into a sanctum, where it will sleep for a thousand years."

"The lake, Myles. They can't follow."

Myles gestured to the mountain. "No, this way." He sprinted across the beach on his two bony stilt-like legs. I raced after him.

"Myles," I called after him, "I've heard things as though our minds can exchange thoughts. I heard you speak, though you didn't make a sound."

"We haven't any flesh, mate," he hollered back to me, "so we can't shield our thoughts. Our souls are bare to each other."

Myles led the way into a cave at the base of a cliff and then down a dark passage. We ran deep into the mountain before the stone corridor broke into two separate paths. Myles couldn't decide which to take. Prodded into a quick decision by the screeching of the approaching beasts, he jabbed a bony finger at the tunnel on the right.

"This way," he said.

A few steps further, the trail ended at the edge of a vast canyon. We were trapped.

"My mistake." We retraced our steps and bolted down the left tunnel. Behind us, alarmingly close, came the whines of the beasts and the sounds of their metal weapons scraping stone.

With each step, the granite walls closed in on us and I feared we were approaching another dead end. The farther we pushed, the narrower the passage became until we had barely enough room to squeeze by. Yet Myles gave no hint he wished to abandon this route and continued pushing his bones between the rock walls. He sprinted well ahead of me. I struggled to follow, forcing my body between the ever-narrowing walls.

The clamor of beasts faded behind us. We were out of

their reach, their large frames unable to slip through the constricting passageway.

The trail ended abruptly against a stone wall. Confused, I slapped my hand against the granite. The thought of retreating filled me with dread. I was trapped. "Myles, where are you?"

My voice reverberated around the confining stone passage. I had reached another dead end.

CAPTAIN MYLES EDWARDS

I heard my friend's voice call from a distance. "On your knees."

The sound resonated at my feet. I knelt and discovered a cylindrical tunnel two-feet in diameter, a deliberate passage hewed for people half my size. I slid into the tunnel and pulled through on my stomach.

The passage emptied into a high, vaulted chamber that reminded me of the ruins of a grand cathedral, an ancient place of worship. I let out a long, low whistle, while my eyes, wide and wondering, cast about the remarkable cavern. In the center of the chamber rose a massive altar carved from rock. Perched above it was a magnificent bird-like creature made of stone, its angelic wings spread for flight.

Myles stood at the base of the altar, tending a fire in a cauldron-like vessel that provided the chamber's light.

"Where are we?" My voice, distorted and eerily amplified, echoed off the high, arched ceiling.

"The crypt of Aruka," he said, poking the fire with a rod. The play of light cast huge dancing shadows across the ceiling as though the ruins were alive and restless. "Aruka bore children that became known as the Lenites."

I gazed at the magnificent winged creature made of

stone and wondered. Myles picked up an ancient urn, shook its liquid contents and emptied it into the fire. The flames grew higher. I drew closer, welcoming its warmth.

"This Aruka—what became of it?"

"Aruka left this realm a long time ago," he said, stirring the flames in the vessel, "or most of it did, anyway. This flame is all that remains of its ionized flesh. It's been burning here for countless millennia after Aruka's soul left the sanctum."

"Sanctum? I don't understand."

"A soul sanctum is a tough shell made of matter from both the physical and astral worlds. Very tough, very resilient. A soul migrating back to the physical world sometimes chooses to stay in a sanctum, unconscious for millennia—a very long hibernation of the spirit, awaiting the right age to be reborn. Aruka ultimately chose not to return to the physical world and shed what he couldn't take to the higher realm. That residue is what's now burning."

"You know much about this place."

Myles sat on the altar's bottom step. "I've been to the higher realms and have beheld the vast Sacred Knowledge that awaits us there. This is my sanctuary when I return to the lower world, and I come here when I want solitude. But never mind all of this. Aruka is not of your world or your time. I brought you here so we could talk about your destiny." He pointed the rod at the ground in front of him, and I sat where he indicated. "Tonight I must warn you about this dangerous world."

At a much younger age, my brother and I often gathered by a fire while Myles told grand stories of his sea adventures around the world. This reminded me of those days. By the firelight, I noted that his face had changed. Instead of a pale and shriveled corpse, his face appeared whole, and his eyes alive and bright. He had a week-old beard. I began to see him as he was, not as I presumed.

"It might help," he said, "if you think of this as a world within your mind—a dream from which you cannot awake."

His words sent a shiver through me. "A nightmare, you mean. Are you saying the forest, the beasts, you, are not real?"

"Our souls are real—as is the evil. Fear casts a black cloud. It confuses and will allow the evil to corrupt and control you. Fear is your real enemy here, not the beasts."

"How can I not be afraid of a world—real or not—as hostile and terrifying as this one? The pain is real."

"He has lured you to this primitive realm beneath the earthly plane where pain, when experienced, is more intense. You must keep your vibration level high and your thoughts clear. I will teach you to focus. Only then can you accept the Sacred Knowledge."

"Sacred knowledge?"

He waved the smoldering rod as a teacher would a pointer. "Knowledge from the Source that will liberate you and make you whole. This you must discover on your own, mate. In time you will understand everything. You have the character to achieve complete liberation of the spirit—man's highest destiny. You can succeed, I am sure of it."

His eyes held a disturbing intensity.

"This liberation you talk of," I asked, "is it heaven where we sit in the presence of God?"

"God in heaven?" He belted a hearty laugh. "Liberation is so much more than that. I have seen it, but the subject is vast. I cannot begin to tell you."

This intrigued me. "Why must I undergo this torment? Why am I not liberated immediately?"

Myles thrust the rod at my face. "Patience—the Plan will reveal itself when you are ready."

"Plan? What plan?"

"There is a reason all this happened in the manner and order that it did. There is a reason Vanessa disappeared and why your obsession to find her got you and your brother killed. Those events led you here to me at this moment—it's part of the Plan we all agreed to before we were born."

"What does any of this have to do with Eben?"

"All our destinies are tied together to defeat a man whose earthly name is Rudler. Alive, none of us possess the power to destroy him—certainly not on his island where only an army can take him. His defeat must be managed very carefully, lest his soul escapes to this world where he will grow stronger as he plots his return."

"But he is just one man," I said.

"He is not a man. He is Belial—a terrible demon incarnated."

I stiffened. *Belial*—that name has haunted me since Africa. I looked up to see Myles staring intently at me, his expression grave.

"The man you know as Rudler is merely a physical form that allows the demon to walk the earth," he said, once again reading my thoughts. "Belial intends to turn all nations against each other in a bitter global war. Rudler used his warships to accumulate vast wealth. Now he will declare war on the world. Nations will assemble larger armies and build more powerful weapons to defend themselves against an evil that will destroy mankind. There can be no mortal victor because the evil is not of the earth. When he succeeds, the world you remember will change. Belial will take possession and begin a new order among the living—a world of darkness, chaos and suffering." Myles stood and stirred the flames with his rod. "You can see it in the fire."

The flames flared, and an image appeared within the fire, a moving picture. I saw an execution chamber. Two soldiers were strapping a victim into the death chair, an older man with noble features wrought with dread—the Cambridge professor I met on the steamer to Royale.

"The demon continues his carnage," Myles said.

Myles continued stirring the fire, forcing a different image to appear. I saw the open sea. Rudler's twin steel vessels opened fire on an armada of more than twenty British warships. A fateful battle was imminent.

I felt a burst of hope. "Rudler's vessels can't possibly defeat the firepower of a fleet of warships."

"The outcome of this single battle will not decide mankind's fate," Myles said. "If he loses his ships, his armies, his plundered wealth—even his flesh—he will take possession from other sources and begin again. We must defeat him in this world. It is your charge to lure him here where his soul can be trapped. That is your purpose. Once you've brought him into this realm, others will put his soul into a sanctum where he will remain dormant for at least a millennium. My life's purpose was to prepare you for that duty. I pray I haven't failed you, that I haven't failed humanity. Mankind must be rid of Belial."

"So why me?"

"There are a thousand answers to that question, and none would satisfy. Why you? Why any of us? Do you possess great wisdom? Strength? Resources?"

He watched me for a reaction. Before I could respond, he blurted, "None of that matters here. Know that you were simply chosen—a single soldier summoned to fight a battle of which he understands little. You have no choice, nor does your Vanessa, or your brother. Nor do I. We all agreed to this plan before our births."

I stood, my head spinning in revelation. "Vanessa ... Rudler used her as the lure to bring me to the penal islands. Gabrielle told me I couldn't save her. She will die, and I will kill Rudler for it. So that's your so-called plan?" My anger surged. "I will not allow her to be used—"

There came a low rumble, and then the mountain began to shake. We both were on our feet, staring. A loud cracking filled the chamber, and a great shower of dirt and debris poured down over us.

He looked at me and said. "I pray you are ready."

"For what?"

Myles sprang to the tunnel from which we entered, knelt down and peered inside. "To experience your earthly death."

I remained by the altar, watching him intently. A blast deep within the mountain forced a thick cloud of dust through the shaft, and I could hear the approaching screeches of the guardians.

Myles' anxious eyes met mine. "They've found a way in."

"Can we fight them?" I doubted he could hear me over the growing clamor.

"There are too many. He is desperate and will try to overwhelm you with his soldiers in great numbers." My friend pointed to the altar. "That way."

The altar hid another tunnel, much like the first. I followed Myles into the opening just as the floor of the temple behind began to crack.

"Keep moving."

We pressed into the dimness on hands and knees as great billowing clouds of dust obscured what little light the tunnel provided.

"A bit farther," he said over his shoulder.

We emerged into another chamber—an enormous sphere. This was no natural cavern. Someone or something with a vast knowledge of engineering had hewn this compartment from the center of the mountain. The tunnel from which we emerged was but one of a thousand shafts leading into the sphere. The holes were subterranean passages, each leading in a different direction deep inside the mountain.

To reach the lowest point of the sphere, we were forced to climb down its curved wall. Myles watched my descent as we slid down the steep slope, concerned that I might slip into one of the dark tunnels and vanish. "This place once was a nest," he said, "a beehive of sorts, created by a species bearing an uncanny resemblance to the cricket. But very smart."

"Those forest beasts, Myles—you called them guardians—how can we be rid of them?"

"We can't. Belial fears you. This man, Rudler, is keenly aware that once you're dead, you will be in a position to do him real harm. He is obsessed with a desire to either imprison you here or lure you back to the living where he can keep you in his power, thereby removing the final obstacle to his destiny."

We reached the bottom of the sphere, and I found a safe spot next to my friend and sat down. Myles had shed the last vestiges of his corpse-like appearance, and I could see him as a whole man, though younger than I remembered. He looked anxiously at me, his manner restless, and I sensed his doubts and fears, not for his safety, but for mine. My unease mounted. Before I could say anything, a terrible hissing filled the sphere—the guardians' battle cry.

I jumped up and grabbed Myles' arm. "Let's keep moving."

He shook his head and made no effort to follow me. "There is nowhere else to run. Very soon it will be your time. When you return here, I want you to find your way to the graveyard where we first met in this world."

A legion of beasts, each brandishing a weapon, charged from several tunnels at once. I scrambled blindly backward, taking refuge in a shallow crevice. But my friend had no time to move before the beasts pounced on him.

Myles shouted to me, "Seek out his fortress—"

A beast severed his head with an ax, silencing him. I watched helplessly while a dozen guardians dismembered my friend with their grotesque weapons until only a bloody pulp remained.

More beasts, one more fearful than the next, charged from a dozen shafts at once. They kept coming—thirty, forty, fifty—all of them armed.

Myles' severed head rolled into the crevice next to me. A ceaseless wail poured from his lips, a noise lacking any human emotion. I stared at his disembodied head, frozen by what the beasts had done to him. A voice within my mind, Myles' voice as clear as if he were standing next to me, said, *"Listen to me, mate. The Fortress of Belial is not far from here. Inside, the veil between the world of the dead and the living is thin—"*

A spear pierced the upper calf of my leg from behind, its tip sticking straight through. I cried out more in surprise than from pain. I spun around. There, glowering over me with a cutlass in hand, stood their leader, half again as tall as the others. The thing's snout drew back in a grin, showing me rows of merciless fangs. It shook its full mane and bellowed a frightful caricature of arrogant laughter. A second beast, toting a stone club that could pulverize a bear, appeared at its side.

I had only the spear rammed through my leg. I twisted it free much too roughly, tearing away part of my leg. The crude spear, a good ten feet long, was awkward to handle, but deadly nonetheless with a lethal tip made of iron.

With one wild swipe, I went for the club-toting beast. My aim was off, but the spear's tip managed to clip the beast's wrist. The thing yelped as the club spun away. The others drew back in surprise.

"So you cower when your prey fights back," I shouted, anger pushing aside my fear. "I will make you pay for what you did to my friend."

A chaotic blur of movement swirled around me, but I dared not chance a look, not even for a second. This fight required my full attention.

The leader and I circled each other, each watching the other, each avoiding the holes that threatened to swallow us. The thing let out a growl from deep in its chest, while its crimson eyes remained fixed on the spear's tip that I held pointed at its face. "You unsophisticated swine," it said. "You cannot win here."

Its speech surprised me. I lowered the spear and plunged the tip with all my strength through its leg joint.

The leader went down with a deafening howl.

The second beast stepped over its fallen leader, eager to take over the fight. I pulled the spear free, releasing yellow sap from the fallen beast's wound. I swung the spear like a club at the second creature, striking it hard against the side of its head. A blunder on my part. The blow split the shaft in two, leaving me unarmed.

My eyes darted about, assessing my predicament. Countless beasts formed a circle around me, howling as though this was a grisly spectator sport. My spine froze into a wretched, twisted column of ice. They greatly outnumbered me. I couldn't fight them—I was doomed.

Don't be afraid—

I raised the broken shaft above my head with a yell, ready to strike another blow. The gesture must have struck the beasts as amusing, for they began whining, laughing and taunting me. I whirled around, fending off dizziness. The sphere took on a dream-like quality as I lost hold of my sanity. My eyes drifted down to a hole directly in front of me.

I heard Myles' voice say to me, "The tunnel, mate."

A beast sprang for me, its claws extended, its jaw open. I had no time to consider where this shaft might lead—it offered my only route, my one hope. Before the beast could reach me, I leaped into the abyss.

Down, down I fell, watching the rocky walls rush by. Darkness enveloped me, and the beasts' howls faded far above. The air blew past me in thick sheets.

I closed my eyes and prayed: *Lord, please end this horror and allow me peace the instant I strike bottom.*

But there was no bottom.

THE CHAIR

"**I** am disappointed to find you sleeping on the most important morning of your life," said a voice I first thought was part of my dream.

I opened my eyes to a painful light above me. If someone spoke, my mind could not yet sort the meaning of the words. I squinted up at Rudler, dressed in a tailored white suit, holding a lantern over me. Two streaks of dried blood on his left cheek marked where Vanessa had nearly gouged out his good eye. Dr. Dane, standing at his side, refused to look at me. In the gloom behind them, I could see the outlines of two guards standing at attention.

"Shall we begin?" he said.

I stirred uneasily, shaking the heavy shackles on my wrists and legs.

"Are you not curious to know what will happen to your brother and your lady in moments from now?" he asked.

I stared at him coldly, refusing to show him the fear he sought.

"Two years ago," he said, "I installed on this island a pair of alternating current generators to aid in the construction of my warships. I soon discovered more creative uses for it." Rudler's eye widened. "You will see what happens to a man who is electrocuted."

"Electrocuted? You can't be serious. I won't listen to this rot—"

"You will do as I *order*." His protruding eye blinked spasmodically as he struggled to keep his rage under control. After a moment, he settled into a controlled, all business look.

"You need us alive," I said, hoping this was true.

Rudler touched the scratches on his cheek and winced. "Just you, Mr. Finsbury." He waved the guards forward. "Remove him so that he may bear witness."

Several pairs of hands bundled me out into the corridor where I stood stomping the cramps out of my calves and thighs. My side with the broken rib ached.

With the rattle of keys and a creak of hinges, the guards removed Eben from his cell. His eyes, deep and desperate, met my own. I wanted to reassure him somehow, but I feared this would be our final walk together. What have I done? My brother did not belong here. He belongs in Potters Bay, attending school.

"Take me instead of my brother. He is just an innocent boy, a hired hand aboard my ship. Hardly a crime punishable by death."

Rudler reached into the pocket of his suit coat and withdrew the handsome pipe he was so fond of. He touched the tip of the pipe to his lips as though testing an oboe's timbre and tuning. "You decided your brother's fate when you brought him along on this desperate hunt of yours. And so it is you who killed him."

With a suddenness that startled everyone, Eben lunged at Rudler with his galley knife. Before he could deliver a blow, a guard, all hair and muscle, wrapped a tree-like arm around my brother's neck and yanked him backward. The knife clattered to the stone floor. Although bound in chains and restrained by the guard, Eben expelled a blast of spittle into the warden's face.

For several frightening seconds, no one moved while the guard awaited the order to snap the bones in my brother's neck. Eben began to giggle, a mocking laugh full of glee that threatened to burst into hysteria.

With a slight wave of his hand, Rudler signaled the guard to relax his death hold on my brother. "I should warn you," he said to Eben, drawing out a silk handkerchief and dabbing his cheek, "that I alone control the current that will pass through your body. I can kill you in an instant or I can introduce the electricity slowly until you feel your blood boiling." He inspected the handkerchief and grimaced. "Let us proceed."

The guard shoved Eben forward. Dane retrieved Eben's knife and considered the crude weapon that had almost claimed his employer.

Rudler led the way down a stone corridor that seemed to run the length of the small island. Several more soldiers, their carbines held ready, joined our procession. Any hope of making a run for it evaporated.

I peered into the first cell and saw a figure hunched in the corner—the Cambridge professor from the steam tub. His sallow face bore the look of the condemned. A dead man. As we passed the other cells, I saw the rest of the elite group of men who arrived with us on Royale, destined to also walk this corridor.

With the solemnity of a priest about to begin High Mass, Rudler led our procession under a stone archway and into a vaulted chamber. At the front of the chamber, atop an altar-like dais, sat Rudler's instrument of death—a lone chair, squarely built of oak. A single incandescent lamp above cast a harsh light down upon it. Leather straps hung from its arms and legs, and a thick cable trailed from its back like a black serpent. The wall to the left of the platform hosted a panel of meters and switches.

Eben gasped when he saw the chair, and the last of the color drained from his face. His dread grew so intense that I thought he would collapse with convulsions.

"Let us pray," I said to him. "Our Father in heaven, sacred is thy name—"

A rifle butt struck my back. "No talking."

I nearly passed out from the blow, but two guards held me upright, dragging me forward. We stopped before the platform, the guards at our backs. Eben jumped when a metal door beside the dais opened with a bang, and a stream of men began to file into the chamber. The general who presided over my tribunal entered first, leading a contingent of officers who filled the three pews facing the platform. The general looked smugly at me as he took his seat before the dais. I longed for a single blow to rid him of that arrogant look.

A pair of soldiers escorted my Vanessa into the chamber, the left side of her face blue with bruises. Still, she projected an air of fearless grace, even in the face of her own imminent defeat. Seeing Eben and me, she bowed her head to hide tears of regret. My poor Vanessa. She would die too, and I could do nothing to prevent it. I cannot describe my bitterness. How could I have allowed this to happen? How could I allow the woman I love to die in such a horrid fashion?

I pulled forward as far as the chains would allow. "For the love of God, let them live—" Two guards jerked me back.

Rudler ignored me and ascended the dais. His gaze bore not a trace of compassion, only the dull, dark look of a mind possessed.

Like the crack of a whip, he ordered, "Bring him."

Eben's eyes were wide and wild while several soldiers dragged my brother to the top of the platform and unfastened his chains. He looked back at me, desperate, and cried, "Don't let them do this to me, Andrew."

Rudler removed from his coat pocket the official order of execution: "The prisoner, having been found guilty of crimes against the Imperial Forces of this colony by the honorable Tribunal of Guiana, is hereby sentenced to death by electrocution, to be carried out this twenty-third day of April, in the year of our Lord, eighteen-hundred and ninety-four."

Rudler returned the paper to his coat pocket and faced the pews, allowing a smile to soften his expression. His audience fell silent with anticipation.

"Gentlemen," he addressed the small group, "today you will observe something truly extraordinary. In France the guillotine revolutionized a swift death. Halfway around the world, but on French soil nonetheless, you will bear witness to the beginning of a new era. Here I have constructed a unique mechanism of execution— death by electrocution." Rudler's voice rose dramatically, driven by the passion of his sermon. His congregation stirred with excitement.

"The condemned," he explained, "will be given a shock of sixty-cycle alternating current at a starting point of five-thousand volts. I can assure you that death will be instantaneous with the first introduction of current through paralysis and destruction of the brain. As the electrocution proceeds, the temperature of the body will rise to one-hundred forty degrees Fahrenheit. This alone will rule out any possibility of resuscitation. Dr. Dane, medical officer of the merchant ship *The Raven*, will serve as medical counsel."

The ship's surgeon rose from among the spectators and

bowed awkwardly. He still refused to look at me.

"Let us begin."

A buzz of whispers erupted from the observers while the soldiers manhandled my brother into the chair. Eben, his mind riding on the shredded edge of madness, sobbed uncontrollably. His eyes were screwed shut, and his arms trembled so violently that I did not think the soldiers could contain him. Two guards made fast the straps that bound Eben to the chair—one on each wrist, one on each ankle and one around his chest. Another soldier fitted a cap-like electrode over the top of Eben's head, and then fastened a second metal clamp around the calf of his right leg.

When the guards finished, the warden moved to the master control panel and pulled down a switch. A crack of sparks startled the attendees, followed by the rising whine of the dynamo. The soldiers fled the platform as though running from a burning keg of black powder.

Eben struggled against the straps in a violent spasm of terror. "Andrew, don't let them do this to me."

"Ebby," I shouted.

Rudler stood ready by the control panel, one hand gripping a second lever, his eye fixed on my brother in great anticipation. The inevitable moment had come. I could feel my heart throbbing in rapid, hard beats, forcing a surge of blood through my brain. A steady whine filled the chamber—the death song of the dynamo.

"My Jesus I love you," Eben shouted, spitting white flecks of foam over his chin. Our eyes met for the last time, and I knew he still hoped I would save him. I never felt so impotent.

In one quick, fluid motion, Rudler pulled down the lever, allowing five-thousand volts of electricity to pass through my brother's body.

God help me forget the terrible scene that followed.

"Andrew—"

A blue spark leaped from the electrode atop his head, followed by a crack of thunder that shook the chamber. Eben's torso jerked outward from the seat, threatening to tear the straps from the chair with extraordinary power. The observers gasped.

"Nooooooooo," I cried.

The dynamo shrieked, protesting the murder of an innocent boy, while the lamp overhead sputtered and dimmed as the chair greedily drew all power for itself. The only illumination came from the glow of Eben's grossly contorted face.

The chair, weakly mounted, began to rock frightfully as if Eben were straining to free himself. The cords of his neck stood out like metal rods. One of the leather wrist straps broke, allowing his left hand to thrash about as though he were fighting off an unseen attacker. The unbridled limb, a bright red, flowed with a strange life of its own, beckoning the warden to come forward and experience this horror. Rudler, in a rare display of alarm, signaled frantically for the guards to contain my brother's arm. But no one dared approach the platform.

The odor of burning flesh made my stomach constrict violently. My mind reeled with revulsion and rage. I shouted with all my strength for this carnage to end, but my words were lost in the roar of the dynamo. I averted my eyes to the rows of spectators. The sight of the slaughter visibly shook even these morbid witnesses, several of them turning away in revulsion. My poor Vanessa—two soldiers fought to contain her cries of protest.

Finally, Rudler broke the current to the chair, signaling the end of this atrocity. The dynamo dropped to a murmur. Eben's body fell limp, held in a sitting position by the remaining straps. His face resembled melted wax, and a purple fluid oozed from his lips and ears. A thick stench of burnt flesh filled the room.

For several long moments, everyone sat in stunned, miserable silence. Rudler alone bore a look of satisfaction. Impatient, he motioned the guards forward. Two soldiers mounted the platform and approached Eben with the prudence of those inspecting a beached shark, careful not to touch the carcass for fear of being bitten. One of them braved a quick touch of Eben's hand. Nothing happened. An outburst of relieved murmurs broke the chamber's morgue-like silence, while more guards raced up the steps to assist in the removal of the straps.

Dane ascended the dais and, with keen curiosity, studied Eben's face, lifting an eyelid and feeling his neck for a pulse. After several moments the doctor announced: "I promise this man is dead."

As the soldiers carried my brother's body from the platform, I stood staring at the smoldering fixture, refusing to believe what I just witnessed, refusing to believe Eben was dead. What had I done?

Dane wiped his fingers on his white frock and advised Rudler, "His brain is nothing more than a cinder. I suggest you limit the current to two-thousand volts for one minute. If that is not sufficient, a second shock of the same voltage and duration should follow. The body need not be damaged."

Rudler, scowling, waved him away.

I heard a voice next to me, Myles' voice, whisper into my ear, "It's done. Don't fret what just happened—your brother is now liberated as planned. He is safe with us—"

"No." In a rage, I swung the chain dangling between my wrist cuffs in the direction of Myles' voice, catching the closest guard hard on his temple. The blow had all my strength behind it. The guard grunted, spun sideways and collapsed onto both knees. Enraged, I went for the tribunal general standing to his left, my chain whistling towards his head. He leaned back to avoid the blow, but the chain caught him square on the jaw. His teeth flew everywhere.

Soldiers rushed forward amid the clicks of carbines being cocked. I heard Vanessa scream.

The general removed a hand from his bloody mouth and ordered, "Shoot him."

Frantic, I swung the chain at another soldier with a pistol drawn. Once, twice. Each time he leaned back beyond its reach, forcing me to take another step forward, then another. I stumbled on my leg irons.

A hard blow knocked me forward. In the next instant, I was on my face, surrounded by leather boots. A searing pain bore down on the base of my skull.

Several hands jerked me from the stone floor. The room swirled with lights and faces. Bewildered, half-conscious, I saw the general, his face bloated with rage, standing before me while a stream of blood flowed beneath the hand clasping his mouth. He withdrew his revolver.

"*I forbid it,*" Rudler roared, scrambling down the steps of the dais.

But the general would not be dissuaded. Sneering, he thrust the gun into my face. I closed my eyes. A thunder-like blast exploded in my ears.

In the roar that followed, I hear Vanessa cry out my name.

THE GRAVEYARD

My eyes opened with a start. I stared up at a deep scarlet sky—the same crimson heavens I had seen from the forest.

But the land had changed. I sat up in the midst of tall, neglected grass that had grown to seed. I knew this place— the old graveyard where I first met Myles after his death.

. . .

"Take him to the table," Rudler ordered. *"Quickly."*

Two guards lifted my body from the stone floor and carried me from the execution chamber. Dane followed. Vanessa, her face ridden with anguish, stood from her pew among the soldiers and watched them carry me away through an archway.

"Andrew!"

The general produced a soiled handkerchief to wipe his broken and bloody mouth. "He would have killed one of us," he insisted, spitting out blood.

Rudler faced the general, his eyes cold and steady. He swung his fist with a snarl and hammered the general on his injured jaw. The officer, caught unaware, landed heavily on the floor at the feet of several of his soldiers.

Rudler stepped over him and roared, "You have no idea what you've just done."

The general, a hand on his jaw, stared up at the warden in stunned immobility. His other hand moved to his holstered revolver and stayed there.

Rudler thrust a finger at him. "If he dies, I will destroy your miserable soul."

Rudler stormed from the death chamber and entered an anteroom where the guards had taken my body. There were no incandescent lights in this room, and Dane lit a lantern. I could hear voices and saw movement around me—not through my senses, but rather muddled through a fog-like detachment from a vantage just above them.

With a sweep of his arms, Rudler cleared several plates from a wooden table large enough to seat a dozen men. "Put him here."

The two guards placed me upon the table. When they finished, Rudler inspected my head wound with the eye of a surgeon. Grimacing, he grabbed Dane by his shirt and yanked him to the table.

"Save him," Rudler demanded.

The doctor hunched over my body and, squinting, examined my skull. He shook his head. "The trauma most certainly caused a concussion to the brain." He checked my breathing and felt for a pulse. "This is very bad."

"Will he survive?"

Dane grimaced. "He is in a coma. He is not dead, but neither is he alive."

Rudler pressed a hand to his forehead as though trying to staunch a severe pain. He faced the doctor, his eyes hollow and vacant. "You have one final duty in my employ—see that this man lives. I will not accept failure."

Rudler turned and stormed through the archway.

Dane sat in a chair next to my body, his face a grave

mask of hopelessness. He put his lips next to my ear and rasped: "You are free now. *Stop him.*"

. . .

I scrambled to my feet and surveyed my surroundings. The pine-covered hillside yielded to the face of a tall, dark mountain that reached into the scarlet heavens. My stomach sank. Before me sat the same mountain I had seen from the brackish lake at the edge of the forest. The crypt of Aruka and the strange sphere-like cavern where the beasts butchered my friend lay hidden deep beneath—

A firm hand came down on my shoulder and pulled me around. Startled, I stared up at a tall man dressed in his finest sea captain's uniform.

"Myles," I gasped. "But the beasts … I saw them kill you."

"And so they did—again." His head flew back, and he laughed loudly, as though his foe had fallen for his playful gambit. He gave my shoulder a good-natured slap and looked closely at me, his eyes narrowing. "You don't know how close you are to it, do you?"

"To the forest?"

"To his fortress." Myles' hand went out towards the mountaintop, pointing. "Belial's fortress crowns the top of that mountain."

I shook my head. "I have something to finish … that is, if I'm not already too late."

"Vanessa." It came as a statement, not a question, as though he were reading my thoughts. "I understand. You want to stop Rudler from murdering your lady. Find her and you will find him. That's the Plan."

We were interrupted by a string of muffled curses. The earth next to Myles' cracked and the ground began to rise.

Then, to my astonishment, I watched a man pull himself from the clinging soil.

Charles!

Laughing, I welcomed the sight of my old friend and helped pull him from the earth. Instead of an unkempt bush of white whiskers, Charles displayed a noble face topped with thick, dark hair.

I let out a huff. "Can I believe my eyes? Charles, you look thirty years younger than when I last saw you."

Charles scratched the dirt from his closely cropped beard. "Ahoy, Chief." He cocked his head towards the headstone with a chuckle. "Looks like someone mistook me for dead."

A scream from the next row of markers made each of us whirl. A hand jutting from the ground waved frantically like a storm-blown weed. We rushed to investigate. A large, flat headstone had toppled over, trapping someone beneath. I knelt beside the grave and tried to lift the weighty marker.

"It's Joseph."

The three of us grabbed the stone and heaved it aside. Joseph sat up in the loose soil, his dazzled eyes blinking to adjust to the light. Like the others, his features were unspoiled, and he looked younger than I remembered.

His eyes brightened in recognition. "I'm grateful to see you. I couldn't get a grip."

Joseph reached up and shook each of our hands, more for his own reassurance than from gratitude.

"We have one more grave to find," I said.

We scattered among the headstones, reading inscriptions. There were unfamiliar names, centuries-old dates, and stones whose markings the weather erased long ago. I used my mind to reach the souls buried here. What I heard—disembodied cries—unsettled me. The old graveyard was alive and restless, with an ululating chorus of buried fear and anger emanating from below.

I weaved among the stones, reading each name. Thirty headstones later I found it, a worn marker barely readable:

Here lieth the Remains of Ebenezer R. Finsbury,
a gifted Student and loyal Brother...

The grave sat still and silent, with no sign that Eben wished to rise. I tried to reach him with my mind. Nothing.

I called to the others. "Over here."

They came quickly, and together we used our hands, spade-like, to uncover my brother's grave. We removed a fair-sized mound of dirt before reaching the top of a wooden coffin. Then more digging. We cleared a path beside it just wide enough to allow me room to descend. I slid next to the coffin and had little difficulty breaking through the warped and rotted pine lid. I reeled at the sight within. Brown and charred rags, ruined by age and decay, hung loosely from a corpse roughly Eben's size, and here and there the rags had dropped away, revealing an empty skeleton.

Something metallic gleamed beneath the bones of its hand. My lips tightened as I retrieved a knife. I turned it over in my palm—Eben's galley knife.

I looked at the others. "Where is he?"

"It's not your brother," Charles said. "It's only a shell he discarded a long time ago. Leave it be."

Joseph turned away, shaking his head.

"I found this in his hand." I passed the knife up to Myles, then grabbed Charles' hand and climbed from the hole.

Myles weighed the dagger in his hand, considering it.

Then he smiled, amused by the crude, yet lethal weapon. "Wherever he is, he wants to protect you."

There came a shout from a nearby grove of pines— Joseph, announcing another discovery. I led the others into the grove and, pushing through the bramble, found Joseph kneeling by the edge of a pond, staring into the shallow water. I knelt beside him. The sunken eyes of a long-dead corpse stared back at us from beneath the surface. My heart missed a beat and then settled into a hard, rapid thudding.

Williams.

Those staring eyes—a dull hue, like those of a dead fish—blinked. Joseph and I scrambled back with a start.

Williams rose shakily to his feet like a drunkard, while water poured from green silt that had once been clothing. He looked ghastly, his bloated skin as pale as flour. The others drew back in revulsion, and Charles blessed himself with the sign of the Lord's cross. Williams' wrists were bound behind his back, and a length of frayed rope dangled from his stretched neck. He had been hung and thrown into this pond.

Williams twisted his elongated neck around to inspect his wrists and swung his eyes back to me, pleading for my help. I waded into the pond and, splashing behind him, loosened the binds. Grim business, but I had little difficulty unraveling the old cord. Once free, Williams waded ashore without the courtesy of acknowledging me. I scanned him with my mind and encountered an obstruction, like a stone wall, which prevented contact of this sort. The strange vibration emanating from him unsettled me.

I trudged ashore after him and said, "Williams, I had hoped you, at least, would survive this awful business."

Williams frowned, his dark and sunken eyes staring

vacantly at some disturbing event in his past. "Died the first night on that rock you stuck me on, Cap'n."

"How did it happen?"

His dull eyes shifted to mine. "You know I gots no money. But some dog spread lies I's carryin' pockets of cash. That night whilst I slept, two of them came to my bunk and murdered me for what they thought I'd hidden in my empty pockets. Tied me helpless and strangled me with this here rope." He unwrapped the frayed cord from around his neck and flung it angrily into the pond.

"You'll get your revenge," I said. "There may be a way to return to the living through a fortress on top of this mountain. It belongs to a demon called Belial. We intend to trap him."

Williams smiled without humor and showed me a set of rotted teeth that had once been unnaturally white. "So that's what you's up to." Then his expression darkened and anger flared from his soul. "Stop it. Stop it right now. No good'll come of it."

What happened to the selfless fighter and friend? Before I could respond, an unsettling chorus of voices rose from beyond the pine grove. We glanced at each other, puzzled. As we listened, the macabre sound grew louder.

Charles pointed through a gap in the pines. "Yonder they come."

Hundreds of men marched up the hillside, each chanting in unison a strange, unholy song. The others followed me into the clearing, where we watched in wonder. A procession of delirious bodies streamed from the wooded valley below—an army of walking dead men—marching like beaten soldiers to the top of the mountain. From their vast numbers rose a pitiful chant—a song of mourning, harsh and haunting. Their chorus sent a chill through me like a strong tide. They were urging me to join them.

"It's the devil's work," Charles said. "Don't listen to them."

Williams screwed his eyes shut and he, too, began wailing that woeful song of the dead. I hated to listen to it.

I shook his arm. "*Stop it.*"

He continued that ghastly wailing, and a hard slap across his face finally silenced him. Williams looked at me, his eyes glowing with anger. Responding to some unspoken command, he pushed roughly passed me and began walking towards the procession. I started to follow, but Myles pulled me back by my arm.

"Stand easy, mate," he said.

"Who are these men?" I asked. "Why is he joining them?"

"The poor bastards are lost souls," Myles said. "It's the fortress that beckons them. They believe the way to their eternal reward is up this mountain. I'm afraid we've lost your friend."

I broke Myles hold. "Our paths are the same."

Before Myles could object, I dashed towards the ghoulish procession, an army that now stretched ahead and behind as far as I could see, with unnumbered hundreds still pouring from the forest below. The corpses of earth had been given leave of their graves to walk this mountain. I felt no fear walking among them.

There were fresh corpses whose bodies were torn and mangled, as though they had been crushed beneath a great avalanche. Warriors killed in battle? Dead only a short time, they still bore expressions of bewilderment.

There were dead men bound with rope and chain, marching with an air of mockery. Murderers executed for their crimes? They rolled their sunken eyes from side to side, watching the others with suspicion, a look of revenge etched on their criminal faces.

There were corpses whose bodies long ago had become one with the earth, with little flesh remaining on their cracked and crumbled bones. Others were little more than twisted sticks of bone, assisted in their march by unseen crutches.

There were those who marched quietly, patiently, accepting their fate as the natural order of things, while others were full of anger, suggesting their souls would never know peace.

I found it eerie the way these dead men heeded so readily to the voice beckoning them. But to what end? Perhaps Williams could give me some answers. I moved through the crowd and caught up with my friend.

"I'll walk with you," I said.

He looked at me, annoyed. "I believe in the power that calls me up this here mountain. My travelin' through this wicked land is almost over. 'Tis wrong what you're doin'."

God gave new, virile life to the rest of my crew—but not Williams. Why? I watched him carefully, searching for clues on his stony features.

"Don't walk with these men," I said. "We'll make our own way."

Williams gave me a queer look. "We's strayed a long way from God's glory. Now we all march together. Soon we's all be at peace. You too, Cap'n. You'll see."

I glanced back at the long procession of corpses still streaming from the valley. My crew followed several paces behind, the only living faces among a sea of walking decay. Myles signaled me to give up and leave the procession. I shook my head, insisting on ascending the mountain at Williams' side, hoping to find a way to break the power that possessed him.

As we neared the summit, the foliage vanished, leaving a field of jagged rocks. The corpses became increasingly restless the higher we climbed. Their pitiful chanting grew louder. Another voice deep within me, the voice I came to trust, told me that we were nearing the end of our journey. But I didn't share Williams' belief that this mountain was sacred. On the contrary. The voice warned me of great evil here.

The trail leveled off just below the mountain's summit, where the way took us along the edge of a vast crater filled with fire. Instead of a peak, an almighty hand had carved the heart from the mountain, leaving a cauldron of molten rock. From the center of the hellish moat rose a dark plateau on which sat a twisted castle as wide as a hundred ships.

The Fortress of Belial.

Far from the majestic palace I envisioned, here stood a black, impenetrable keep, all battlements and towers, rising to a grotesque peak against the scarlet sky. A magnificent creation, utterly dwarfing man's mightiest achievements.

The army of dead men marched across a vast stone bridge—the single road to the fortress—and proceeded up a steep flight of steps that took them under a giant arched transom. On each side of its threshold stood a mammoth statue, giant specters of evil guarding the bastion against all who dared approach. The stone figures were feline beasts with thick manes, terrifying eyes and snouts filled with angry fangs. They were the same warrior beasts— guardians, Myles called them—that had stalked me through the forest. This mountain belonged to them.

Williams paused at the foot of the bridge and, gazing at the fortress across the crater, let out a sigh of awe. Our minds met briefly, and I heard a string of French superlatives.

What? Williams barely commanded English, but in

death he mastered French? All at once I knew. He had lowered his mental barrier for an instant, long enough for me to discover the truth. This wasn't Williams. We had been duped. One of Belial's spies masqueraded as a friend I trusted. And I told him our plan to return to the living through his master's keep.

He saw my incredulous look and, realizing his mistake, lunged at me with a howl. Caught off balance, I stumbled back onto the gravel trail and rolled dangerously near the rim of the crater. A blast of scorched air blew past the back of my neck.

The beast in Williams' body straddled me, pinning my arms. He lifted a brick-size rock above his head with both hands and brought it down hard. I swung my head to one side as the rock shattered next to my ear.

With a cry of surprise, Williams grabbed his neck and rolled off me. Myles stood behind him, Eben's knife in hand, his arm cocked for another plunge.

The imposter disguised as Williams scrambled to his feet and bolted into the crowd.

"That's not Williams," I shouted.

"Stop him," Charles yelled, "—before he summons Belial's army."

Myles and the others stormed after him. The imposter charged across the bridge with sheer weight and ferocity, knocking down one corpse after another, leaving them to fall under the herd of marching feet. I scrambled to my feet and fought the crowd in an attempt to reach the others.

Once across the bridge, Williams bounded up the flight of granite steps that led to the fortress' regal entrance, brushing aside corpses like a wild horse storming through bramble. Nothing could stop him. I caught up with Charles and Joseph, and together we made a mad scramble up the steps after him. Twice I stumbled in my haste, and only the quick hand of my mates prevented my being trampled by the mob.

The imposter did not look back, nor did he slacken his pace. At last, he cleared the steps and charged under the fortress' high arched entranceway. There came a terrific roar. He disappeared inside the edifice as a mammoth stone door fell closed with a crash, shaking the mountain and crushing the bones of those unfortunates caught beneath. Whoever this was, whatever his intentions, he was gone.

Myles bounded back down the steps to join us, his eyebrows raised in apology.

I stared up at the sheer face of the fortress' stone door. Our plan appeared hopeless. An army of titans with winches and chains could never raise that massive slab of stone. How could we gain entrance?

"Looks like we peeved the lot of them," Charles said, pointing back down the steps.

The great chanting of the dead ceased. I turned to see the army of walking corpses now standing motionless, unable to proceed, the bridge now jammed with dead men with nowhere to go. There would be no returning the way we came. Each corpse stared at us with rueful expressions, accusing us of denying them their salvation.

"I suggest we adjourn to higher ground," Myles said.

THE FORTRESS OF BELIAL

"Myles," I implored, "is there another way inside this place?"

He shrugged. "Belial built this bastion to keep out the likes of us—"

"Over here," Joseph called from the rampart above us.

Our eyes followed his outstretched finger to a giant tower rising from the corner of the fortress.

We charged along the rampart and gathered at the base of the tower where Joseph stood staring up at the distant battlement. I spotted a tiny vent-like opening about two-hundred feet above. I considered the sheer wall with its large, jutting stones separated by wide gaps of mortar. An easy climb. I hoisted myself up onto the first stone, the toe of my boot feeling for a foothold between the rocks. I moved from one stone to the next, climbing up the tower, keeping a wary eye on the small opening above me. The others followed likewise.

I reached the vent, barely the breadth of my shoulders, and squeezed onto a spiral stone staircase within. I stood inside Belial's fortress, letting my eyes adjust to the dimness. The place reeked of ancient decay, the air thick and musty. The walls and narrow stone staircase dripped with undisturbed moss. No one had climbed these steps in centuries. The stairs coiled up until it vanished in the sheer height of the tower.

One by one the others squeezed through the aperture and joined me on the steps.

"By all of God's angels," Charles marveled, gazing upward, "this tower has no top." His voice echoed eerily around the curved walls.

"Which way?" I asked.

"Down," Myles said.

I led the way down the circular staircase as quickly as the moss-covered steps would allow. We passed through layer after layer of ropey cobwebs as large as ship sails, while our padded footsteps created an appalling dust cloud as we descended, making it difficult to see. At the bottom stood an old oak door strengthened with iron grills. I put a shoulder to it and pushed, but it would not yield. I rammed my boot against the planks with a solid thud. Nothing.

"A dead end, Chief," Charles said.

There came a rasp of a bolt from the opposite side of the door, and then the handle turned. I motioned the others back and signaled Myles for the knife. The door opened wide with a protesting crack. Across the threshold stood a petite, Latin woman dressed in a white, flowing robe. Her eyes, luscious brown and bright on a face as striking as any princess, met mine, and there stirred in me a warmth bred of familiarity.

"Gabrielle," I gasped. "How...?"

We exchanged gazes, and her soul showed me a vision of what happened. Gabrielle had been murdered after locking herself inside the bordello to save us. The barman she called her father broke her neck with a single, vicious blow with the back of his hand.

"Gabrielle ... I'm so sorry—"

"Introductions are in order," Myles said with a grin, pressing in beside me.

"Please," she said, beckoning us out of the tower. "You must hurry. And be very quiet."

Gabrielle led the way into the castle and waved us against a shadow-cloaked wall. I expected the fortress' interior to be as stark and foreboding as its exterior. But not so. The dazzling sight astonished me. The interior was a single room the size of a grand amphitheater with a high vaulted ceiling supported by impressive pillars and arches. Despite its antiquity, the castle's intricate mosaic floor was free of the ancient crust that sullied the tower from which we had just emerged.

Someone had filled this incredible room with items that suggested a museum of sorts. We were surrounded by an astounding collection of art objects and treasures, arranged in neat rows that stretched in every direction as far as I could see. The high walls were covered with weaponry and implements of war, ranging from ornamental broadswords and crossbows to huge projectiles and machinery with wings whose purposes and function I could not fathom. We stood within the grandest armory of heaven and earth.

Though lacking windows or skylights, a bright light filled the room. I shielded my eyes from its peculiar source radiating from the center of the chamber.

"We are in Belial's refuge," Gabrielle said, her voice hushed, "a keep for his plundered wealth from all the worlds. When cast off the earth, Belial and its minions come here to feed on the power of a dreadful crystal." She glanced uneasily over her shoulder at the strange light.

Before I could question her, Charles cried out with excitement. We moved along the wall and found him gazing longingly at a collection of firearms arranged neatly in a case.

"She's a beauty," he said, fondling a double-barreled shotgun. "Well oiled and never been fired."

"You must keep your voice low," Gabrielle warned.

The others filed past me and began their eager investigation of the firearms.

"Tell me about this crystal," I said to Gabrielle.

Her eyes, full of fear, locked with mine. "It blocks the way to the passage leading to the world of the living. I will take you to see it. Bring one man with you. And come armed."

I said to Myles, "Let's go."

Myles spun the chamber of a fine revolver he found and, satisfied, stuffed the piece into a holster around his waist. He also removed from the wall a splendid crossbow and a satchel of metal arrows. There weren't many weapons ancient or modern that Myles couldn't wield with keen competence.

I selected a loaded revolver from the case and slid it into my waistband. Before I could seize a shotgun, Gabrielle grasped my arm and led me to an aisle lined with urns that held priceless gems of every size and color. In their midst stood an ornate glass case holding an odd sickle-shaped implement on a satin cushion.

"This will serve you," she said.

I opened the case and removed the implement. The weapon felt heavy, made of what appeared to be platinum, with razor-sharp edges and an exquisitely carved ivory handle adorned with jewels.

"Remarkable."

I ordered the others to remain behind while Myles and I followed Gabrielle to the source of the peculiar light. We moved down a long aisle lined with priceless idols of every century and civilization—Aztec, Grecian, Phoenician, Egyptian, Tibetan and scores more I did not recognize. From beyond the aisle came that bizarre chanting of dead men. A thick stench of burning flesh accosted us. Gabrielle led us into a deep shadow cast by a jade statue of an animal with a long neck and high, pointed ears—a shelter that afforded us a broad view of the center of the keep.

I crouched beside its pedestal and watched the procession of walking corpses caught within the fortress. A regiment of well-armed guardian beasts stood sentinel over them, keeping the dead men in a neat, orderly line. These souls had no choice but to march like cattle to the top of an alter-like dais on which sat an amazing boulder-size gemstone. A tangible light radiated from its facets, a clear, blinding luminance that revealed every decaying fiber on each dead man's face. I couldn't tear my eyes away from its shifting orbs of light. So this was the source of power that summoned the corpses from their graves and brought them here. But for what purpose?

Each corpse, in turn, stepped through the gem's corona, head bowed, and vanished in a spasm of light. Above it, a wispy column of smoke, foul and oily, spiraled to the ceiling, bringing to an end their journey through the otherworld.

I whispered to Gabrielle, "The gem cremates what's already dead. Why fear it?"

"The crystal is more dangerous than you can imagine," she said, her voice a husky whisper. "It separates a soul from its shell and locks the pure life-force within its facets. Belial feeds on this energy and grows stronger, forever united with the souls it consumed."

"And the crystal blocks a way out of here?"

Gabrielle nodded. "Its aura hides a tunnel through which Belial and its minions return to the earth."

Myles put his lips close to my ear and pointed out a

giant of a man, all whiskers and hair, standing atop the dais. "Isn't that frightful fellow the slaver who brought you to the islands?"

Indeed. There was no mistaking Marart's bullish head, chillingly bear-like, surveying each corpse with a slaver's eye before it stepped into the crystal's corona.

"He must know we're here," I said. "Our spy would have warned him by now."

Myles gestured farther down the procession. "There's your impostor. He hasn't reached the dais yet to tell him anything."

The corpse masquerading as Williams couldn't leave the procession under the beasts' close guard. Each time he stepped from the line to protest, a sharp crack of a whip and the sweep of a cutlass forced him back. When he reached the next beast, he again implored it to let him pass, also without success.

"The beasts are too stupid to let him through," I said. "Still, when he reaches the top of the steps, he'll inform Marart of our presence here and our plan."

"Not if we take him out first," Myles said.

He told me his plan, and I readily agreed. Myles twisted in a fetal position by the edge of the aisle and moaned softly. His first groans attracted no attention at all. So he moaned louder, feigning more pain. The closest beast turned towards him, curious. A second beast, farther down the procession, noticed his comrade's attention and also left its post to investigate.

Myles continued to groan, unaware that he summoned two beasts instead of one as planned. Gabrielle gestured to the weapon I held at my side. The two guardians, huge driveling things, entered our aisle of artifacts, swords hissing from their sheaths and clattered to a halt over Myles. I motioned Gabrielle back against the base of the shadow-cloaked idol before moving nimbly away from the statue.

The first beast extended its cutlass and emitted a growl from deep within its chest—the last sound it ever made. Myles spun onto his back and, using a precious second to bring his crossbow to bear, sent a metal arrow with a thud straight through the beast's throat. The thing went down with a gargled croak. While Myles fumbled to reload his crossbow, I took the last several steps in a single bound. Using both hands, I swung my sickle-shaped weapon with a great *whoosh* at the second beast's unprotected neck. The weapon's unnaturally sharp blade sliced through without the slightest resistance. The monster's head flew off with a yelp and spun end-over-end into the shadows.

Myles twisted to his feet and surveyed the heap of armor and fur. But we had no time to revel in our quick victory. On cue, we bolted straight for the procession of corpses, where we grabbed Williams by his arms and dragged him back into our darkened aisle, while the other corpses continued their catatonic walk towards the crystal. We dumped our prize unceremoniously onto the floor.

Myles put his mouth to the traitor's ear. "You can start by telling us who you are."

The corpse, surprise still etched on his spoiled features, babbled a few unintelligible words of protest. When he recovered enough composure, he uttered in a thick French accent: "Your ridiculous display of force will accomplish nothing."

Myles raised his crossbow club-like and hissed through clenched teeth, "Then I'll take the satisfaction of smashing your skull."

Williams' face darkened. "You are not so clever as you pretend. When we first met, I had little trouble deceiving you to sink your ship." His reedy voice became teasingly familiar.

Myles lowered his crossbow as the revelation sank in.

The traitor, grinning maliciously, removed a musty logbook from beneath his shirt and tossed it at Myles' feet. "You are an easy man to fool." The name *H.M.S. Timonium* was inscribed on its cover. Myles stared incredulously at the logbook's worn and weathered leather.

"Fascinating reading," Williams giggled. "I will never forget your face just before you died, a frightened and foolish captain in command of a doomed ship. I laughed a long time, *monsieur.*"

Myles' gaze shifted from the logbook to the man with Williams' appearance. Only it wasn't Williams anymore. There sat Henri La Gallienne, grinning up at the befuddled sea captain.

"*Bastard.*" Myles jerked his crossbow and fired an arrow into La Gallienne's chest, pinning the slight Frenchman to the floor like a moth to a display board. The little Frenchman laughed at him, a piercing noise that threatened to draw attention.

"You cannot kill me," he cackled. "I am already dead."

I swung my silver sickle across La Gallienne's neck and sliced his head neatly from his body. The eyes in his trunkless head stared impotently up at me.

"I still can warn them." His mouth opened and out came a chillingly sustained shriek of alarm. I jammed the toe of my boot into his mouth, muffling him. He bit down hard on the leather. I winced and felt his teeth coming through.

Gabrielle passed me an oriental urn stuffed with a silken tapestry.

"Perfect." I yanked La Gallienne's head off the end of my boot and, careful of his gnashing teeth, stuffed a piece of tapestry into his mouth, stifling him. I pressed his head deep inside the urn and buried it beneath the layers of fabric. Gabrielle hid the vessel in a crevice beneath an idol.

"You debase this sanctuary by coming here," said a cold voice behind us.

The three of us whirled. There, half silhouetted at the entrance of the aisle, stood another corpse of a man with a mocking grin and coarse black hair draped over his shoulders. I recognized Francis Moore, *The Raven's* last captain.

"I will see that you are imprisoned here for eternity," he sneered.

I took several steps towards him. "Listen to me, Moore. Rudler hung you for trying to save *The Raven* and its men. Yet you still hold allegiance to this abomination?"

Moore's dull, corpse-like eyes stared darkly at me. "I do not serve men. I give my loyalty to a far greater power that will not be denied." He turned to leave.

"Wait, Moore," I said, rushing to him. I grabbed his arm. "Join us, and you will have your revenge against the demon who killed you."

Moore considered me for a moment. Then his lips stretched into a grin that revealed decayed teeth. As I watched, his face changed, and his body grew to twice its size until I peered up into the eyes of a savage feline beast.

With a growl, he swept his giant paw down across my face and sent me sprawling. "Yes, I will take my revenge," he roared. The beast turned and signaled someone out of my view.

Myles raised his crossbow, but the beast that had been Moore bolted out of his range. I staggered to my feet and rushed to the edge of the aisle. The beast joined a group of fellow guardians, cackling and gesturing back in our direction.

He had given us away.

THE SLAVER

My body jerked and spasmed. Dr. Dane, who had been sitting slumped in a chair next to me, stood quickly to check my breathing. This was the moment he feared, the moment of my body's death. He had no choice but to summon Rudler.

"Convulsions," Dane shouted from the death chamber's archway. "He has gone into convulsions."

Rudler turned from the death chair, his eyes wide with alarm. He thrust a finger at Vanessa still seated in a witness pew and ordered, "Bring her."

Rudler followed Dane into the anteroom, where my body lay racked with convulsions, foam spilling from my mouth. A guard dragged Vanessa into the room by her arm. Seeing me, she broke his hold and rushed to the table where she swept her arms around my neck.

"Oh dear God," she cried.

"Talk to him," Rudler ordered. "Give him hope. Give him a reason to live. If you succeed, I will spare your life. If he dies, I will put you in the chair."

Vanessa, her eyes eager, ran a hand through my hair. "Andrew, please, if you can hear me, I need you to come back to me. Don't give up. You are strong. Fight the clutch of death that means to take you from me."

My body continued convulsing, and nothing she could say, and no force I could summon, would make it stop. I watched helplessly as my body died.

"Please, Andrew. Stay with me!"

My body slumped back onto the table, but my lips continued to move. She leaned over me and put her ear close to hear.

"What is he saying?" Rudler demanded.

Vanessa turned to the warden, puzzled. "He is talking to someone. He thinks his brother is there with him."

Rudler swung his fist in a rage. "*No.*"

Dane stood and did nothing to conceal the knowing smirk on his lips. "It appears, Warden, that you blundered by killing the boy. Their souls will become powerful allies."

Rudler, his face a block of stone, shifted his dark eyes from the doctor to my body. "I will not allow that to happen."

He placed his hands upon Vanessa's shoulders, a gesture that caused her to shudder with loathing. "I will summon his soul here. And then I will destroy him."

. . .

There came creaking and rumbling from the opposite end of the aisle of artifacts, like a wagon approaching. The three of us remained frozen, watching.

"Yo," came a familiar voice.

I breathed easier—Charles.

He emerged from the shadows carrying over his shoulders a matched pair of double-barreled shotguns and several belts of cartridges. Joseph, also heavily armed, followed, pushing a Napoleon III bronze field cannon on its two large wagon wheels.

Charles threw me a quick salute and chirped, "What's wrong Chief? Never seen a cannon before?"

Myles rubbed the barrel of the artillery piece. "Clever fellows," he said. "Perhaps you've given us a way into that tunnel. This cannon will blow that crystal clear off."

"Then use it—quickly," Gabrielle urged.

I helped Joseph wheel the cannon into position at the edge of our aisle, a vantage that offered a clear shot at the gem. There I discovered the first complication to our plan—the procession of dead men stood in our line of fire.

"They'll be carnage," I said to Myles, indicating the line of corpses.

"Never mind them," he said. "We're doing the poor souls a favor."

He was right. Besides, we had no other option. Thanks to Moore, a contingent of beasts were marching towards us, their weapons unsheathed, their eyes scanning each aisle of artifacts searching for us.

Myles let out a snort. "They aren't giving us much time."

I slapped the cannon's barrel. "Load and run out fast."

Charles shoved a triple shot of powder down the barrel, but instead of an iron ball, he heaved up a large urn filled with diamonds ranging in size from several carats to fist-sized rocks. "Stuff's much harder than buckshot. She'll make one hell of a shotgun."

"Brilliant!"

He emptied the urn into the smoothbore barrel, and Joseph jammed the concoction home with the ramrod.

"Aim for that crystal," I said to Charles. "Blow it clear off."

"Better lash her down," he said, scraping the sole of his boot over the tiled floor. "The recoil will turn it over."

"Forget the recoil," I said. "We have one chance."

There came a terrible howl as a beast, its cutlass raised, charged into our aisle. Myles spun on his heels, his crossbow coming up in the same instant, and discharged an arrow with cold competence. The steel projectile buried itself with a hiss in the center of the beast's forehead. The force of the blow hurled the monster onto its back in full view of its comrades. Seeing their fallen warrior, the other beasts came charging.

"Bloody hell," Myles muttered.

Gabrielle's eyes met mine. "You must hurry!"

Their leader, a vicious thing with a coal-black mane, stormed into our aisle and let out a battle howl. Myles, his expression strained, fumbled to place another arrow into his crossbow.

Gabrielle helped herself to one of Charles' shotguns, brought it to bear and discharged simultaneous rounds from both barrels. The blast tore away the beast's gruesome armor and with it a good portion of its chest. Beyond, I saw Moore's beastly figure clawing its way up the steps of the dais, pushing past dead men in his haste to alert Marart.

"Fire this thing," I shouted.

Charles leaped behind the cannon.

I waved the others away. "Stand clear."

Joseph took up a defensive position between two pedestals. Gabrielle and Myles fled into the shadows.

A contingent of beasts charged into our aisle. My heart—or some reasonable facsimile within me—pounded heavily, painfully, in my chest. I crouched behind a large trunk filled with gold ingots and swung my weapon as a signal, my voice a desperate cry.

"Fire!"

Charles lit the fuse. An instant later the cannon

belched a great geyser of flame and precious stones that cut through the monsters and struck the dais. The recoil hurled the gun backward, end-over-end.

The effect of the blast, fueled by the crystal's energy, was devastating. The dais exploded in a spectacular upheaval of gravel and bones. Corpses burst into unrecognizable bits, while stone pillars shattered into rubble. Beasts and corpses alike, well out of the line of fire, fell as the explosion's shock wave radiated outward in a lethal arc.

The cannon's roar faded, and the terrible wailing of corpses echoed away, leaving a strange stillness. There were no signs of life on or near the steps, only a moment of frozen, unbelievable silence. The crystal, however, remained undamaged, its bright, shifting orbs alive and eager to consume more souls.

I swung my arm and cursed. "By God, is there no way past it?"

The others stepped tentatively forward, their faces mirroring astonishment at the destruction wrought by the blast, amazed by the crystal's power and resilience.

Gabrielle emerged from the shadows and said to me, "I know another way." Then she simply vanished.

I stared in awe. "Gabrielle?"

'I am here.' Her voice, a sound within my mind, came from somewhere nearby. My eyes jumped from one statue to another, but I saw no one hiding there.

A magnificent bronze goddess, standing on a pedestal above me, began to move. I jumped aside before the falling piece could crush me. But the statue did not topple. The robed figure—as tall as three men—stepped down from its perch and stood before me, unsteady, with a hand on the pedestal for support.

A gasp caught in my throat. "Gabrielle...?"

The bronze goddess twisted its massive head downward to look at me, and I heard her say, 'This metal shell will protect me.'

I scanned the giant artifact and felt an intelligent presence and a compassionate heart. Gabrielle had sealed her soul inside.

'Stay behind me.'

The bronze figure began walking stiffly forward, its massive metal feet pounding the tiled floor with each step. The others, astonished, rallied around her. I expected her to topple under the awkward weight, but she continued, determined, towards the dais.

Several beasts regrouped at the bottom of the steps to stop our advance. Charles, a shotgun braced against his hip, laid down covering fire. The beasts scattered. My men, screaming and shouting, charged the dais. Joseph followed Charles' blast with a steady volley of fire from his repeating Winchester rifle. Myles discarded the awkward crossbow and drew the handsome revolver from his waist holster and spun it around his finger. I stayed close to Gabrielle, my revolver in one hand, the blade in the other.

She began her arduous climb up the remains of the dais, taking the first step with a clang and pulling her metal shell up to the next. The beasts mounted disorganized attacks from several directions at once. Myles assumed a crouched position, pointed his revolver at two spear-toting beasts, waited for the range to close, and then shot point-blank until his revolver clicked empty. The beasts fell. He hollered for a shotgun. Charles obliged, tossing him a piece and a belt of cartridges.

The walking corpses were everywhere now, clumsily resuming their march up the steps and putting themselves in our crossfire. Beasts and corpses alike fell. I met the assault of an ax-wielding monster, as swift as a lion and twice its size. Its massive two-headed blade whisked over my head. I lunged, my weapon upraised, and drove the precious blade through its armor without resistance, gutting the beast like a fish. The thing toppled with a howl.

The carnage and appalling confusion grew to a furious pitch as the beasts mounted one failed attack after another. My men, caught up in the excitement of the unimaginable battle, advanced steadily up the steps behind Gabrielle. I, too, felt no fear, only a fervent exhilaration. Charles drove onward, firing his shotgun and reloading, firing and reloading while dragging a spear that had passed through his upper leg.

A beast jumped into Gabrielle's path, its snout drawn back in a snarl, and swung a mighty broadsword at her with all its monstrous strength. The blade struck her bronze neck with a clang and shattered at the handle. Gabrielle didn't waver. The monster stared dumbfound. Gabrielle's metal hand, as wide as a shovel blade, flew out in an arc and caught the beast just below the temple, snapping its neck like a brittle twig.

A swirl of light and smoke, unbelievably hot and foul and blinding, covered the top of the dais. I held up a hand in defense and felt a violent energy streak my palm.

Gabrielle hauled her bronze frame up the last step and continued her awkward gait to the crystal. My men formed a defensive line across the top steps behind her and fired the last of their ammunition into the terrible noise and confusion below. I fired my revolver into the fray below until its chambers were empty.

Moore's beastly hulk broke through the line, pounced on Gabrielle and struggled to wrestle her massive metal hulk to the ground. She continued unimpeded, dragging the snarling beast with her into the crystal's aura.

"Gabrielle ... don't—"

A terrible flash, white and blinding, consumed both statue and monster. I heard Moore's shriek as his body disintegrated into shards of ethereal matter that sparkled like a thousand stars before fading to ash. It took several seconds before my eyes, blinded by the afterimage, could again focus on the crystal. The bronze statue remained upright and intact, bathed in the fountain of osculating light.

The metal shell protected her.

Gabrielle lumbered to the crystal, touched it and reeled back from its heat, her solid expression fixed in a grimace. She screwed her lifeless eyes shut and, summoning incredible resolve, covered its facets with her huge hands, this time holding them in place. And there she stood, rigid. The dancing orbs of light retreated into the crystal until its corona vanished. The heat dissipated and the dais grew dark, save for an orange glow emanating from her metal hands. She had trapped the crystal's deadly energy within itself. But for how long?

'The tunnel,' she urged me. 'Please hurry.'

Embedded in the stone wall beyond the crystal stood a massive iron door with large hasps and handle. My mouth felt dry, my heart racing. I wove carefully past her searing frame and depressed the door's scalding handle. It would not move.

'Break through it.' Her tone was sharp, urgent.

I looked at her hands. The anxious energy trapped within the crystal was melting away her fingers in a fountain of molten bronze that bubbled and flowed down the sides of the pedestal. Gabrielle's metallic hands could not take much more. I had seconds.

Wielding my weapon like an ax, I chopped away at the metal door, sending metal shavings away like wood chips.

It took little time for the extraordinary blade to carve out a fair-size wedge where the handle had been. I stepped back and jammed my boot against the door. It flew open with a bang. A cold draught of air, damp and stale, blew past me. Beyond the transom, a flight of steep stone steps led down into a dark, subterranean tunnel.

I shouted to the others, "I'm through."

My men refused to give up their defensive positions at the top of the steps. Charles tucked the shotgun against his shoulder, took general aim and fired. "That's the last of the cartridges," he hollered.

"Inside, all of you," I shouted.

"We can't, mate—just you," said Myles, wielding his empty shotgun like a club. "Bring Rudler's soul onto this battlefield."

"How?"

"Raise your vibration level," Myles said. "This will allow you to interact with the living. It's not difficult—"

"Come with me."

Charles said, "We'll hold this position so they won't follow you," adding with a wink, "Say ahoy to the good earth for me, will ya?"

"Her hands, Captain," Joseph warned, pointing.

Gabrielle's hands, now a burble of melted bronze, could no longer contain the crystal's energy. Its peculiar light flowed dangerously outward, and I could feel the temperature of the air around me rising. I had to go, with or without the others.

I turned back to the door. And there I froze. A club-toting figure, huge and menacing, stood glaring at me from across the threshold, blocking my way.

Marart.

He had transformed into a large animal, his rugged, beast-like face terse and frightening, his black eyes implacable in their hate.

"I will never let you pass," he said to me in a deep, evil voice that stopped my blood.

I had no choice but to rush him, my sword against his club. His weapon outreached my blade by an arm's length, and he delivered a blow that sent me sprawling.

He laughed wickedly. "You will be my prisoner for all eternity."

The torrid air washed over me like a great wave. I couldn't retreat. I had to get past him *fast* before the gem's corona consumed my soul.

Marart raised his massive club to deliver a lethal blow, and there it hung for a moment, its weight pulling him back a step. In the same instant, Gabrielle swept a hand off the crystal and flung a puddle of bronze across the dais. Her aim was impeccable. The molten metal flew over my head and spattered with a sizzle in the giant's face. Marart let loose a bone-chilling shriek and dropped to his knees, his hands clawing his burning face.

'Go!' Gabrielle ordered.

I launched myself over the giant's shoulders and hurtled through the doorway. I fell onto the steps behind him and tumbled headlong down to the floor of the tunnel, dropping my weapon in the fall. Gabrielle stepped back from the crystal, freeing its deadly energy. The virulent corona flared and swallowed the top of the dais with its fire-like field, sealing the entrance to the passage with its dangerous power.

Marart, his face charred and steaming, beat the corona through the doorway. He stood glaring at me from the top step and let out a loud, drawn growl, like a bear provoked to attack. I scrambled for my weapon. With his hands pressed against each wall for support, the giant began a labored descent down the steps, his dark eyes filled with sinister vengeance.

"You will never escape me—"

He froze, his ruined expression riddled with surprise. Something clasped him by the ankle. He strained his neck around to see the remains of Gabrielle's bronze hand, reduced to thin ribbons of metal, grasping him firmly by the ankle, fusing him to her frame.

Marart shrieked and thrashed about the steps like a wild animal caught in a death trap. *"I will have your soul."*

For all his ferocity, he could not break her metal grip. With deliberate slowness, Gabrielle dragged the twisting and screaming giant back through the doorway and into the crystal's aura. Marart's eyes met mine for the last time before a flash as bright as the midday sun swallowed the dais. His flesh peeled away, exposing muscles, arteries, tissue—until his bones exploded into countless glowing particles. Bare seconds later, his final wail died with him.

I rose stiffly to my feet, shaking, and blinked uncertainly at the tunnel's beckoning darkness. I had no choice but to go on.

Alone.

HIS MESSENGERS

D r. Dane turned away from the table, his face reflecting genuine sympathy. "Your prisoner is dead."

"*No.*" Vanessa clutched the front of my prison shirt. "Stay with me. *Stay with me.*"

I could not raise a finger to console her. Alas, my body grew still. My life torn from it.

Vanessa collapsed onto my chest and began sobbing, her fingers still clasping my shirt. "Please, God..."

My poor Vanessa. I wished to hold her. I wished to tell her that I stood with her at this very moment. But I could not.

"Your love is a weak elixir," Rudler said to her in disgust. He summoned the guards. "Put her in the chair."

Noooo!

Two guards grabbed Vanessa's arms and dragged her off my corpse.

"Let go of me!" She fought them with all her strength, but her resistance proved pointless against the soldiers who had little difficulty taking her from the room. I listened in despair to her retreating sobs.

How could I stop this? How could I?

There came the distant sound of thunder, a deep, intense rumble that shook the island. What was that? The sound came again, closer. A rain of loam began to fall. And then I knew—mortar fire. The island had come under attack.

Soldiers gathered in the archway awaiting Rudler's orders. But he ignored his officers and remained rooted by my corpse.

"Sir?" Dane said.

Rudler grasped the front of my shirt and pulled my body into a sitting position. "You will return here very soon. When you do, you will find your woman dead. You will spend eternity searching for her soul, and I will be rid of you."

• • •

Rudler's voice faded into the blackness of the ancient passageway. I rubbed my eyes, struggling to focus. I must move on.

In the retreating half-light, I passed one tunnel offshoot after another. This wasn't a single corridor, but a black labyrinth of caves.

With each step, the air grew fouler, staler. The passage's aura felt dead—old Charles would have said haunted—and I heard the constant rumble of the sea through the walls and ceiling. At any moment I expected an onrushing torrent of water to sweep me away.

I heard whispers all around me. Echoes. Taunting me. Beckoning me. Warning me. I crouched in the nitrous corridor, listening to the strange voices, watching. I could see nothing definite. Yet I sensed movement everywhere, forms twisting in the darkness as though the living rock were breathing, exciting my wildest fears.

I heard an infant wail. Startled, I remained still and

waited. A white pedestal appeared before me, not unlike a baptismal font, with narrow curved sides that opened to a bowl-like top. The crying came from within.

I approached the font and peered inside. At the bottom lay an infant whose delicate features were teasingly familiar to me. When I laid a hand upon the marble opening, the font fell dark and cold. The crying ceased. My hand groped about the interior but touched only stone.

I heard another sound, a heavy shuffle interspersed with desperate wheezing. A chill swept through me when a contorted figure struggled from the gloom and staggered towards me. I jerked back and stared at an old man with white wisps of hair above a shriveled brow—an image of my father on his deathbed had he lived to see one-hundred years. Each step of his hunched and twisted body took considerable effort. This ancient man gave me a toothless grin and raised a trembling finger to touch me.

Then I knew. This wasn't my father. Like the infant, this specter was an image of me.

I reeled beyond his touch. The man's grin exploded into a shrill laugh at my fear of him. So intense did his laughter grow that I expected him to collapse from exhaustion.

I backed away and stumbled over a bundle at my feet—a corpse leering up at me with holes for eyes. I stiffened. My own features were stamped upon those last shreds of flesh. The corpse was my own.

I dropped to my knees beside the remains, my hands trembling with a deep sense of my earthly mortality. My corpse would soon look like this—a bag of dried bones buried in some unmarked grave.

The corpse's brittle fingers grabbed my wrist with the strength of a virile man. I cried out in surprise and struggled to pull free. But the thing's grip was stronger. With a swiftness that startled me, the grisly remains wrapped its other skeletal claw behind my neck and pulled me down to within a breath of those holes that had once been eyes. Its jaw opened and out poured a ghastly wail.

"Corr ... corrrr ... corruptionnnnnnn," it groaned. "The child is corruptible..."

A violent wind poured through the tunnel and swept away the bones, leaving me kneeling alone on the stone floor. I held my wrist. The area where the corpse touched me left a burning I couldn't shake.

Then, from somewhere deep within the mountain, came the distant din of a large machine. I knew that sound—the dynamo in Rudler's death chamber. Could I be that close?

The sound stirred within me an urgency that would not be denied. I grabbed my weapon and rushed into the smothering darkness. I sensed the walls fall away from me as though I had ventured into the infinite gulf of nothing-ness, save for the solid floor beneath my feet. Each step brought the sound of the dynamo nearer. I let my vibra-tion level build as Myles instructed, and my mind grew more lucid, my senses more acute. I basked in the promise of great knowledge flowing just beyond my awareness, waiting to be revealed to me.

Several hundred paces farther a rippling light breached the blackness. Through this portal came the distant voices of men. I hastened towards the sound.

The light radiated from an underground pond fed from the core of the mountain. I could see movement deep beneath its surface. I knelt at the edge and placed my hand into the water. It felt neither cold nor wet. I let the liquid flow from my fingers and felt a low, tangible current cross my palm.

I stared down into a large, cavernous room with people rushing about. And then I knew—this was Rudler's death chamber on the Isle of the Devil. The thick mist of innocent victims who died in that hellish chair filled the chamber, reminding me of the haze of dead men flowing from the Beliel's crystal.

My vantage placed me directly over the death chair. Rudler stood by the controls, his hands moving with cold competence over the switches and knobs.

Next to him sat Vanessa, strapped to that hideous chair, pulling at the binds in helpless frustration. My throat swelled with emotion. I shouted down to her, "Vanessa!"

Neither she nor Rudler reacted. My voice could not penetrate.

I stepped into the pond and let myself sink. A strange current enveloped me, lowering my vibration level and inhibiting movement. My ethereal body felt denser, heavier the farther I sank. I tried to hasten my descent by waving my arms as though swimming, but my movements did not produce any reaction. I wasn't sinking so much as hovering, like a feather drifting down over a ripple of air.

The room's atmosphere had changed. Instead of strict military order, guards rushed about in a panic. The handful of morbidly curious officers who came to watch my brother die were on their feet at the base of the dais, arguing among themselves.

I came to rest on the dais in front of Rudler. He seemed oblivious to the commotion and stood undistracted by the instrument panel, immersed in the business of killing. Vanessa strained against the binds.

Rage boiled within me. I raised my weapon to him. My arm felt heavy, my movements sluggish. I swung my blade awkwardly across Rudler's throat. It whizzed harmlessly through him—alas, I was not part of his world and could not touch him.

Rudler pulled down one of the panel's levers. The overhead lamp sputtered as the dynamo drew more power, building its lethal current. Vanessa struggled in fear of it.

"Stop this," I shouted. But my voice carried nowhere.

Rudler peered through me, his eyes fixed on the chair, his fingers curling around the fatal lever. I stared at him in stunned immobility as my doubts surfaced in great waves. Could God be so cruel as to bring me all this way so that I could do nothing but watch this demon murder my love? At that moment I understood the hopelessness of my presence here. This so-called divine plan would not allow me to save Vanessa. Her death—my lure here—had already been fated. Could I summon no power in heaven or hell to stop him?

Someone shouted up to us. "This is madness." I recognized the general who had presided over my tribunal, appealing to Rudler from the base of the platform. "You are a fool to kill her. We need her to bargain."

Rudler refused to divert his good eye from the chair. "Because of your blunder, he is here with us," he said. "I will finish this so her soul will take him far away from here where he can do me no harm."

"You *are* mad," the general said through his broken and bloodied teeth. "Your warships have failed to stop the armada. Put an end to this carnival before we all die beneath your miserable island."

Dane appeared at the general's side. "Sir, there is only one passage out of this dungeon. A collapse of the tunnel will trap us."

Rudler shifted an intimidating gaze to the pair. "The British fleet cannot touch us down here. You are safe."

The British fleet? Here? I spun and knelt beside

Vanessa, my mind spinning with a desperate plan. "Don't let him kill you. Stall him until Uncle arrives. *Do it NOW.*"

Her eyes lifted and I saw something, the slightest softening of her expression. Perhaps my spirit could somehow touch her. Maybe she could hear my voice like a distant echo in her mind.

I placed a hand upon her forehead and struggled to raise my soul's vibration. I let my thoughts and feelings flow into her mind. "He needs you alive. *Make him stop.*"

Vanessa twisted her neck around to look at Rudler. "Your warships have left you defenseless," she said to him with as much defiance as she could summon. "Now the British will sink this grotesque island of yours. You have lost."

Rudler removed his hand from the lever. I stood up before him, blocking him. He looked directly at me; his expression suggested he could see something. He wasn't sure.

There came a low rumble in the distance, and then the platform began to tremble. The lights sputtered.

A soldier shouted from the stairwell, "The Armada is within attack range."

There erupted another outburst among the officers.

The general swept around to the others and shouted, "I am ordering an evacuation. We will take this woman with us to negotiate—"

Two shots rang out, twin explosions that echoed like thunder through the subterranean chamber. The general, surprise etched upon his face, swiveled to look at the warden. Rudler held a service revolver, ready to squeeze off another round if necessary. It wasn't. The general let out a gasp of astonishment before collapsing face down in front of the dais.

The room fell quiet. Dane, pale and shaken, knelt beside the general's body and ran a trembling hand over his white wisps of hair.

Rudler waved him away. "I forbid you to attend to him. His soul is mine." He pointed his revolver at the other officers. "The rest of you will do as I order—"

A loud banging filled the chamber, and a great shower of mortar and dust rained down on everyone. The subterranean chamber shook as one blast after another rocked the island. An explosion brought down part of the limestone ceiling at the far end of the chamber, crushing a group of guards gathered there. The remaining officers scrambled for the exit.

Rudler emptied his revolver at the retreating soldiers. *"Cowards."*

The cannons continued their unrelenting shelling. Rudler ignored the chaos and returned to the chair. He rubbed a lingering finger along Vanessa's cheek. "Yes, a farewell kiss. Let him see what we shared together."

She squirmed with repugnance.

Rudler removed the electrode from Vanessa's head and grabbed her by the hair, forcing her to look into his good eye. His mouth buried her cry of protest in an ugly kiss. She squirmed and hissed and screamed beneath him.

Another salvo of explosions rocked the island. A boulder-size section of ceiling crashed down behind the chair, splitting the planks. A brick grazed Rudler's head. Dazed, he stumbled backward and touched a neat gash creasing his forehead. He blinked incessantly, surprised by the wound. Shaking the oozing blood from his eye, he staggered to the controls and groped for the lever.

"Don't ... I beg you," I shouted.

His eyes scanned the dais as though looking for me. "You and she will soon share this world—" His fingers found the lever and pulled it downward. "—forever."

"NOOOOOO!"

The dynamo shrieked, and the light above the chair flared. An appalling shower of sparks erupted from the cables behind the chair, hissing and spitting flame, threatening to ignite the wooden platform. Vanessa hid her face from the sparks that snapped at her like rabid wolves.

I approached the chair, astonished—she was still alive. The death apparatus was not working. The electricity failed to complete its circuit.

Rudler, his expression darkening, disconnected the switch. The sparks ceased, and the dynamo sank to an idle. He wiped a paste of blood from his forehead and staggered to the chair—his child. The cap, he realized; she wasn't wearing the electrode.

From his awkward position behind the chair, Rudler grabbed the steaming cap and struggled to place it over Vanessa's head. She resisted, throwing her body across the chair, fighting him.

"Keep away from me," she shouted.

Rudler grabbed her hair and pulled her head back against the chair.

She jerked free of his grip. "Don't touch me!"

Enraged, Rudler swung the metal cap at her, trying to deliver an immobilizing blow to the side of her head, but it landed awkwardly, brushing her temple with no force. I lunged at him, passing my soul through his body with no effect.

The struggle with Vanessa threw him off balance, and his free hand groped the back of the chair for support. Perhaps the blow to his head contributed to Rudler's carelessness at this critical moment. Perhaps my presence here distracted him. Perhaps he had gone irrevocably mad in his obsession to kill her.

Rudler's free hand inadvertently grabbed a live cable. He teetered behind the chair, at once realizing his folly. His desperate eye locked with mine as he attempted to push himself away. Too late. Five thousand volts of electricity completed the circuit between the chair's cable and the electrode cap in his hand.

The room swam with light. A blue flame joined his hands, and his legs jerked and twisted convulsively in an odd dance of death, his features frozen in a ghastly mask. His good eye popped from its socket and turned bright red. I would have sworn the current lifted him off the floor.

The gruesome spectacle lasted seconds. Rudler's fiery remains flew backward with a dull snap and dumped in a heap against the cinder wall. Two switches tripped on the control panel, breaking the circuit. The lamp above the platform flickered and popped, while the dynamo sank in a sad diminuendo, an almost human cry of despair for the death of its master.

There followed a cold, death-like stillness. Even the shelling above stopped.

I hovered over Rudler's smoldering remains. His scarlet eyeball, resting on his cheek, fixed on me with wicked intensity.

BELIAL

Vanessa twisted free of the chair's straps and stood from the smoldering chair, visibly shaking. My soul basked in waves of relief—he failed to kill her. I did not want her to cross into this base netherworld. I wanted her safe in Uncle's care, far away from this horror.

Vanessa hesitated by the edge of the dais and clutched her abdomen against severe pain. She sat wearily on the top step, her breathing labored, and drew up her legs into a fetal position. A stream of tears flowed down her drawn and pale cheeks. The pain crushed her.

I knelt by her side. "What is it, my love? Tell me."

She shook her head as though she could hear me. "Please help me, Andrew."

A foul, demonic odor assailed me. A shadow more imagined than seen drifted overhead and shrank into the chamber's shattered masonry. We were not alone. I sensed an evil watching us, lurking, waiting to be discovered.

Then, from the gloom of the chamber, came a low, guttural laugh of someone taunting me. My eyes scanned the rubble while my heart sent rhythmic tremors through me. I could see nothing.

I snatched up my precious weapon and scampered

down the steps of the dais, ready to give my immortal soul to protect Vanessa. I walked the perimeter of the chamber, my darting eyes searching. A sudden wind spiraled through the chamber. I shielded my eyes and watched a silhouette with a flowing cape scuttle through the chamber's deep shadows, hiding from me.

I followed, bounding from shadow to shadow, keeping a prudent distance, ready to strike if something threatened Vanessa.

"You have met my Messengers of Life and Death," a voice boomed through the chamber. "Your fate is set."

I touched a severe pain in my wrist. The burning where the corpse touched me intensified.

The entity floated up before me, rising like a great wave from the sea while emitting a deep laughter chillingly amplified by the chamber. I stared up in wonder. Before me stood a giant, thrice the size of a man, clad in black armor with spiked fists. Perched atop his shoulders sat a grotesque helmet with a single horizontal eye-slit out of which glared twin orbs of fire that scrutinized me with hideous intent.

I grabbed the handle of my weapon and stood ready. Those spiked hands grasped both sides of the black helmet and lifted it off, revealing the head of a feline beast engraved with a look of evil born from the deepest bowels of hell. Its penetrating eyes, sunken beneath black overhanging cliffs of whiskers, regarded me with contemptuous amusement. The creature grinned, displaying knife-like fangs that could bite through steel.

This abomination from hell's deepest valley was Belial, king of the otherworld.

REBIRTH

B elial unsheathed his mammoth sword and thrust its tip to my throat. I remained rooted and still. However, the demon did not advance. Instead, he removed his hand and allowed the sword to float free. With one fluid motion, the sword swooped down on its own power and shattered a boulder sitting between us, expelling pieces of shrapnel-like gravel.

Belial, snorting, snatched the hovering sword from the air and sheathed it. "So, pauper of hell, my will alone can assail an army."

Belial had migrated to the battlefield of the other-world, as Myles foretold. But how could I fight this creature? I raised my precious sickle against him, a feeble weapon against such a powerful opponent.

Belial threw back his massive head and let out a howl of laughter that shook the chamber. "*Fool.* You dare challenge me? I am stronger than all of Earth's armies. You are nothing." Belial's voice rose to a roar. "All of Earth's miserable creatures will kneel before me." He thrust his spiked fist at Vanessa. "Your woman will be the first. Her body will give my soul safe passage back to your home."

His words incited a fury within me. "I will not let you touch her."

Belial's nostrils flared, and his snout stretched into an arrogant grin. The demon swept around and ascended the steps of the dais, trailing an echo of mocking laughter. His foul spirit passed through Vanessa huddled on the top step, and then he dropped his hulk into the electric chair, which grew to accommodate his size. The demon gazed down across the ruined chamber from this blasphemous throne—a dark monarch reigning over a kingdom of misery and death. He raised his right hand in a slight, summoning gesture.

I heard movement behind me. Four guardian beasts dressed in military uniforms advanced towards me. Belial had resurrected the slain soldiers to fight his battle.

The first beast, wielding a two-edged battle axe, came at me swiftly and deliberately, like a seasoned soldier who has no doubt as to the outcome of his attack. I didn't wait for it to move within striking range. I lunged forward and swung my weapon with a neat hiss, amputating its arm at the shoulder.

The beast did not falter or stop its advance. Even its severed arm clawed forward, dragging the ax with it.

A second beast, clad in an officer's uniform I recognized as the general's, stepped to the lead to continue the attack. I raised my sickle and focused my full attention on its steel claws.

A deep, grating sound erupted from its throat and grew in timbre until it resembled human speech. "The prisoner will not speak unless addressed by this court," the thing mocked.

I stepped in fast and drove my weapon up between the beast's legs, hard. The blade sliced an effortless canyon from groin to jaw. The general went down with a roar.

Two more beasts loomed behind.

"You surprise me," I shouted to Belial. "Why do you

send weak minions to fight in your stead?"

Belial, frowning, made another slight gesture with his right claw. The two remaining beasts retreated into the shadows.

"This is no fight," Belial said. "I can slay you however it amuses me."

I mounted the stairs of the dais and stopped before Vanessa. Belial watched me intently. I raised my weapon, ready to confront this monster regardless of the consequences.

Suddenly, my hand was empty, the precious weapon gone. I whirled, my eyes searching the dais for it. A point of light gleamed off the blade in the demon's grasp. My heart sank.

"I take back what is mine," he bellowed. "You are a thief as well as a fool."

I watched in dismay as the demon slid the weapon into a sheath on his belt. As I watched, his face changed, and I stared, astonished, at Phillipe Rudler.

His eyes—whole and without scares—flared at me. "I am less of an opponent now? Perhaps you think you have a chance?"

"You won't leave this miserable cavern of yours. I will see you are caged here forever."

His shoulders jiggled with amusement. "Mr. Finsbury, you are in my house, my world. Whatever happens here will be because it is my wish."

"You fear me," I said. "You lured me here out of fear so you could lock me away and do you no harm."

Ruler, ginning, spread his arms palms up. "I fear nothing. I have a great destiny to fulfill. Nothing will stop me." He thrust a finger in anger. "Least of all *you*."

Rudler sank back into the chair and shook his head, a mock look of sympathy on his face. "You are beyond pathetic." He gestured to Vanessa. "You have lost your so-called true love forever. You and she could have shared all eternity together if that so pleased you. Instead, you chose to intrude in matters that are far beyond your witless comprehension. And what will be the divine reward for so brave a soldier? *Oblivion.* I will wipe your memories. You will begin a new life of the flesh, never knowing who this woman is or what she once meant to you."

I took a step forward, a movement that startled him. He feared me. My touch? Why?

"The process begins," he said.

I took another step forward.

Rudler recoiled slightly. "Your hand. It pains you?"

I extended my hand to him. "You fear my touch—"

I stood root still and stared at what once had been my hand, the appendage reduced to a swollen and featureless mass, inflated to bursting.

Rudler's head flew back with a healthy laugh. "You are a ridiculously weak opponent. A pity. So quick an end to what could have been an interesting meeting."

The air grew close and hot around me, welding me to the spot. I wiped my perspiring brow. Instead of sweat, a thick mucus dripped from my hand. And then I knew—the rebirth process had begun.

What have I done?

"I owned your soul the moment you let one of my Messengers touch you," he said.

My head pounded. My mind worked to digest this new turn. Rudler—Belial—intended to imprison my immortal soul through the rebirth process, as he tried once before on Marart's ghost ship. The corpse I encountered in the tunnel had the power to deliver me to the womb. *And I let it touch me.*

"Men of simple minds succumb to simple tactics,"

Rudler laughed.

Convulsions racked my spirit body. I dropped to my knees and tumbled down the steps of the dais. A viscous substance formed a puddle beneath me. A network of tissue weaved an intricate web, imprisoning me within a jelly-like shell that throbbed in rhythm to my new, physical heart. My head fell back in a swoon, and I saw everything through a strange, fluid veil.

"You will be born from your own seed of the woman you love," Rudler said. "Flesh of your flesh. I will take possession of your woman's body to again walk the earth in human form. You will suckle at my breasts, and I will nurture you as my son, always at my side."

"No..."

Rudler stood behind Vanessa and placed a hand on her shoulder. I felt myself slipping deeper into the physical world. My strength dissipated, my memories fading. *Fight him.*

"NO."

Rudler's laughter tore at the foundation of my soul.

"Your woman is the perfect host—quality, distinction, breeding. When your uncle returns her safely to England, he will not know that she possesses a soul that will destroy him and his great navy. He will die at her hands. In the final moments of his wretched life, he will learn how he delivered a plague into the world that will mark the end of mankind."

The horrible turn of events swirled within my mind, drowning the last of my sanity in the darkest pool of despair. I couldn't let this happen. I must do something. *Do something.*

"I have sown the seeds," he droned. "The fruit of that harvest will be bitter. I will watch with glee as your people destroy each other with hatred and venom. No mortal will emerge the victor. The world is mine."

My soul's vibration continued to slow … I could no longer control it. I fought back fear and revulsion, struggling against the descending blackness. My mind could not yield a plan for escape.

Think.

I watched, helpless, as a group of disjointed tubes twisted together to form the umbilical cord, a conduit that would serve as my sole source of nourishment until my birth. The umbilical cord—my lifeline. I moved my embryonic hands through the fluid. Perhaps I had one chance.

I forced my arms through the thickening pool. The effort was exhausting, the pain excruciating. My retreating finger stumps slipped around the cord and pulled it to me. I clenched my jaw and twisted the cord noose-like around my neck.

The embryo went into spasms. With each contraction, the cord drew tighter, strangling my emerging physical form. A muffled cry ripped from my throat. Vanessa writhed in agony. I was the cause of her pain, a fetus dying inside her womb. But not without a terrible price. *I was killing her as well.*

Through the clouding murk, I saw Rudler look of confusion as he clamored down the steps and stared in at me. The death of the embryo would defeat his plan and return my soul to the battlefield of hell. And I would not be duped again.

He again assumed Belial's beastly form. "Scum," he roared. "I could have subjected you to centuries of agony. Instead, I allowed your miserable soul to return to the living. And this is how you repay me?"

The demon raised his sword, ready to split the shell in two. But he did not. Belial knew that destroying the embryo would hasten my release and thwart his plan for safe passage in Uncle's care. The demon swept around, his eyes wild and flared, searching for a way to stop my escape. But he found nothing.

The beast stepped over me and drove a spiked fist through the shell's membrane. Belial clawed deep into the thick medium and grabbed the cord from around my neck. I was too dazed, too weak, to make any real effort to stop him. With one, swift jerk, the beast pulled the cord free.

But I wasn't finished. With the last of my dwindling strength, I grabbed his spiked hand and let him pull me through the womb.

"You don't dare." The demon twisted his arm to dislodge me.

Desperate, I wrapped the umbilical cord around the beast's exposed wrist to hold him.

"You don't dare—"

The demon let out a howl as the cord fused to his astral forearm with an appalling cracking sound. The sword fell from his grip. Belial made a terrible mistake. Belial, me and the embryo were now inseparable, fused to this conduit of life.

The demon dropped to his knees and began kicking and thrashing like a rodent caught in a trap. But he could not escape. The shell rapidly drew away his unholy strength as it had mine. Belial collapsed in an exhausted heap, helpless. The demon raised a swooning head and looked in at me with dark, sunken eyes. Instead of that arrogant look of strength, his features were drawn and expended, his considerable hulk already shriveled to half his original weight. The demon's lips parted and out poured a long, low moan of anguish.

The embryo began to devour Belial. He sank into the

womb, first arms and shoulders, then his head, finally the torso and legs. The demon slid inside, pushing me against the wall. Would we be born twins? The very notion utterly sickened me.

I had little time to ponder the situation. Blackness descended. My mind began fading, taking with it memories of who I was … memories of Vanessa ... of Rudler ...

Something began shaking me violently.

I felt a pair of strong hands under my arms. In one swift motion, these hands wrenched my soul free of the embryonic matter and laid me on the chamber's floor. I felt my soul's vibration immediately begin to build. These same hands shook me from my exhausted stupor. Feeling returned to my extremities. I pried open my eyes and looked up through gummed lids at the figure kneeling over me.

"I warned you about this," Eben said by way of greeting.

His handsome features broke into a warm smile. With a note of pride, he set down between us the homemade knife he used to extract me. He still possessed his boyish features and winning smile. But he had undergone a profound change. I saw in his face a look of deep wisdom that humbled me.

I raised a weary hand and touched him. He felt real and we embraced as never before. His touch filled me with strength, and I no longer felt afraid. Tears streamed down my face.

He looked deep into my eyes and said, "It's been a long time, brother."

I wiped a sleeve over my eyes. "But just a short time ago..."

"I waited a very long time to be with you again," he said, his eyes filled with compassion. "Vanessa summoned me here. Your bond with her is extraordinary. Your unconditional love for her saved you."

I rolled my head and looked at the boulder-sized shell beside me. The incision Eben made to release me was healing. He helped me into a sitting position. I looked at Vanessa, whose pain had subsided. Some color infused her cheeks, and she stood up, testing her returning strength.

"Ebby..." I groaned.

"Genius, dear brother," he laughed. "A stroke of genius."

"What have I done?"

Eben, grinning, said, "Belial's soul can't be destroyed. But you have imprisoned him for a generation. It's been eons since Belial was born of a womb. Unlike possession of an earthly body, the demon now must undergo the rebirth process and will have only the vaguest notion of his past. Belial will need a lifetime to relearn who and what he is. Genius, Andrew."

I watched Vanessa descend the steps of the dais. I couldn't bear the thought of that thing inside her. "I cannot allow this ... not to Vanessa ... not to my son. This isn't the way. We were to imprison him inside a sanctum."

"The plan changed," Eben said. "When you were inside the womb, you lacked the strength and skill to imprison him, a skill that requires a lifetime to master. This is the way now."

I rose unsteadily to my feet and saw the dark, nightmare shape inside the embryo. Belial's scarlet eye stared out at me, unblinking. "I'll cut that monster from her."

"No," Eben snapped. "She's in no danger. Belial is helpless now, his strength gone—you trapped him for one lifetime. This is a great victory, Andrew."

But I could not—would not—allow the demon to

grow inside Vanessa and become my physical legacy.

I grabbed Belial's sword.

"What are you doing?" Eben demanded.

I lifted the huge weapon onto my shoulder but lacked the strength to use it.

Eben pushed me away. "You mustn't touch it. *You mustn't free him.*"

The sword began to throb. Its blade grew hot in my hands until I had no choice but to drop it. But it didn't fall. Instead, it floated upward, parrying, wielded by an unseen swordsman.

"He means to cut himself free," Eben shouted.

The sword swooped down in a fencing thrust and knocked me to the floor with the flat of its blade. It assumed an offensive position, ready to impale anyone who dared advance. No one could stop it. The sword swept over the sphere, point downward, and there it hovered, ready to slice through the membrane to free its master. Belial's unblinking eye stared out at me.

Eben threw himself between the blade's tip and the embryonic shell. Belial's eye snapped sideways to look at him.

The sword drove down through my brother's chest, pinning him to the shell. Vanessa stumbled and cried out in pain. A crimson fluid erupted from Eben's chest. He twisted and groaned on the skewer as an unseen hand tried to wrest it free. The blade began to withdraw. Eben, his face a stone mask of resolve, grabbed the blade with both hands to prevent its retreat. The sword fought to free itself, but my brother's hold was stronger.

With methodical slowness, Eben sank into the womb. He watched me, his eyes glazed, still clutching the blade. I grabbed the weapon's handle with both hands and, with grim determination, tried to pull it out.

"Don't," he wheezed, his energy spent. "Don't...."

I fell back onto the stone floor and watched, helpless, as the womb devoured my brother as it had Belial. He watched me, his expression resigned, and allowed himself to sink inside. Finally, he closed his eyes and nodded. A moment later he was gone. The sword clattered to the ground.

I sat there, breathless, staring in stunned disbelief. What had Eben done? Was he now destined to be reborn to age and suffer to keep Belial imprisoned?

I spotted Eben's knife on the floor, grabbed it and forced myself to my feet. I intended to free him as he had done for me. As I approached, I saw Eben's silhouette inside, his hands working feverishly. What was this? I crouched to watch him. He manipulated Belial's nascent life form, spinning it one way, then another, like a spider winding a silk cocoon around a captured fly, only much faster. What was he doing?

As I watched, the mass that had once been Belial began a transformation. Instead of a human embryo, it became a perfect crimson sphere. A large shell. Then I understood—Eben was sealing Belial inside a soul sanctum.

I couldn't control my laughter. "Brilliant, Ebby."

When the metamorphosis completed, the sphere vanished from inside the womb and reappeared beside me. Belial's sanctum had migrated back to the world of the dead.

I touched its hard, peculiar surface. "Absolutely brilliant, Ebby."

I vowed to guard the sanctum for countless millennia—that was my purpose. But with Eben at my side. I raised the knife to free him.

But I never got the chance.

There came a deep rumble as though in the next instant a locomotive would roar through the chamber and crush me. I looked up, terrified. A point of light pierced the chamber's darkness and sped towards me, exploding in a searing brilliance that blinded me. Stranger than any radiance I had ever seen, the light appeared simultaneously white and blue, and something much more, like a diamond transformed into pure energy. The strange illumination opened to reveal an eye.

An almighty entity was scrutinizing me.

BEYOND

The otherworld shared only two more of its secrets, denying me revelations reserved solely for the dead. I remember only the barest fragments of a journey to the far rim of eternity. A merciful Wisdom allowed me to forget this last episode of my extraordinary adventure, lest I spend the remainder of my days ranting in an asylum.

I do, however, recall the "eye" enveloping me in a giant channel of energy. I fell into its eddy, moving slowly at first, then faster. The walls were bright—remarkably so—more brilliant, more glorious, more radiantly splendid than the purest light on Earth. Soon I was falling at a velocity faster than I thought possible; I dreaded an awful smash at any moment.

A terrifying noise shrieked past my ears. Several stunned moments passed before I realized the strange sound was—*music!* Not a funeral requiem, but a brilliant symphony played on a thousand instruments unheard of on Earth.

The infinite was speaking to me. There stirred in me a belief that something of profound importance was about to be revealed.

The faster I traveled, the more translucent the dazzling

tunnel became until it eventually vanished. I rode atop a great wind that carried me across the vastness towards a pure, divine light that encompassed everything. I closed my eyes and surrendered totally to the experience.

When dawn broke, golden and glorious, my soul arrived at the walls of a grand city whose terraces dripped with amazing flowers of every hue, tended by skilled and loving hands. I felt eternal serenity of love and peace.

I became aware of a time eons ago when all souls were part of the Source awaiting their birth. I saw all of humanity dwelling in an enormous valley of light, untouched by the scars of earthly existence. I longed to become one with them, pure and wise again as before my birth, a spirit without the clouding of my life. I felt humbled, dazed and exalted all at once.

The gates to this magnificent city opened to me, and I beheld grand architecture of astonishing variety and forms. And, yes, there were people here, and in large numbers. Who they were and how they behaved towards me, a stranger here, I have no recollection.

All other memories of my visit elude me, save for two: I remember entering a great marble temple. At its center sat a strange tree of fire that burned with images of my life like fruit on branches. Five beautiful entities adorned in long, regal robes formed a circle around me. Light radiating from their faces obscured all features, yet I could discern their smiles. They spoke in a language made of musical tones, yet I understood their meaning. I sensed that they were infinitely wise, unbelievably ancient and enormously compassionate ambassadors to mankind. I knew why I had been brought here—these beings would celebrate the arrival of my immortal soul and allow me to evaluate my life, specifically how my life affected others from their viewpoint. As I watched and became aware of my shortcomings, I felt ashamed and realized I had much to atone for.

I remember no other details of this encounter, save for its outcome. They gave me a choice to stay in this sacred city and travel to farther and more fantastic realms, or return to the mortal world and finish the life I left behind.

I thought of Vanessa, and of the day she would bear our child. I desperately wanted to be by her side. The choice was easy. Yes, I was grateful to go back and spend the remainder of my life with her.

Finally, I remember vividly entering a sunny chamber adorned with exotic furnishings and remarkably colorful flowers arranged in precious vases. I felt warm, sensual energy fill the room.

I was not alone. A petite figure, veiled in the purest white silk, stood by a window waiting for me.

"Do I know you?" I asked.

She walked to me and raised her veil. The woman was Gabrielle.

"Greetings," she said to me, her eyes bright, her voice musical. "You have given humanity an immeasurable gift. Generations will owe you a profound debt." She lowered her eyes and bowed to me.

"No—I am in *your* debt," I said. "I could have done nothing without you and the others."

"We followed you. Only you could get close enough to the well of absolute evil through your love of Vanessa. Everything in your life, every friend you made and every encounter that befell you, prepared you to meet Belial. You will understand in time."

I didn't want to understand. "I thought I would never see you again."

She looked deep into my eyes. "We met in many life-times. Often our journeys have taken us down the same paths. And perhaps they shall again if that is what we decide. This is true of your friends as well. It is love that joins us. This is the lesson life teaches us—the lesson we must accept to grow closer to the source. Above all else, the power of unconditional love to all as part of ourselves allows our souls to transcend to higher energies."

"What will become of Eben? I couldn't pull him from the womb as he had for me."

"He is where he should be—safe and soon back in your care. He will once again grow to love and celebrate life with you."

I had so many questions to ask her. "Tell me how you escaped Belial's fortress."

"That is not important. Just know that Belial's keep is barren and shall remain so until the day evil emerges from the sanctum."

The sanctum. "I vowed to stay and guard it with my soul."

"That is not your task," she said. "Your place is among the living where you still have much to learn and give to the world."

I looked at her, puzzled. "Then who will guard it?"

She smiled. "I will."

Gabrielle replaced the veil over her face and walked to an arched, glassless window that overlooked a quiet pond. "You have made a wise choice, and now you must go to her." Then she spoke her final words to me: "I promise we all will meet again."

I put out my hand to her. Before we could touch, the beautiful room vanished. My soul grew heavy as my vibration slowed, and I plunged like an anchor down a dark tunnel that delivered me into a container of flesh— my earthly body.

THE ARMADA

The sun bathed my face with its warmth, and a breeze rustled my hair. I opened my eyes to a bright blue sky. I drew in a deep breath and released it slowly, savoring the sensation.

I was alive.

I lie still, staring skyward, letting another wave wash under me, gently lifting me. The sand felt vibrant beneath my fingertips. The Earth appeared new to me. My eyes focused on a piece of flotsam bobbing in the surf beside me. One end of the twisted stick was a human hand, tangled in a shredded burial sack. I lifted my head. The surf was awash with human rubbish.

I pushed my palms against the sand and sat up slowly. My arms felt like great weights, and the change in position made my head swoon. I felt my forehead and found a tender area from an apparent bullet graze, but no open wound. Had I even been shot?

Behind me, the beach yielded to a stark and foreboding mountain—the Island of the Devil. I now understood. The flotsam were the remains of the murdered prisoners who had been buried with me in the island's shark-infested waters. I looked away.

The breeze carried a black, noxious cloud. I twisted my

head towards its source. There, blocking the beach several hundred yards from me, lay one of Rudler's wrecked warships, a black cloud billowing from its interior. The burning hulk lay on its side, half-submerged in the surf like a lifeless whale. Its pocked and bent steel plates, many of them missing, couldn't save it from a pitiless salvo of twenty-four pounders from Uncle's Armada. Such was the end to Rudler's indestructible navy.

I became aware of sounds. The even rush of the sea. Distant shouting.

And gunfire.

I saw a contingent of island soldiers huddled on the beach, a woefully small resistance against the invasion from the sea. Scores of British troops were disembarking from longboats, grabbing ammunition, readying their rifles and quickly falling into position on a beach that offered little cover. These landing troops came from more than twenty British man-of-war ships anchored beyond the reef.

With a shout, the British troops advanced, their bayoneted rifles held in the firing position. Two island guards who had no stomach for combat deserted their comrades and began running down the beach away from the fight. They didn't get far. Plum-size spots appeared in the center of each of their backs, dropping them face down onto the sand.

Despite their best efforts to organize a defense, one island guard after another fell to a barrage of bullets. A retreating guard bolted through the surf and fell dead before me in a bloody pool. I heard more splashing behind me. A dark figure stepped over me, grabbed the dead man's carbine and used it club-like to deliver a lethal blow to the head of another retreating guard racing passed us.

I shielded my eyes and looked up at a powerful Negro. The man standing over me was my friend Williams.

"By God's glory..."

He tossed the carbine aside. "They no guards left to keep us. 'Tis all men for hisself."

Williams grabbed my arm and lifted me over his shoulders. "You gonna get shot if'n you stay here, Cap'n."

I choked back the pain that spread throughout my body like an unchecked fire. But he was right. At this range, I doubted the British soldiers could discriminate our gray prison clothing from the island soldiers' khaki uniforms.

Williams stepped from the sucking surf and staggered towards the boulders at the edge of the beach. For several precious seconds, we moved unchecked. Then, with a chorus of yells, the advancing British troops let rip another storm of fire. Bullets plowed into the beach around us, throwing up bursts of sand.

A bullet clipped Williams' leg, forcing him viciously onto one knee. He gritted his teeth and rose onto trembling legs. Step by difficult step, he struggled to deliver me to the relative safety of the boulders beyond the beach.

A grenade landed behind us. Williams dropped to his knees and flung me forward off his shoulders. A bone-shattering blast whipped a storm of sand over us. I heard the shouts of approaching soldiers.

"Go," Williams cried. "Go. GO!"

I struggled towards the boulders, my arms all but useless. I didn't get far. A row of black boots formed a tight circle around us, and I heard the clicks of a score of rifles being cocked. I propped myself on one elbow and stared up at a line of barrels trained at my head. I raised a hand, a useless gesture of surrender.

"Prisoners," I managed.

For several long, heart-stopping moments, the stillness was absolute. No one said anything, no one breathed. My eyes moved from one British gun to the next, to one intent soldier's face to another. Then I heard a gruff voice shouting orders.

"Keep one alive for interrogation," the voice commanded.

Several soldiers were pushed roughly aside to make room for an officer. I shaded my eyes against the sun.

Admiral Joshua Finsbury, dressed in his finest double-breasted Navy blues, loomed over me like a monument. His stone eyes scrutinized me as though pondering how to end the misery of a crippled horse. The troops kept their rifles pointed at us, awaiting his next order. Uncle rubbed a finger through his smooth, white beard, beautifully trimmed for the occasion, while his eyes shifted from Williams back to me.

"Lower your weapons," he said. "These men are family."

His troops stood at ease.

I let out a long, loud sigh, while Williams blessed himself.

Uncle grimaced when he saw Williams' leg wound. "Fetch the medical officer—*in haste.*"

A sergeant standing next to him bolted down the beach.

"The two of you could have been killed charging down here like this," Uncle said. "You know the drill. Why in God's name didn't you stay in your cell until we took this island?"

How could I explain? "If you've come to reclaim your compass—"

"I wouldn't be here at all if I hadn't received your messages from Freetown. Your report gave me the piece I needed to complete this dangerous puzzle. Now I'm looking forward to hanging a French admiral who I mistakenly believed died under the guillotine a decade ago."

"Too late," I said. "His body lays in a dungeon beneath this island."

Uncle scowled in disappointment and barked an order to his lieutenant. The officer ran off with several men to investigate.

"Where's your brother?"

I lowered my eyes and shook my head. Uncle's expression sank into a hollow look of loss, a look a commander of his experience wears too often.

I heard a woman shouting. The line of soldiers opened to reveal a group of prisoners trudging up the beach to the longboats. A slender figure broke away and ran towards us. A thrill rushed through me. Her hair, uncombed and lustrous, framed a face on which despair yielded to surprise and joy. She wasn't yet sure.

I rose to my knees and reached for her. And as she rushed closer, I took in her beauty, afraid she would forever linger beyond my touch.

"Vanessa—" Emotion silenced me.

"*Andrew.*"

The woman I loved with all my soul ran for my waiting arms. I let the tears flow freely from my eyes. I vowed that once I held her again, once I felt her eager and silken arms around me, nothing and no one would ever again separate us.

Far out to sea, a hundred cannons fired rounds of victory.

"He went like one who hath been stunned,
And is of sense forlorn:
A sadder and a wiser man
He rose the morrow morn."

Samuel Taylor Coleridge

"And now abideth faith, hope, love, these three;
but the greatest of these is Love."

1 Corinthians 13:13

EPILOGUE

And so, my dear Eben, I'll bring this narrative to an end, satisfied that I have shared with you the essence of my adventure all those years ago. Suffice it to say that we returned with the Armada to England aboard the Admiral's ship. Your mother and I never left Potters Bay to raise you in the States as planned. I hope you agree that we lived full and happy lives here together. I harbor no regrets.

What am I asking you to accept about this admittedly extraordinary account? Very little. Whatever you choose to believe, be assured that you are a gifted individual with unique talents and experiences.

I wish to leave several ideas for your consideration. There is life after death. I know this to be so with every fiber of my being. I believe that the "real" world with which we are familiar is merely a difficult place to learn and prepare our souls for a greater, more wondrous future. A future without limits.

The dark realm of the afterlife, which my account describes, is but one of many worlds below the physical. It is in this realm that we confront our sins and answer for the choices we make in our lives. We are haunted not for our sins but rather by them. Whatsoever a man soweth, so shall he reap.

I believe there are still deeper and darker worlds. And I cannot imagine the anguish of those forced to dwell there. Evil, which walks the earth in many guises like a plague, is borne of these base realms with the corrupt purpose of keeping us from the Source. Reject these forces totally, my son. Focus instead on the higher worlds of love, wisdom and abundance that await us. Each of us will find our own way through a life of enlightenment, striving always to grow to higher levels of awareness. By rejecting evil, we learn and accept what it means to forgive all with unconditional love. We learn to become one with our neighbors. That is your life's purpose, as it is every man's.

And finally, I have left you a relic of my past—a well-traveled knife taken from the galley of *The Dolphin*. Ask your mother where I keep it. Its original owner weighted the handle and sharpened both edges; indeed, you will see that it has become a formidable weapon. I wanted to give it to you long ago, but I could not bear to part with it. Nor was I ready to answer the questions it certainly would bring to your mind. I now have told you how I came by it. Please honor it as a symbol of love between brothers, and now between a father and his son. May it protect you in your travels as it has done for me.

When you read this, God will have taken my soul for the final time, and so I bid you farewell—for now. I look forward to the time when we will again be together. And perhaps you will remember to bring this most useful item with you.

With love,
Your Father

ACKNOWLEDGMENTS

I am truly grateful to my special friends who shared their time, talents and sympathies with me to realize a dream that began way back in 1979. For their counsel and suggestions, I thank Daniel Barbier, Darlene Bissonnette, William Burns Jr., Sandra K. Donaldson, Ellen Feig, Mike Holladay, Stephanie Johnson, Lenetta McCampbell, Donald Merz, Daniel Needles, J.R. Provost, Roger Rittner, Toni Rommel, Keith Seewald and Sheila Stevens.

*Four strangers become inextricably bound when they put
their lives on the line to help a mysterious old man complete
a harrowing journey to avert mankind's extinction.*

AMAN

A NEW THRILLER BY JOSEPH MASSUCCI

Turn the page for a sneak preview

AWAKENING

Zbol, Iran

Young Jalal found herding sheep through the gorge a far more difficult task than anything he had ever tried before. There were no wells along this route, and the unforgiving sun rising between the towering hillsides stole his breath as it baked him. He could think only of water.

His father coaxed the animals along the rocky path with a constant stream of curses, whipping their legs with his staff. Jalal struggled to keep up. He had grown weary and parched from chasing strays back to the flock.

Despite the challenging terrain, they had no choice but to follow this twisting trail. Much was at stake. The sheep were worth twelve pounds each at the Bedouin market, possibly more if the region's drought continued. Jalal turned ten only last week, and he had already betrayed his father's trust for the flock's safekeeping. Eight wandered off into the gorge during the night under his watch. Another failed test of his manhood.

Jalal's father thrust a finger up the hillside, his leathered features stretched into a rare smile. "You are a very lucky boy."

Jalal shielded his eyes with two hands and saw eight sheep grazing on the hillside high above.

His father gave no instructions, and Jalal needed none. His elder settled cross-legged under one of the path's few trees with their bottle. Jalal knew his father would share its contents only after he returned with the strays. Water would be his reward.

Jalal secured his leather pouch over his shoulder and struggled up the hillside.

"Faster," his father shouted. He laughed.

His father took a long swallow of water, a sight that made Jalal's throat ache. The sooner I am back, the sooner I drink, he thought.

The way up the hill was steep and rock-strewn, and Jalal exhausted his last breath by the time he reached the strays. He felt his father's eyes boring into him, judging him. He vowed not to show his fatigue and fail yet another test.

Jalal chased after a lamb that had strayed from the others and gathered it into his arms.

He froze. Something was wrong. The earth groaned with a strange deep sound he had never heard before. The ground began to shake, sending small rocks tumbling from above. A rumbling like distant explosions boomed down the gorge. The devil was coming.

Frightened, Jalal stumbled down the hillside with the lamb. "Papa!"

Far below, his father was on his feet while the flock scattered as in a panic. The mounting tremors made it difficult to stand. Jalal never felt anything so violent, and it terrified him beyond reason. The lamb in his arms squirmed and thrashed. He drew it tight against his chest.

Jalal heard his father shriek and saw him running down the gorge away from the hillside. The youth's hammering heart choked off the last of his breath. *Don't leave me!* He was too frightened to cry out.

The bottom of the gorge suddenly disappeared in a massive fireball. A deafening burst of thunder followed. Jalal eyes widened. His father and every trace of their flock vanished into the inferno.

"*Papa!*"

Thick black smoke erupted high into the air and turned the bright sky into night. In seconds, fire consumed the bottom of the gorge. The devil's callous breath encompassed him, burning him.

Jalal could no longer distinguish the ground from the sky. Surely he would die on this hillside. He hid with his lamb behind a boulder, horrified, as outlines of larger rocks crashed past him in an avalanche and disappeared into the flaming abyss below. His heart pounded. Behind the thick shrieking storm of dust, he caught glimpses of trees, uprooted and thrown aside like sticks. Tendrils of fire raced up the hillside, hunting him. He hugged the lamb like he once hugged a stuffed animal, burying his face in its singed wool. What did it feel like to burn while alive, he wondered?

But Jalal did not die.

He did not know how long he sat there perfectly still, covered with a thick coat of ash. When he finally stood, a layer of ash had settled over the hillside, cloaking the landscape in a dull gray sheet of death. An acrid fog lingered. The floor of the gorge was gone. In its place lay a deep, charred canyon with no bottom.

The devil had awakened. And he was angry.

. . .

Global Consciousness Project
Princeton University, New Jersey

Dr. Irving Weissmann loved numbers more than any person. He caressed them with his mind, calculating, manipulating, arranging, collating, studying and showcasing them. And when he looked closely enough, numbers revealed secrets to him—the universe's secrets.

The morning sun poured through his office window, and with it came voices of the campus coming to life. He settled back into his abundant leather chair and frowned. A chronic insomniac since turning sixty almost a decade ago, he preferred the place to himself, free of noise.

"Go away and leave me alone," he ordered the window.

Weissmann turned to the bar graphs he had monitored for the last three hours—the output from the project's global network of random number generators. Sixty-six units scattered around the world. They relayed the behavior of random numbers, recording proof of an emerging collective intelligence called the noosphere, mankind's next evolutionary step after the geosphere and the biosphere. The implications of a single mind for humanity were staggering, their results always intriguing.

The computer applet produced an audible heartbeat every second as it processed new chunks of data from the network. An occasional bell signaled deviations from normal random values. The rhythmic heartbeat often put Weissmann into a meditative state. He closed his eyes and listened to those deviations, subtle signs of mankind collectively reacting to global events. The early morning transcendental experience helped make up for his lack of sleep.

A series of bells suddenly began going off like a pinball machine winning streak, jarring him from his trance.

The alarm gave way to abrasive gongs, signaling the most extreme deviations.

Weissmann grimaced, annoyed. Surely a software malfunction. He put on his reading glasses and squinted at the display's bar graphs. No system fault—the figures showed a steady influx of new data. Yet the alarms, irritating and insistent, heralded that all sixty-six stations were reporting extreme non-random number variations.

Weissmann stood from his desk and stared, unbelieving. His breathing came rapidly, and he felt his heart racing. His blood pressure must be through the roof, he thought. Could this really be happening? Had something awakened mankind's collective consciousness in a fundamentally profound way? He needed to verify the data's integrity.

And if he found no malfunction, a cataclysmic event had just occurred the likes of which the world had never seen.

• • •

South Dakota foothills

He did not recall waking. The old man simply found himself standing in the first light of a new day, barely upright, his ancient eyes struggling to focus on a patch of violet windflowers at his feet, assuring him that life could still bloom from this depleted soil.

He felt no pain. There was, however, an unusual sensation like a low-grade current running through his skeletal fingertips. As the sun cleared the mountaintops, his shriveled lungs inflated with the foothill's warm air. It smelled so sweet, so full of life. He indulged himself like a famished man, filling his lungs again and again.

Only six days.

The old man squinted against the dust spiraling off the plains. He saw no trace of the village that once flourished here with its tall dome-shaped dwellings, clay streets and roasting pits. Gone were the children who invariably ignored their elders to play with their puppets among the graves. What had become of the land's people so vibrant with life and love and hope? And what of the wife and two children he had left behind so long ago?

The *Paha Sapa* mountains, rising behind him like eternal sentinels, had seen everything, yet told him nothing. Impressions of the land's past flowed through his consciousness, mingling with the music of the wildflowers as they sang to each other. The tribes had moved on and vanished, their dances still. He shook his head. The earth had long forgotten his people. He listened for the slightest whisper of his wife's voice. *Speak to me, my love.* But even her lingering memories had faded. The wind and the elements, but mostly time, had taken everything.

The old man looked away with sadness, his throat swollen with grief. But his withered eyes could summon no tears. All that remained to mark the place where he had slept lay a deep hole in the rough shape of a man. A handful of sandstone pebbles disturbed its perimeter.

His eyes turned skyward. The rising sun promised a very hot day. He must begin his journey.

Before him stretched a boundless prairie—the way to a new world he knew little about. Staring uncertainly at the gravel path ahead, he wondered if his old legs would support him. Or would he collapse with the first step, his brittle bones shattering into a thousand fragments? There he would lie forever, his journey ended before it even began.

He took a tentative step. To his astonishment, his legs did not buckle. As he placed his full weight upon the desiccated bones, he felt neither feeble nor aged. His legs were firm. The barest smile stretched his thin parched lips, and he began walking along the trail with a slow but deliberate pace.

He had much to do in only six days.

Available from Amazon.com,
Barns & Noble
and other quality book retailers.